THE ROAD IS A RIVER

NICK COLE

THE ROAD IS A RIVER
Copyright © 2013, 2019 by Nick Cole

All rights reserved. No portion of this work may be reproduced in any form, except for brief quotations in reviews, without the written permission of the author.

This book is a work of fiction. Any references to real people, events, locales or organizations are used fictitiously. Other names, characters, places, and events are imaginary, and any resemblance to actual places, events or persons, living or dead, is entirely coincidental.

ISBN: 978-1-949731-09-5

Published by Galaxy's Edge Press

CHAPTER 1

Can you let go?

The Old Man is sick. The Old Man is dying.

His fever is high in him and the days pass long and hot, as though having no end to them. The villagers come one by one, and it seems to all of them that what's left of the Old Man will not be enough. Though there are no goodbyes, there are words and looks that mean just as much.

Yet she will not let him go.

"No, Grandpa," she says to him through the long days and even longer nights. "I need you."

Can you let go?

He has told the villagers as much as he can of Tucson through the ragged flaming trench that is his throat. The security of the Federal Building. The untouched mountain of salvage. The tank. The villagers are going there.

That could be enough. They have Tucson now.

He lies back and feels that swollen, fiery ache within every muscle.

Just rest.

Most of them, most of the villagers have gone on to Tucson and all that he has promised them of a better life waiting there. A new life, in fact.

Can you let go?

The Old Man is sick.

The Old Man is dying.

My wife.

He thinks of her olive skin.

Will I be with her again?

Soon.

He is glad he thought of her when the wolves were beneath him and his hands were burning as he'd crossed over the abyss. He is glad he still loved her when he needed to remember something other than the burning pain in his fingers.

"No, Grandpa. I need you."

The Old Man thinks, in the darkest moments when it seems as if he is crossing from this life to the next, that there are things worse than wolves snapping their jaws beneath you as you pull yourself across an abyss while thinking of your wife.

And he can hear the worst.

What is the worst?

His eyes are closed.

His granddaughter, Emily — she is his best friend, he remembers — is crying.

"No, Grandpa. I need you."

And he is going. Almost gone. Fading.

He hears her sobs. Weeping. Weeping for him.

His failure to live just a little longer.

She needs him just a little longer. "Forever," she tells him.

The worst is when you imagine the grief of your loved ones after you have gone.

'When you are sick in the night,' he thinks, 'you imagine the worst. To hear my granddaughter in grief for me… that is the worst I can imagine.'

Can you let go?

'Not yet,' he thinks. 'For her I will stay just a little longer, and maybe I can die later when it won't matter so much. She still needs me now.'

That is the love of staying when you know you must go.

And the Old Man lives.

CHAPTER 2

What follows are moments.

Individual moments, each one like a picture. A photograph before there was digital. Just before the end. Before the bombs. Snapshots of the hot days that follow.

The Old Man lies in his bed. When his voice returns, he is surprised. He didn't even know it was missing, he'd been so many days gone to the wasteland. He tells them of Tucson.

He tells them of the tank.

The wolves.

The Horde.

Sergeant Major Preston.

When he is finished, he is so tired that his words merge into a dream of nonsense. When he awakes, he sees stars through the openings in the roof of his shed. He hears the voices of the villagers outside. He feels his granddaughter's tiny hand holding his old hand, and as he drifts back to sleep he hopes that he will not have that terrible nightmare again. The one in which he is falling and he can hear her.

No, Grandpa. I need you.

Snapshot.

It is morning. The cold wind blows across his face as they carry him out from his shed.

Am I dead?

But he can see his granddaughter. She is holding his rucksack, the one from the tower in Tucson, stuffed with the treasures that were once lost and now found.

They are taking me out to bury me.

"The book is for you," he hears himself mumble across cracked lips. His granddaughter turns to him and smiles.

I love her smile. It is the best smile ever. There is no good thing like it.

Maybe her laugh too.

"I have it with your other things, Grandpa. Right here." She pats his rucksack proudly.

All the villagers above turn and smile down at him hopefully.

The sky beyond them is gray. It is still monsoon season.

"We're taking you to Tucson now, Dad," says his son who has now bent down to adjust the blankets high about the Old Man's thin neck. "Hang in there, Dad. You're the last. We're leaving the village for good."

Sadness overwhelms the Old Man and then he thinks of his granddaughter and her smile as weapons against the darkness. Against a dragon that is too much for any mere man. He thinks of her perfect, lovely, best ever smile as sleep, fatigue, and a tiredness from so many days in the wasteland overwhelm him.

Her smile will keep the nightmare away.

Snapshot.

The red desert, east of Tucson.

We must be near the Y where I found the staked-out bodies. The warning the Horde had left. Please…

Snapshot.

He feels her hand.

It is a darkness beyond anything he has ever known.

Like the night I walked after the moon had gone down. The night after the motel.

It is quiet. Thick and heavy. Familiar.

He wakes with a start.

He is back in the office. The office where he found the last words of Sergeant Major Preston. He is lying in his sleeping bag.

I never made it back. I've been so sick I've stayed here too long.

In the hall outside he hears voices. A bright knife of light cuts the carpet on the floor.

"Dad?" says his son.

"It's me," replies the Old Man.

"Are you okay?"

Am I?

"Yes."

"Are you hungry?"

If I am, it means I am well and that I'll live.

"Yes."

"I'll get you something to eat. Be back in a few minutes."

"Thank you."

And he falls once more into the pit that almost took him and he does not have time to think of her, his granddaughter, or her smile. And so the nightmare comes and he has nothing with which to defend himself.

The snapshots fall together too quickly and soon become a movie.

He sees the blue Arizona sky, wide and seemingly forever, play out across the high windows. For a long time he watches the bright white clouds come and grow across its cornflower blue depths.

He hears an explosion. Dull, far away. It rattles the windows of the building. When he stands up and moves to the window, he sees a far-off column of black smoke rising out over the silent city. For a long time he stands watching the smoky, dark column. He feels unconnected and shaky. Occasionally he sees his fellow villagers moving down a street or exiting from a building. It is too far away to tell who each one is. But they are dressed differently than he has ever known them to dress. Almost new clothing, found here in this treasure trove, not the worn-out and handmade things of their years in the desert.

Time has resumed its normal pace. The sickness and fever fade. But not the nightmare. The nightmare remains, waiting for him.

What will become of us now?

Down the street, he sees a man pushing a grand piano out onto the sidewalk.

CHAPTER 3

Sam Roberts leans his blistered head against the hot steering wheel. Every ounce of him feels sunburned and sickened. He'd torn off the rearview mirror of the dune buggy three days ago. He couldn't stand seeing what was happening to him.

The dune buggy rests in the thin shade provided by an ancient building, part of some lost desert gas station. Now that he's running on electric, the gas within the buggy's small tank is useless, dead weight now that he has escaped. He'd only needed it for speed in the brief run through the gauntlet of crazies lying in wait outside the blasted main entrance of the bunker.

The sun hammers the dry and quiet landscape of hard brown dirt, blistered-faded road, and sun-bleached stone. The yawning blue of the sky reaches away toward the curvature of the earth. There is no wind, no movement, no sound.

Sam Roberts has spent the morning allowing the solar cells to recharge while patching the large rear tire. His sweat pours through the radiation burns on his skin. He feels it on his head where there was once hair. His eyes are closed. Even with the visor down, it is too bright at noon.

'But I can't drive in the dark,' he thinks.

He was born underground.

He has lived his entire life, other than the last three days, underground.

He is dying of severe radiation poisoning.

He is twenty-three years old.

He is a captain in the United States Air Force.

He moves his bleeding fingers to the ignition. The act of grasping the key and simply turning it feels as though it will kill him.

"I was dead the moment I left," he says to the dry air and the southern nothingness he must find his way through. "I was dead the moment someone turned on that radio station."

He laughs to himself and begins to cough and that leads to the rusty blood he spits into his glove.

He looks at the charging gauge. The plastic cover is melted. Even the seat vinyl is peeling.

He moves his hand to the switch that will engage the electric motor.

"Well, I've got lots of solar. Lots of that…" And he stops himself because he knows he will laugh again.

CHAPTER 4

The Old Man has been up for a few weeks. In the mornings he tries to help at breakfast. Tries to see if anyone will need assistance with their various projects. But when he does, they smile politely and tell him he needs to rest more. Then they disappear when he is not looking.

He returns to the office and watches them working in the streets below. Fixing up their new homes, salvaging in the afternoons farther out.

He takes walks at the end of the day. After the heat has given its best to destroy them all. He always walks first to see where his granddaughter is working. He tries to remember how thirteen-year-old girls spent their time when he was her age. In gymnastics and soccer and… boys? No, that was later. Or maybe I didn't notice when. Finally, he decides, maybe they, all those long-gone girls from his youth, didn't want anyone to know how they felt about boys when they were just thirteen years old. Her father, his son, is trying to start a farm. Their community will need fresh produce. Most of her work is done by the early afternoon and together they walk the streets and see what each neighbor has done that day. A new fence. A newfound treasure. A new life.

Look what I found today…

An antique double-barreled shotgun with scrollwork engraving.

Fifty feet of surgical tubing.

This beautiful painting. Each day at breakfast there are fewer and fewer of the villagers who come and eat in the dining hall at the Federal Building.

They are making their own lives now behind their fences in the houses where they store their treasures rescued from Before. Not like in the village where we all ate together in the evenings and the sky was our painting.

At night he returns to the Federal Building. The sentry gun, waiting on its tripod, its snout pointing toward the entrance, waits like a silent guard dog. He pats it on the head-like sensor, like he might pat a friendly dog, and returns to his room.

For a while he listens to the radio, their little station that Jason the Fixer had up and running in a day, playing the old programmed music from Before. Even Jason cannot figure how to change that. But, if they ever need to, they can interrupt the program and broadcast a message. Each night one of them takes a turn at the station. Watching the ancient computers. Just in case there is an emergency. Then all the radios in all the new homes of the once-villagers can be used to summon help.

We can still help one another that way. We are still a village.

So the Old Man leaves the radio playing softly through the night just in case there is some kind of emergency that will bring them all together again. Every so often he hears the voice of the villager whose turn it is to watch the station, saying something as the long dark passes slowly into dawn.

And he reads.

He has read the book once more.

He is glad he had his friend in the book, Santiago, there with him out in the desert. When he reaches the end of the book he is glad for Santiago, that he made it home to his shack by the sea and for the boy who was his best friend. Again.

He thinks of his granddaughter.

She is my best friend.

But for how long?

Girls become women.

He remembers being sick and hot and hearing her voice calling him back from wherever he was going.

If I think of the sickness, I will think of the nightmare and then it will come while I sleep and I will wake up to get away from it.

So he goes down to the library.

He tries to pick a new book. But so many of the modern books, books from right before the bombs, seem like they might remind him of people and times that are now gone.

I'll pick a classic.

How will you know which is and is not a classic?

The Old Man stands before the quiet, dusty shelves inhaling their thickness and plenty, then sighing as the burden of choice overwhelms him.

A classic will be something from a time I never lived in. That way I will not be reminded of war and all that is gone because I never knew it. I'll read about the Roaring

Twenties as told by a southerner or the London fog of Dickens or even the Mississippi as it was.

I have not seen a river in forty years.

Nothing with war.

In a corner between other books he finds one that he knows is a classic, knows it from school though he cannot say whether he'd ever read it. But he knows it was a classic.

He takes it back to the office, his room, and lies down on his sleeping bag. He watches the night sky for a moment and listens to the radio playing softly on the other side of the room.

It will play all through the night, even while I am asleep. Like Before.

He opens the first page and begins to read.

CHAPTER 5

Sam Roberts had a few more hours to live.

He wanted to know how much radiation he'd absorbed in escaping the front entrance of the bunker, but the dosimeter had stopped working by the time he was clear of the massive door and the freaks in front of it.

Still, he would've liked to know how many rads he'd soaked up.

It was just before dawn.

He could see the lights of Tucson far off to the west, lying on the southern side of a gigantic black rock that heaved itself up from the desert floor. The pinpoints of light twinkled softly in the rising pink of first morning like tiny jewels set amid gray pillars of sun-bleached stone.

Earlier, outside Hatch, a small town that had collapsed into the drifting sands and rolling weeds, he'd stopped to scribble a message onto a piece of paper, his hands badly shaking.

'Wouldn't that be something,' he'd thought. 'To come all this way and I'm too sick to tell them the message.'

As he threw up again he tried to say, "Help me!" But no sound came out. His voice box was gone. Either scorched by the acid his stomach seemed to churn up, and that came out of him constantly, or fried by the radiation of two high-yield Chinese nuclear warheads deposited at the front door of his lifelong home forty years ago. Either way, he would never speak again. So he wrote the note. Then he added, *Please stay away from me. I'm contaminated with radiation.*

He watched the far city. Morning light opened the desert up to Captain Roberts. There were so many different colors. The golden sand. The pink rock. The blue sky. The red earth.

'Best day of my life,' he thought. 'And I saw it all at least once'…

He blacked out.

When he came to, it was noon.

His heartbeat pounded throughout his entire body, but it was slow and intermittent. Captain Roberts reached into his chest pocket. He took out the emergency syringe and jammed it into his thigh. His vision cleared as his heart began to race.

'Last one,' he thought.

On the horizon, Tucson looked gray amid the shimmering heat waves that rose above the road. Already his vision was starting to blur. 'These injections aren't lasting long,' he thought.

He started the engine. The cells were below half full. He'd forgotten to set them to charge. I don't know if it's enough, but it's all I have.

He took a safety pin out of the medical kit that lay sprawled across the passenger seat. He'd done a bad job of bandaging his own blisters. He pinned the message to his jumpsuit. 'All I gotta do now,' he thought, 'is get close enough for them to find me.'

He gunned the engine and felt the acceleration press what was left of his thin body backward. He did his best to keep the dune buggy on the road with what little time he had left. The road shifted and swerved in the heat and sweat as his dying heart thundered out its last.

It was tough going but he did his best.

CHAPTER 6

The Old Man walked to the wide window of the office. Below he could see the villagers congregating in the park. Or what had once been a park. Now someone was hard at work down there preparing the ground for crops. That someone worked with a hoe, turning the bleached and hard, forty-year baked mud over into dark soil, waiting and ready for rows and eventually tiny seeds.

The Old Man watched them for a long while. When the discussion seemed to grow in intensity, he closed the book and took the elevator down, passing the silent sentry machine-gun dog, patting it as he always did, and walked through the lobby and out into the heat of the afternoon.

It will be a hot summer this year. It's good we have these buildings. If it gets too hot I can sit down in the bottom of the garage near the tanks and it will be cool there. I can even read if I bring a light.

When he reached the discussion, he saw his son and the others debating over something one of the younger villagers had found. A man he remembered once being a boy was now waving a piece of paper in the air.

"What'd you do with him?" asked a kid the Old Man thought looked more like his father, who had not survived the first ten years, and less like his mother, who had.

He's not a kid. He's a man now. Even though they were all once children. They are men and women now.

Time is cruel that way. It erases us. It erases the children we once were.

"I left him there!" whined Cork Petersen.

That's his name. We'd called him "Corky" and he would follow Big Pedro and me sometimes. Now his name is Cork.

Time.

"He's dead anyways," mumbled Cork.

The Old Man sidled up behind his son.

"Dad," his son acknowledged without looking at him.

"What's all this…" began the Old Man, and the words he knew he must use to complete the sentence escaped and ran off into the desert.

His son looked at the Old Man and then turned back to the discussion, which seemed to be about the piece of paper Cork Petersen held on to.

I'm not old. I just couldn't… I just got lost in the middle of my words. It's because I am still recovering from the sickness that almost took me. But I am not old.

"Cork Petersen found a dead man in a dune buggy out in the desert," whispered his son.

The Old Man waited.

"I say we do nothing." It was Pancho Jimenez. If anyone led the village now, it was Pancho. He had been the strongest and best at salvage in recent years.

I remember him also as a boy.

"But the note says…" grumbled Cork.

"Take care," interrupted Pancho. "Take care of what the note says." His voice was enough to silence the discussion as they all turned toward him. Ready to listen.

When Pancho had their attention, their full attention, he began.

"You saw the bodies along the way. You heard the Old Man's tale of the desert. Those savages called the Horde."

Everyone turned to look at the Old Man for the briefest moment. Uncomfortably he smiled back at them and saw in some a look of pity.

They're surprised you're still alive.

I also am surprised.

"We've found paradise." All eyes were again on Pancho as he continued to speak. "We have found paradise now. We're planting our gardens, late, but we are planting. We have houses, each family their own. We have an entire city to salvage from. And what happens? A man dies in the desert. Is that any of our concern? No, none at all. We have much to be concerned with and little time in which to accomplish those things we must."

"But the message is for us," interrupted Cork.

Pancho, patient, strong, confident in who he was, smiled.

"And that, Cork, is who we must take care of. Us."

Everyone began to murmur.

The Old Man turned away, looking down the street, searching for his granddaughter.

Maybe I can find her and we can go salvaging in the afternoon. That would be fun if I feel up to it.

"There are worse than those people called the Horde," proclaimed Pancho above the clamor.

"How do you know that?" someone asked.

"How do you know there isn't?" replied Pancho.

Quiet.

"We do what that note says and we open a door we may not be able to close."

Quieter.

"Even now," continued Pancho, "you are saying to yourselves 'we have weapons, the tanks, some guns left by the Army.' Well, you don't have an endless supply. And do you want to go down that road? Do you want conflict? No, none of you do. You want tomatoes and lemons and homes just like I do. Right now, our greatest weapon is not the Old Man's tank or our few rifles. Right now our greatest weapon is our invisibility. Whoever sent that man wants to confirm that we are here. They picked up our broadcast, which I advise we turn off immediately, and now they want to know who we are and what we're doing out here. If we respond to that message, who knows who we'll be talking to. All I ask is that you consider this. The world isn't a nice place. It hasn't been a nice place for a long time. We answer that message and we would be unwise if we did not expect the worst. In fact, we would be stupid."

"Says they need our help," said Cork.

"We need help!" shouted Pancho.

More murmuring. A few comments. Cork handed the note to Pancho in defeat. Villagers drifted away. Only a few remained, all in agreement with Pancho. In agreement as he tossed the note into the wind and the paper fluttered down the street.

And then they were all gone and only the Old Man remained, invisible and unconsidered.

He went to pick up the note.

On it was written a message.

To whomever is operating the radio station at Tucson. Please tune your receiver to radio frequency 107.9 on the FM band and send us a message so that we can communicate with you. We are trapped inside a bunker and need help. Beneath that, *Please stay away from me. I'm contaminated with radiation.*

CHAPTER 7

That night the Old Man snuck out of his room and made his way to the radio station the villagers had set up inside the Federal Building.

"Are you sure, Grandpa? Are you sure we should try to contact them?"

He raised a finger to his lips.

His granddaughter nodded, excited to be playing the game of not being found and doing things that should not be done in the dead of night while others slept.

When they reached the radio room they found it unlocked. Inside all was dark. The equipment had been turned off. The Old Man closed the door behind them and for a moment the two of them listened to the silence.

The Old Man switched on his flashlight.

"How does it work, Grandpa?"

"Power. Electronics require power. So we must find the switch or the button or the toggle that will turn it on."

"Toggle," she pronounced and laughed softly.

The Old Man searched and just when he had given up ever finding out how to turn on the power, his granddaughter's thin hand darted forward.

"Is this it, Grandpa?"

The Old Man didn't know if it was.

"Do you want to try it?" he asked.

She nodded.

"Okay then. Try it."

She hesitated for a moment and then with only the confidence that the young possess in their movements, she flipped the switch. Soft yellow light rose behind the instruments. Green and red buttons illuminated. There was a faint scent of burning ozone.

The Old Man watched power course through the ancient technology.

After the bombs I never thought I would see such things again.

He found the frequency keypad and typed in the numbers from the slip of paper.

"Grandpa?"

The Old Man stopped.

"What if…" She hesitated and began again. "What if my dad and the others are right?"

The Old Man could hear the worry in her voice.

"They are right."

"They are?"

"Yes. They are. But that doesn't make it right to do nothing."

"I don't understand."

"It's right to be afraid. It's right to be afraid of what you don't know. What could hurt you, you should be afraid of that, right?"

"Yes."

"But sometimes you have to do a thing even if you are afraid to do it."

"Because it's the right thing?"

"Yes, and because the world has got to become a better place."

For you to grow old in.

"Okay then, Grandpa. We'll do it."

You're very smart. And brave too."

"You're brave, Grandpa. Like when you were in the desert."

"I was afraid too."

"But brave also."

If you say so.

"So do we do this? Do we try to help whoever sent the message?" he asked her.

The young girl watched the power coursing through the machine as buttons lit up and needles wandered and settled. The Old Man watched her eyes. Watched her reach a decision.

"Yes."

The Old Man hit ENTER and a green button lit up. Stamped in black letters upon it were the words "Active Freq."

The Old Man moved the speaking mic close to his mouth.

"What do I say?" he asked his granddaughter.

She reached forward and pointed at a button.

"You have to push this when you talk."

"How did you know that?"

"I've watched others."

Of course you did. Nothing escapes you.

"All right, then, what should I say once I push that button?"

She touched her tiny chin with her thumb and forefinger, which was her way of thinking and was a gesture he remembered her first making when she was only three turning four.

"Tell them, 'we are here.' "

"Just that? 'We are here'?"

"Yes, just that."

The Old Man cleared his throat. He moved closer to the mic again and this time took hold of it. His finger hovered over the button his granddaughter had indicated he should push.

He pressed the button.

"Hello," he began. He looked at his granddaughter. She nodded.

"We are here," said the Old Man.

"Let go of the button now, Grandpa," she whispered.

They waited.

And then they heard the voice.

"Who am I speaking with?" The voice was a woman. Older. But clear and crisp. A voice used to giving commands and having them obeyed.

"Us," said the Old Man who had needed to be reminded that he must touch the button to reply.

"All right," said the voice cautiously. "Are you operating the radio station that just went active a few weeks ago in Tucson?"

"Yes," replied the Old Man. "Who are you?"

"My name is Brigadier General Natalie Watt. I'm the commander of forces at Cheyenne Mountain Complex and we need your help. We're trapped inside our bunker and we need to get out very soon."

The Old Man and his granddaughter looked at each other in the thick silence of the radio room.

"Are you still there?" asked the General.

"Yes."

"Can you help us?" she asked.

Pause.

"Yes."

"Will you?"

Pause.

"Yes," said the Old Man.

CHAPTER 8

The Old Man watched from the high window as his granddaughter slipped back through the quiet streets of Tucson to her family's home. It was well after midnight.

If I go on this journey, I must go alone. It is too dangerous for her to come with me.

He thought of the route. All the way into California, then back to Nevada, through New Mexico, and up to Colorado Springs.

It is over a thousand miles. The tank can only hold two hundred and sixty-four miles' worth of fuel according to General Natalie Watt. She said I could scavenge. Tanks can draw fuel from many sources. Even kerosene. There are no guarantees of fuel and then there is the radiation. Well, that would be why you need to go to California for the extra gear. And after I cross all that desert, I am to aim a laser at the back of a mountain surrounded by unknown enemies. A Laser Target Designator. And who are these enemies? The General doesn't know. She only knows they are trying to tunnel into the bunker and that when they do, they will flood the complex with radiation and kill everyone inside. They only opened the main door once so that the dead man, Captain Roberts, could drive his dune buggy out of the complex.

There is too much for just an old man like me to think about. This is too much for just me.

A one-way trip, my friend. He'd volunteered.

General Watt said the radiation is so bad at the front entrance that Captain Roberts probably absorbed a lethal dose in just the few minutes it took him to drive away. So I cannot take my granddaughter with me to such a place.

The Old Man watched the night.

In my nightmare she is crying for me. I am dying. Just like I almost did after the last time I went into the wasteland alone. She is crying and there is nothing I can do to make it better. The last thing I will ever hear is her grief for me.

It's just a nightmare, my friend, heard the Old Man as though his friend from the book were with him and they were discussing some problem of fishing or salvage together.

But it is my nightmare.

Everyone dies. What would you have her do? Laugh about it? Of course she will weep.

I was hoping it would be later. When she has her own family and everyone is tired of me. When I have become such a burden to them all that they will be glad to see me go. Then, that would be a good time to die.

She will still cry for you.

Of course.

The Old Man felt the night. Felt its emptiness was only a lie and that all the world and the places and dangers hidden in it were waiting to devour him.

I need to leave soon. In the dream she says, *No, Grandpa. I need you.* It's terrible. I never want to disappoint her. I never want to hear her say those words. I never want her to have to say them. Is it too much to ask to just fade away and have no one miss me until I've been gone for a long time?

And yet you must leave, my friend. Soon.

Yes. If I leave when no one is watching, just as I did last time, then I will not hear her grief.

Still, you will know. You will know she'll say that which you do not want to hear. And even if you don't hear her, in your heart the nightmare will lie to you and tell you that you did all the same.

Yes, that is the thing about nightmares. They embrace us when we are vulnerable, telling lies that seem very real. Like an older child who teases a younger child by making the child believe things that aren't true.

In our nightmares we are all children.

The Old Man looked down. In his nervousness he had picked up his copy of the book. The one he had read for those forty years in the desert. The one with his friend inside.

The Old Man settled into his sleeping bag. He held the book in his hands and watched the ceiling.

So we will go together, my friend?

Yes.

The Old Man listened to the soft howl of the wind outside the large windows.

Soon I will be asleep and tomorrow all this might have just been a nightmare. Things will be different by the light of day, right, Santiago?

They are trapped in the bunker, my friend. They need someone to come and help them.

Yes.

She said she was going with you.

Yes.

And you must leave soon.

Yes, that too.

CHAPTER 9

The Old Man gathers the supplies he will need. There are only a few people inside the Federal Building now. Most have staked out homes and are busy salvaging throughout Tucson. Hours pass before any one person might encounter another in a city so large and the villagers so few.

There are only eleven rounds left for the main gun.

But there are the smoke grenades still in their canisters alongside the turret. You could use those when you need to run away from trouble, my friend.

Yes, Santiago, what I don't think of you will, my friend from the book.

Yes.

He takes a large map that covers all the places he must go and folds it down until it fits in his pocket. He takes a hunting rifle and two boxes of ammunition. Canned and packaged food. Plastic drums full of water. He places his crowbar inside the tank.

When his granddaughter finds him in the late morning, he is exhausted and sweating from his efforts. She takes hold of the box of food he has been carrying and together they take it down into the depths of the garage and to the tank waiting in the darkness.

"When are we going to leave, Grandpa?"

"I don't know. I haven't made up my mind yet."

They went ten more steps toward the tank.

"Grandpa, are we going to leave tonight, or in the morning, or when?"

"I'm not leaving tonight," says the Old Man. "I'm too tired."

"That's why you need me, Grandpa."

He looked at her for a long moment.

I need you more than you'll possibly ever know, not because I can barely do it with the hoist and winch, but because you are the most important person in the world to me.

"That's why," he said simply and turned to check the heavy straps they'd used to secure the fuel drums to the side of the turret.

The tank is loaded by nightfall. She takes the keys and stuffs them in the pocket of her cargo pants.

I'll get another hundred miles out of these drums at best. Taking her would be the most selfish thing you could do.

It would seem so, my friend.

"If you go without me, I'll follow you, Grandpa."

If I keep her with me, then maybe the nightmare will be powerless to harm me.

Do you think so?

Yes. And I hope so too.

"All right."

"All right what, Grandpa?"

"We'll leave in the morning."

And maybe in the night I will just leave without her.

"Why not now, Grandpa? You drove most of the route we'd cover tonight in the dark last time."

I'm tired.

Do you think you will actually sleep tonight?

No.

Then maybe it's better to be done with the waiting. You know what you must do. Now do it, my friend.

I feel like I haven't thought everything through.

Did you the last time? Did you have any idea what you were getting into the last time? And yet you survived.

Barely. And now I'm even considering taking her with me. Do you want the truth?

Yes, my friend. Always.

Besides not wanting the nightmare to torment me… If I admit to myself a truth I do not want to hear, then yes I am taking her with me because I feel too weak for this. Not as strong as I was Before. The others should do this, but they won't.

Those people are trapped.

The Old Man sighed.

"Climb aboard then," he said to her.

Her face, tiny, elfin, perfect, exploded in a brief moment of joy and was quickly replaced by determination as he helped her up onto the turret.

After all, we'll be inside this thing. What can possibly hurt us?

"Thank you, thank you, thank you, Grandpa."

Only the young are excited about going anywhere.

Maybe it is because they are too willing to believe in what they will find where they are going, my friend. That something good might happen at any moment. Expecting it simply must.

"You must do everything I say, no matter what. Promise me you will do that."

"I will, Grandpa."

"Promise?"

"I promise. And you have to promise me you'll never leave and go salvaging again without me, Grandpa."

"I promise."

Someday I will die and you will remember that I promised. Please forgive me when I must break that promise. I won't want to, but death will make me. I hope you'll understand then.

Inside the turret they strapped on their thick green helmets and plugged communications cords into their stations, the Old Man in the commander's seat, his granddaughter in the loader's station below him. He turned on the auxiliary power unit, the APU. He could hear their breathing over the soft dull hum of the communications net.

"I'm glad you're with me this time," he said and squeezed her shoulder tightly.

"Me too, Grandpa."

Her eyes shone darkly in the red light of the interior as she stared about at all the equipment. He started the main turbine and the tank roared to life in the dark garage.

"Here we go."

CHAPTER 10

In the night, the headlight of the tank flooded the streets with bright light. Only one woman, out late and coming home with a pushcart of salvage, saw them as they turned onto the overpass and headed north into the midnight desert. He expected someone, anyone, all of them maybe, to come rushing out and stop him. To save him from himself and his foolishness. But they passed only the woman with the pushcart and no one came out to stop them.

Are you really going to do this?

The Old Man looked down at his granddaughter. She was smiling as the tank bounced over the crumbling remains of the interstate.

It seems I already have.

The night covered them all the way past Picacho Peak, where the Old Man could no longer smell the rotting bodies of the Horde above the exhaust and heat of the tank.

But they are out there in the dirt and the scrub all the same.

"When can I see where we're going? asked his granddaughter over the intercom.

"It's too dark and there is nothing to see right now."

"Here," he said. "Move to this seat below my knees and do not touch anything. It's where the gunner sat."

She unplugged her helmet cord, and after squeezing by the feet of the Old Man, she found herself looking out onto the desert floor through the targeting optics.

The Old Man drove on toward the fire-blackened remains of Gila Bend and felt they should stop, but he knew the road and knew their village was just another few hours beyond the charred dust of the place.

We can stay in our village one more night. At least it will be familiar.

When they arrived at the village, the Old Man shut down the tank and stood in the hatch looking at the collection of shacks in the darkness. He turned off the tank's headlight and waited to hear the sounds of the desert.

This is madness. In the morning I will wake up and take us back home. Maybe no one will have missed us.

"Grandpa?"

"Yes?"

"How will we get there?"

"Aren't you tired?"

They were rolling out their sleeping bags onto the floor of the tank.

"Not really."

"I suppose we will drive this tank as far as it will go. After that, we will walk."

"The lady said we needed to hurry."

"First we must find fuel at the old fort outside Yuma. The Proving Ground it was called."

It was quiet in the dark tank now as they settled into their bags. The Old Man left the hatch open, and through it he could see the stars above. He thought of closing the hatch but leaving it open seemed to him like a small act of bravery. As though he were preparing himself for other times when he might need more courage. As though giving into fear now would welcome an uninvited guest.

And it is still our village. There was no one here but us for all the years that we lived here and I doubt anyone's come along since.

"That's where you got the hot radio."

The Old Man thought of the desert and the wasteland and the radio that had sent him off on his own. For many nights as he recovered from the sickness, those days in the wasteland had seemed a dream or a story that had happened to someone who was not him.

I was free though.

And you were scared, my friend.

I was that too.

"We're never to go salvaging in the Proving Ground. It's too close to Yuma. Everyone knows what happened to Yuma, Grandpa."

The Old Man was drifting now, thinking of his days on the road and the heat of it beneath his huaraches.

"Was there really a bomb, Grandpa?"

"Yes."

"And you saw it go off?"

"I did."

"Then how can we go to Yuma for fuel?"

Almost asleep now, in fact probably just, the Old Man called as if from down a well, "The fort is far out in the desert, north of the city. I always told them it would be okay to salvage there. But its name was also Yuma and so they would not go."

Soon they both slept.

At first light, familiar birds they'd heard all their lives began to sing in the cool before the heat of the day. The Old Man, lying in the tank, looked up through the open hatch and watched the last stars disappear as morning dark turned into a soft blue above them. He slid silently from the tank while his granddaughter slept.

He walked the streets of the deserted village, his home for forty years, as morning washed everything in clear gold.

We should go back today. This was foolish to start with and it is even more foolish to go on. I was still sick and I got carried away. To go all the way with no promise of fuel is…

He came to his shack. He opened his door. Only the bed and the table remained. Everything was covered in dust.

What is expected of us is too much for just an old man and his granddaughter.

When he returned to the tank, his granddaughter was opening a package of food and kicking her feet on the side of the tank as she chewed, which was a thing she did often when she ate.

I cannot remember when I had so much energy to spare that I could kick my feet as I chewed and smile and think of the day as nothing but a waiting adventure or something to be explored.

"Maybe we should go back," he said standing in front of her.

She continued to chew.

"If we do, then we should call the lady and tell her we're not coming, Grandpa."

The Old Man paced the length of the tank looking for something he had no idea of.

"Would you be mad if we returned?"

"No, Grandpa. I understand. But you should call her. Tell her we're not coming."

"Are you sure?"

She nodded.

The Old Man climbed back into the turret, donned his helmet, and switched the comm channel button near the hatch over to the radio setting. He pushed the button on the cord and began to speak.

"General Watt."

A moment later the voice of General Watt was there in his helmet.

"Yes, go ahead."

"We…"

He paused.

Tell her. Tell her you've left and you're not coming all the way. Tell her you're giving up now.

"We… are beyond Gila Bend and proceeding toward a fort we know of north of Yuma. We think we might find some fuel there."

There was a pause.

"Thank you."

Her voice was tired.

"I wasn't sure if you were actually coming. I didn't think… just, thank you. I'm glad Captain Roberts's sacrifice wasn't in vain."

The Old Man lowered his head. Then he raised the mic to his mouth and said, "Save that until we make it there. We still have a long way to go."

His granddaughter's face, solemn as she considered the morning's breakfast, erupted in the smile he loved. She took off her helmet, put down her breakfast, jumped to the ground, and began to do cartwheels.

"So we'll go to the old fort above Yuma and look for some fuel," said the Old Man.

"I might be able to alter a satellite to search the Yuma Proving Ground for you. I'll allocate my resources immediately. I have limited access to the outside world, but we're not powerless down here," replied the General.

The Old Man thought of the satellite he had once seen in the night.

They are still up there.

"Anything would be helpful."

"I understand," said the voice of General Watt in his helmet. "I can still contact the automated systems of certain facilities. There may be more help along the way."

"Anything would be appreciated. To tell you the truth…"

Words refused to come.

His granddaughter disappeared off into the place where she had been born and where they had lived their entire lives until recently.

I thought we would always live here. I was happy here.

"I almost felt…" said the Old Man.

"Like it was too much?" the General asked.

"Yes," whispered the Old Man.

"I understand that too," said the General.

The Old Man felt tired. Felt like he could let go of a burden he'd never remembered picking up but had been carrying for longer than he could remember.

"I brought my granddaughter with me. She's just thirteen years old. I was afraid this would be too much for just the two of us."

"But you will continue?"

"Yes."

"If you weren't afraid, I'd be concerned you were some kind of idiot."

The Old Man watched his granddaughter run from one shack to another, flinging open doors in the morning light, dust motes swirling about her.

"I won't lie to you," said General Watt. "What you're heading into is very dangerous. If you turned off this radio and went home and never answered it again… I would understand. I have children and grandchildren too. But please don't."

"I'm sorry," said the Old Man.

"Don't be. If you knew my story, you would know that when I was… let's just say it was never considered possible for me to have children. But I have them and they are mine now. I will do everything I can to save them. Sadly, I have done everything and it isn't enough to overcome the one problem we've faced since the mountain above us collapsed down onto our emergency exit. You sound like a good man. Maybe if there had been more like you back before the war, we wouldn't be stuck here now."

"I was only twenty-seven then," said the Old Man. Static rose like a sudden ocean wave cresting and then falling violently onto the shore.

"I know what I'm asking you to do is beyond… reason. But I have to. You are our last hope. My grandchildren's last hope."

The Old Man wiped a sudden hot tear of shame from his eye.

"Don't worry, we'll get you out of there," he said.

Static.

"Thank you," said General Watt just before a storm of white noise consumed her voice.

CHAPTER 11

The Old Man turned to look at the village one last time as it disappeared on the far horizon behind them. The desert, a sandy plain dotted by dry mesquite growing low and close to the ground, swallowed the village and replaced it with more, an endless-seeming supply of itself.

I will never see my village again.

He let the whispering roar of the turbine overwhelm his thoughts, disintegrate them, and turn them into fuel to be spat out the back of the lumbering tank.

You don't know that. Good things and adventures might be just ahead.

Like what?

The noise of the tank filled the Old Man's thoughts as he waited, trying to imagine what good could possibly come of this journey. He could think of nothing.

Rivers, my friend. Rivers that must lead to an ocean.

I cannot remember when I last saw a river. A river — to be on a raft and to float and to fish… that would be heaven. There are no rivers in the desert. Only riverbeds.

Maybe we will find a river and we can make a raft, my friend. She would like that.

"Grandpa," came her high voice over the intercom as they jounced off-road. The interstate was damaged and the outermost remains of the Great Wreck were beginning to clog the highway.

I wonder of my car is still here.

Of course it is, where would it have gone?

True.

Before him the Great Wreck, as they'd called it all those years, lay spreading in every direction. In the distance he could see where the two broken semis that had collided and overturned formed the epicenter. From there rusting cargo vans and sinking station wagons had tumbled away down the road or off into the nearby desert, torn to pieces by the remorseless forces of fearful momentum meeting sudden obstacles. Other cars, hundreds of others, had driven off into the thick sand, becoming stuck as still more and more vehicles, unseen from the Old Man's vantage point, had continued to hurtle themselves into the wall of destruction as they fled the nuclear fireball over Yuma. On that last long-ago day everything had been smoke and screams and rending metal and people rushing away to the east and the fireball in the west where Yuma had once been. Now it was quiet and rusty and sinking year by year into the soft piles of sand that were dunes marching east.

"Yes?"

"Why did you change your mind about going back?"

The Old Man maneuvered the left stick to avoid a rusting station wagon that had fallen backward off the road. The tank clipped the front end and crushed it before the Old Man could adjust their direction.

"Because they need our help and because we must always help one another."

"Even strangers, Grandpa?"

But the Old Man did not answer as he edged the tank closer to the massive destruction of the Great Wreck.

"Let's stretch our legs for a moment and see how we might get around all these old cars and trucks."

They walked a ways from the rumbling tank, heading toward the massive wall of rusting and smashed vehicles that had piled up just beyond the last valley.

It's like coming home… but that doesn't seem right does it?

No, it doesn't. But it all began here. Here was the day after. After what I had once been or was becoming. I can't even remember now. But it was here on that last day when my car died.

"What happened here, Grandpa?"

"Most of the people you know in the village, we all met here on the day of the bombs."

"Did you plan to meet? Like did you know one another before the world ended?"

Before the world ended. That must seem like a strange phrase to her. Strange because the world has gone on.

"No. We were just all here on that day. Or we met on the one that followed as we walked east away from the bombs."

"What was it like?"

The Old Man looked at the two semis around which most of the wreckage centered.

I remember all of us getting out of our cars, trapped by the wreck, turning to see the mushroom cloud rising in the distance over Yuma behind us. I remember a woman screaming and then crying. Men were shouting.

"There was ash and dust. Fires on the horizons. Everyone was afraid."

Like we'd done something wrong. Broken something that could never be replaced. Committed an unpardonable crime.

"Were you afraid, Grandpa?"

"I can't remember."

She laughed.

He took out the map he'd found in the library.

"We can't go into Yuma. It's too hot from the bomb I saw go off there. But if we cut through those plains off to the north, we should pick up the old road heading to the Fort. I found that radio along the road leading there."

"Can I drive?"

"Not yet, you're still too small."

"There's another compartment in front of the tank with a couch where you lie down with a handlebar like a motorcycle. I sat in it, Grandpa."

"Could you reach the pedals?"

"Sort of, yes."

"Soon, though. Soon."

"Yes, soon."

Rusting cars, bashed and torn, crushed by careening fear-driven freight-laden semis with drivers who had watched the world end in their rearview mirrors, remained, spreading across the blistered road.

Into the desert.

Underneath the sand.

Rusting destruction piled long ago during the end of the world.

CHAPTER 12

"This is General Watt calling."

"We're here," said the Old Man into his mic after a moment of fumbling with the communications system.

"I have some good news," she said as a static squall crested and then was gone.

The Old Man stopped the tank.

They were on a small rise far out in the bowl of the desert. Somewhere within all the brown dust ahead lay the Proving Ground, the military base north of Yuma the villagers had avoided simply because it shared the same name of another place they had all seen destroyed.

I feel I don't know everything I need to know about what we're doing. But what am I supposed to ask her? This person, this General, she could be keeping the truth from me. And the others, Pancho, they could have been right all along.

For now, you must play the game according to its rules, my friend.

Maybe I should turn back.

"Our installation keeps a record of all the communications we tracked before the nets went completely offline. I've conducted a data search and found that a convoy carrying JP-9 arrived in the Yuma Proving Ground a week before the city of Yuma was destroyed. There is a chance that you may find the remains of that convoy somewhere within the facility."

"Would this JP-9 be usable? It's been forty years," asked the Old Man.

"If it still exists, then theoretically, yes. JP-9 was a prototype fuel rushed into production in the lead-up to the war. The Defense Department officials foresaw the need for a long-shelf-life fuel replacement and ordered as much of it as they were able to in the months prior to the war. There were some concerns over its use, but at this stage, it might be your only option. Unless someone took the time to use fuel stabilizers and conduct an additive removal process, the chances of finding a completely airtight fuel source are highly improbable. Your only other option will be clean diesel or kerosene. Again, these are not optimal sources, but the M-1 Abrams Main Battle Tank uses a multifuel vehicle system."

"What will these tankers look like?

"They resemble standard military fuel transports and there should be twelve of them. JP-9 had a projected eighty-year shelf life. Though this was never tested, reports indicate the lifespan was achievable."

Our whole journey depends on the word "reports."

"All right then, we'll try and find the tankers."

The Old Man listened to the tank, letting the massive turbine idle in its screaming high-pitched drone as he scanned the horizon once more with his binoculars.

There is no sign of the Proving Ground. We are nearing the end of our fuel. Soon, I'll have to pump our two fifty-gallon drums.

"Grandpa, below that mountain there's a sign sticking out of the ground. Maybe we should go and see what's written on it?"

It's a good thing she has come with me; I never would've seen that sign.

"I can't see the sign," said the Old Man. "Where is it?"

"See that mountain, the low one off to our left that's all shadowy and bumpy and rocky?"

"Yes."

"Right in there."

The Old Man found the sign through his binoculars but it was still too far away to read what, if anything at all, was still written upon it.

He took hold of the controls, pressed his foot onto the pedal slightly, and watched the terrain ahead. I have to keep the tank on the firmest ground. We cannot get stuck. If we do, there is no way to rescue the tank that I can think of right now.

Then maybe you will think of a way when you need to, my friend. Try not to worry about what has not happened to you. And may never happen at all.

"How did you see the sign?"

"I can make this target thing bigger with a dial on the side of it."

"I don't think we should touch those buttons. We don't want to make the gun go off."

"It also sees in the dark if you turn this knob," she continued.

"You're very smart. But we must be careful. We don't know everything yet. Still, you're very smart and I am proud of you. Much smarter than me."

When they reached the sign, the Old Man got down off the tank as his granddaughter watched him from the hatch she'd learned to open on the side of the tank. Again a new thing she understood about the tank and which he hadn't yet figured out.

The sign was sand scoured, and what words had once been written upon it were gone. But the Old Man could feel the hard remains of a road buried beneath the drifting sand under his boots. He took out his map and began to look around.

The Proving Ground must be that way. On the map they are north of Yuma.

There were people all alongside the highway that day, camped out, hoping to get to the airport, onto a plane, and flee. I remember the rumor that airplanes were waiting to take us all somewhere safe.

I remember wanting to believe the rumor was true, which is the terrible thing about rumors.

In his mind he could see Air Force One floating across the sky. Black smoke trailed from one of its engines, coming in to land one last time.

That was a long time ago.

Concentrate! That last day doesn't have anything to do with today. Today you must find these trucks that contain the fuel. If you don't find them, then you have failed.

The Old Man climbed back into the tank and checked the dosimeter.

The needle is still within the green, so we must be far enough away from Yuma to avoid its radiation.

Are you asking or hoping, my friend? Because all your hoping and asking depends on whether the weather compass that is your dosimeter still works.

They followed the mostly buried road as best they could. As it rounded the craggy hill his granddaughter had called a mountain, ahead of them ran the fading, spider silk line of a highway, and off in the distance, the Old Man could see buildings.

"Can you see those buildings through the target scope?" asked the Old Man.

"Gimme a second, Grandpa."

Suddenly the turret began to rotate as the gun barrel came to rest on the far horizon.

In every moment she figures out some new thing.

"Yes, they're brown and dirty. Low and flat."

"Do you see the tankers we're looking for?"

After a moment she said, "No. They're not there."

The Old Man waited, watching the tiny buildings shimmer in the heat of the fading afternoon.

"Do you see any people?"

"No. There's no one there."

The needle in the fuel gauge hovered just above empty when the Old Man finally shut down the tank amid the silent buildings being swallowed by the first low dunes of sand.

If we don't find these fuel tankers soon, I'll need to pump the drums and head back to Tucson.

He took his crowbar and exited the hatch stiffly, his granddaughter already lowering herself down onto the intersection they'd stopped in.

Flat, dust-brown uniform buildings from a different era stretched off in orderly lines down quiet, sand-swept streets. Murky windows hid what lay within. The air was dry and hot.

Signs and street markings had been scoured to meaninglessness. The outlines of once-lawns were everywhere. Within their borders, brown weeds withered under the final waves of the day's heat.

"Hello," the Old Man called out into the silence.

There was no reply and his voice was swallowed by the soft quiet of the dunes.

"It's spooky, Grandpa. I don't think anyone has been here for a long time."

They searched the small streets for any sign of the tankers. But there weren't any vehicles, of any kind.

Inside buildings they found dust-covered museums of life as it had once been. Coffee mugs forever waiting to be picked up lay next to piles of yellowed and desiccating paperwork on dry desks that felt sapped of any sturdiness they'd once possessed.

When the Old Man picked up a newspaper it came apart, and he was left holding only a few feathery scraps. He tried to read the paperwork without touching it. But anything meaningful was lost in a haze of military jargon that he could not understand. He scanned for the words "fuel" or "tankers."

There is no mention of either.

Outside, the day was turning to orange as the sun sank into the dusty west. Gray shadows threw themselves away from the flat military buildings. A light breeze came and shifted the sand a little closer to the surrendering outpost.

"So what do we do now, Grandpa?"

The Old Man stood in front of the largest building.

Probably the headquarters. They picked an idiot. They picked an idiot to come and rescue them. Remember the curse of the hot radio.

The Old Man walked back to the tank. He felt stupid and useless.

It isn't my fault the tankers aren't here.

"We'll camp outside tonight. It seems safe enough. In the morning, maybe we'll have a new idea."

"We're not giving up, are we, Grandpa?"

"No, we won't give up."

She seemed relieved and soon she was back in the tank handing out their bags and sleeping gear for the night.

"Can we have a fire?"

"Yes."

"A story?"

"Yes, of course."

"A ghost story?"

"I don't know any."

"I do."

"I don't like them before I go to sleep."

"Oh, Grandpa." She snorted and laughed.

Later, when their gear was out and they'd made camp in front of the ancient headquarters building, clearing a space along the broad sidewalk that ran through the ghost of the once-lawn, she said, "This is the best salvage trip ever, Grandpa."

"But we haven't salvaged anything yet."

"That doesn't mean it's not the best."

"Yes, you're right, it is the best."

They ate food as the stars began to appear, as the sky turned from orange to purple, then from purple to deep blue.

Night.

The Old Man watched, listening to his granddaughter talk about the tank. He watched for the satellite above. The one that General Watt was using to talk to them.

The satellites are still up there crossing the sky.

Like me crossing this land.

Which is something, if you think about it.

In the night, long after she had drifted to sleep listening to him tell about the time he had seen the fox walking down the old highway, he awoke. The fire was low. There is nothing left to burn but the weeds of this old lawn. Unless I want to pull the boards off these buildings, but the sound would wake her. Besides, the night is warm enough.

The Old Man rose.

Because the ground is too hard and I need to pee. And also because I am not sleeping.

Tomorrow we will have to turn back. Without fuel, it's just not possible to make it all the way. The tankers were most likely in Yuma, at the airport, when the bomb went off. Now, they are gone.

He tried to remember if he'd seen any such vehicles forty years ago on the last hot day of his country.

I can't remember. She will be disappointed.

He turned and crossed the ancient outline of the weed-choked lawn, hearing the dry crunch beneath his feet.

Why would the Army have lawns in the desert?

I guess that was the way the military did things. They imposed order and rules regardless of the situation and location.

They were crazy to try to grow grass in the desert.

But they did. As long as they had water they must've grown these lawns. The world was crazy then.

We were all crazy.

And then he knew where he would find fuel. Or at least he hoped to. Excited, he drifted back to sleep for what remained of the night as though he had found a missing puzzle piece or remembered something good that would happen. Excited that he would not disappoint her. Excited that the best salvage trip ever might go on for at least one more day.

The best ever.

In the morning they found where the military kept its gardening equipment. Ancient rakes, rusty shovels and time frozen hedge trimmers. Dust-choked oily lawn-mowers forever resting in dress-right-dress formation waited at the back of a large dark hangar. And off to one side, an immense storage tank of military-grade kerosene.

The Old Man drew off a little of the kerosene in a coffee mug he'd found in an office where clipboards hung neatly on the wall. He took it back outside as his granddaughter followed with questions, unsure of his game.

"Will it make the tank go, Grandpa?"

"If it's still good, it might."

The Old Man took a match from his pocket. He had loaded up on matches for this trip, remembering the last three matches inside the sewers beneath the hangar the wolves had chased him into. He struck the match and dropped it into the fuel. It caught and made a heavy chemical smell erupt in gray waves of smoke.

They rode the lumbering tank away, leaving the dry and dusty military post to itself and the years that must consume it. Off to the west, sand dunes rose in the afternoon heat.

Soon the sand dunes will arrive here as they march across the desert. Then they will cover this place and the kerosene that still remains inside that big storage tank.

But I will be gone by then.

Now we must hope there will be other fuel sources along the road. We may not find our river, my friend, but in a way the road is like that.

And what ocean will it lead to?

That night, the Old Man dreamed that he and Santiago were on a wide sea, under a hot sun, watching the flying fish leap from the water. Waiting for the big fish they would catch.

CHAPTER 13

Ahead we will find places I once knew long ago and have forgotten since. And I can only imagine what time and the bombs have done to them. I can only imagine that my past memories have changed to present nightmares.

Yes, my friend.

The tank trundled down a long, dirty, brown slope. In the distance they could see a strand of Highway 10 cutting the landscape in two.

It too is still there.

His granddaughter, ahead in the separate compartment containing the driver's couch, steered the tank across the crumbling dirt slope. Often he needed to remind her to slow down.

I feel like we've gone off the edge of something. The edge of everything we've ever known. Did you feel that way, Santiago, as you pulled at the oars farther and farther out into the gulf, watching the color of the water deepen until it was dark and not blue? Did you too feel like you were going off the edge of something?

And yet I knew it all once and long ago.

Memories of the cities of the West began to come and stand around the Old Man like mourners near an open grave.

You must forget all this melancholy and think only of the facts. You have enough fuel to reach China Lake. If you don't find fuel there, then crossing Death Valley into Area 51, will be impossible. You must follow this road until you come to an old tactical outpost set up alongside the highway. General Watt told us we would find it there.

"Grandpa, there's someone on the road ahead."

The Old Man scanned the horizon.

Far to their right, in the direction they must go, he could see the dark silhouette of a human.

It stood, unmoving in the late heat of the day.

The Old Man continued to watch the unmoving man-shaped shadow far down the cracked road as the tank heaved itself up onto the old highway. His granddaughter maneuvered the tank to point west at his instruction. A mile off, the lone figure remained unmoving beside the road they would follow.

I wish I knew how to work these optics like she has already learned to.

"Can you tell me what he looks like?" he asked her.

He knew she would be using her viewfinder.

"He's tall," she said after a moment. "Long dirty hair. Maybe a salvager, but not like anyone from our village. Oh, and he has a hat."

His mind stayed on the words "Not like anyone from our village."

The Old Man felt a cold river of fear sweep through him.

"Out there."

And…

Too many "Done" things.

"Let's move forward. But don't stop unless I tell you to, okay?"

"Okay."

I am afraid of this stranger on the road. Why?

We know why, my friend; it's just that we're not always willing to be honest with ourselves when we must. It is better to admit that you are afraid now than to pretend you are not.

The dark man-shadow, before the setting sun, seemed to lean toward them and out into the blistered highway as they approached. As they closed the distance between them the Old Man saw the shadow revealed. Saw him clearly as one might see something dead beside the road and want to look away in that passing instant of speed. His face was gaunt. Sun stretched by time and all the years since the end of the world. All the years on the road.

Worn rawhide boots. Faded dusty pants. A long coat made of license plates stitched together. A thick staff he leaned on heavily, though his frame was spare. Two small skulls dangled from its topmost tip. He wore a faded wide and weak-brimmed hat under which shining hawk-like eyes watched the Old Man. Had watched since they'd first appeared, the Old Man was sure of that.

He's a killer.

The Old Man could feel the slightest decrease in their acceleration.

"No!" he shouted into his mic. "Keep going!"

The tank lurched forward, and as they hurtled past the Roadside Killer, the vessel of all things unclean, the gaunt man raised one bony arm from the sleeve of his license-plate mail coat and extended a claw-like hand that might have been a plea.

The Old Man knew his granddaughter would be staring, wide-eyed, as they raced past, throwing grit and gravel, drawing up the road behind them.

Do not look back.

The Old Man rose in the hatch, watching the highway ahead.

"Why didn't we stop, Grandpa? He looked like he needed help."

Do not look back.

"Grandpa?"

"Because," said the Old Man after a moment. "Because we must help those inside the bunker."

It was later, in the early evening, beyond a fallen collection of wind-shattered buildings the map once marked as the town of Quartzite, where they buttoned up the tank for the night. In the dark they'd settled into their bags, feeling the tank sway in the thundering wind that had risen up out of nowhere late that afternoon.

"Why didn't we help him, Grandpa?"

The Old Man listened to the sand strike the sides of the tank and thought of some acid they'd once drained from a car battery to weaken the lock on a tractor trailer they'd salvaged.

The wind sounds like acid tonight.

"Not everyone needs our help."

"But some people, the people inside General Watt's bunker, do?"

"Yes, they do."

And I wonder if they truly do. How do I know this isn't some game, a complex game, to draw us all into a trap?

You don't know, my friend.

"How did you know the man today didn't really need our help?"

"I just did."

And how will I teach you to know such things when I am gone?

"So we only help those who really need our help, Grandpa?"

"Yes. Only those whom we can tell really need our help."

I will have to think of a better way to teach her to know how and when to help, but not tonight. I cannot think of a way tonight.

Soon she was asleep and the Old Man lay awake for a long time listening to the sand dissolving the tank, and when he slept he dreamed of the cities of the West and the stranger beside the road and serial killers and empty diners where there was no food anymore.

CHAPTER 14

"You're just two thousand meters away from the last known location of the tactical command post." General Watt's transmission was breaking up within intermittent bouts of white noise. "I have not been able to get a satellite with a working camera over the location. There are only a few operating satellites remaining, otherwise I might have been able to give you better data regarding the container's location."

They were passing through a wide sprawl of ancient warehouses that rose up like giant monoliths from the desert floor surrounding Barstow.

"What will this container look like?" asked the Old Man, hoping General Watt's transmission would be understood.

"Green…" Static. "Size of a box…"

The Old Man asked the General to repeat the description, but the electronic snowstorm he listened within contained no reply. The satellite she had been bouncing the transmission off had finally disappeared far over the western horizon. The General had told them she wouldn't be able to reach them again for another twelve hours.

The Old Man watched the silent place of massive box-like buildings. From this distance they seemed little more than dirty tombstones, but as his granddaughter maneuvered the tank up the road, he could see the telltale signs of time and wind. Metal strips had been ripped away in sections, as if peeled from the superstructure of the buildings. A place like this would have been an obvious choice for salvagers. But this is California. Everyone fled California when all the big cities had been hit. L.A. before I'd even left. San Diego a day later. But there was no sign of the box General Watt said they must find.

And what is in this box?

The Old Man shut down the tank.

They were exactly where General Watt had said they would find the tactical command post. And somewhere nearby would be the container, but there was nothing. No command post.

Dusty, wide alleyways led between the ancient warehouses.

If it was a small box, what would've prevented someone from merely carrying it away?

Then it must be a big box, my friend.

"Maybe it's in one of these buildings, Grandpa."

They left the tank, feeling the increasing heat of the day rise from the ancient pavement of the loading docks.

Inside they found darkness through which dusty shafts of orange light shot from torn places in the superstructure. The Old Man clutched his crowbar tightly, stepping ahead of his granddaughter. *There is a story here. A story of salvage. If you tell the story, you'll find the salvage.* He waited, letting his eyes adjust to the gloom. *You know part of the story. The General told you that part.*

The days of the bombs had begun. Los Angeles was gone. But the Chinese, which was news to me because that must have happened after Yuma, were invading the western United States. The military, the Third Armored Division, or so General Watt said, staged its forces here in the deserts of Southern California. Supplies were air-dropped in as well as tanks and soldiers. They would counterattack the Chinese on American soil.

Imagine that.

At least they were supposed to have. But what happened in those days of bombs and EMPs and the rumors that spread like a super virus is not clearly known and all the General can tell me is what was known. What was known before the jury-rigged, EMP-savaged communications networks that were able to route traffic through the bunker at Cheyenne Mountain collapsed. What was known before everything went dark.

And after?

The success of the counter-attack?

The tanks and soldiers?

The Chinese?

During those first days as we walked east, away from the Great Wreck, I had thought the world had ended. But in truth we knew so little of the story because who really knew everything that was going on and how could they tell us as we carried our possessions in our hands along the highway. The world had gone on ending long after we thought it was dead.

Nothing is known clearly now, and it is no longer important on this hot day forty years later.

The important matter for today is to find a container that was air-dropped and went wide of the landing zone as soldiers and tanks readied themselves to meet the enemy. The container's GPS locator broadcast for years. But even that fading signal ended a long time ago.

"What's inside?" the Old Man had asked General Watt.

"I'll need to explain that later. I only have a limited time to communicate with you before the satellite I'm currently hijacking disappears over the Pacific horizon. Find the container and get it open. I'll explain what you'll need to do once you've obtained the supplies."

Why do I have the feeling bad news has made an appointment?

Because you are cautious, my friend. And right now is the time to be cautious. So if you are cautious, you are doing well.

If we were on the boat I dreamed of last night, Santiago, seeing the flying fish jump, watching our lines, waiting for the big fish that was like a monster to come up from the deep to fight him together, you would say such things to me when my confidence was low.

Confidence can work both ways, my friend.

Yes, there is that.

That is not important now. Right now you need to find this box, my friend. Later you can decide how you feel about the bad news that you fear might be inside.

There is a story here also. A story of salvage.

The Old Man searches the gloom of the warehouse and sees very little. He smells wood smoke and decay from long ago.

Dead animals. Dried blood. Huddled bodies. Decay.

"Go to the tank, please, and bring me back the flashlight," he whispers to his granddaughter.

When she returns, he scans the interior of the warehouse with the beam. Its light is weak and barely penetrates the dark. All batteries are old now in these many years after the bombs.

They walk forward into the gloom. She has brought a flashlight for herself also and he watches her beam move with energy, like her, never staying in any one place for too long, also like her. His beam is slow and searching. He finds the remains of the campfire in the center of the warehouse before she does. It was a large fire.

Around it are storage racks and iron beams, arranged as though many might sit and watch the fire through long winter nights that must have seemed unending and as though the entire world was frozen forever.

I know those nights.

I know those fire-watching nights.

I am always hungry when I think back on them and the howling wind that was constant.

You were very hungry then.

The whole world must have been hungry.

But there is no box here.

They search the building, even shining their lights into the high recesses of the fractured roof. There is nothing.

In the next building, the center most of the three, they find the remains of the same style bonfire, and she, his granddaughter, on the farthest wall, at the back of the massive warehouse, finds the drawings.

Taken in parts they are merely a collection of scribbling.

Stick figure people. A Man-Wolf. Slant-Eyed Invaders waving guns. Mushroom clouds. Stick figure people who wear the wide-brimmed hat. Like that Roadside Killer. Stick figure people with spikes that come from the tops of their misshapen heads. Many dead Spike Heads. The bonfire. The Hat People stare into it.

"Who are they, Grandpa?"

Her voice startles him in the gloom beyond the cone of light he stares into, trying to know the meanings of these scribblings.

"I don't know."

He follows the drawings from left to right and finds no mention of the container.

He finds they are a people. A people who wore hats like the one the Roadside Killer wore. A people surrounded by decay who waited through the long winter after the bombs and stared into fire.

A people like his village. The same and different.

Mushroom clouds.

The Man-Wolf leads them all away.

Leads them toward the Slant-Eyed Invaders who wave guns and trample over other stick figures beneath their stick feet.

"I don't know," he says again, his voice swallowed within the quiet.

And he realizes he is all alone.

"Where are you?" he calls out.

From high above he hears her voice.

"I found a ladder, Grandpa." She is straining to pull herself up. "If it leads to the roof, I can look around and see where the box is."

He shines his light about and can see nothing of her.

His mind thinks only of rusted metal and snapping bolts that pull away from crumbling walls with a dusty *smuph*.

And falling.

A moment later he hears metal banging on metal and knows it to be the sound of a crowbar smashing against a door. The sound is a familiar cadence to him and reminds him for a moment of the comforts one finds in what one does. The music of salvage.

He shines his light high into the rafters and finds her against the ceiling.

She is so small.

She is so high up.

I regret all of this.

Her crowbar gives that final smash he knows so well, when the wielder knows what must give way will give way with the next strike, and a frame of light shoots down within the darkness, illuminating the Old Man.

"I'm through, Grandpa!"

No one will ever stop you will they?

"I'm going up, Grandpa."

Please be safe!

A few minutes later, the longest minutes of the Old Man's life, he can hear her voice shouting down into the darkness in which he stands.

"I see it, Grandpa! It's on the roof of another building. It's very big."

Later, after her descent, in which he can think of nothing but her falling and knowing he will try to catch her and knowing further that both his arms will be broken and that it doesn't matter as long as he saves her so he must catch her, they climb again onto the roof of the other building.

The yawning blue sky burns above their heads as they crawl out onto the wide hot roof.

The roof is bigger than a football field.

Along a far edge, the container, its parachute little more then scrappy silk rags, sinks into the roof.

The Old Man approaches cautiously, feeling the thinness of the roof beneath his feet. He waves for her to stand back and let him go on alone.

When she obeys, he proceeds, one cautious foot after the other, ready to fling himself backward onto the burning floor of the roof.

At the container he finds the heavy lock.

He knows this kind of lock. He has broken it many times and if one knows how to use a crowbar, the design of the container and the position of the lock will do most of the work.

The Old Man knows.

Forgetting the precarious and illusory roof, thinking only of salvage, blinded by salvage, he breaks the lock.

The doors swing open on a rusty bass note groan.

The Old Man smells the thick scent of cardboard.

Inside, stacked to the ceiling of the container are thin boxes, one lying atop another, long and flat.

He takes hold of the topmost and drags it away from the container onto the roof and back a bit where he feels it will be safer to stand.

Bending over the box he reads, seeing his granddaughter's little girl shadow lengthen next to his, as the day turns past noon. He reads the words the military once printed on these long flat boxes.

"Radiation Shielding Kit, M-1 Abrams MK-3, 1 ea."

CHAPTER 15

"By the time communication with the outside world had completely failed," explained General Watt after they'd re-established contact, "fourteen military-grade nuclear weapons had already been used within Colorado alone. I determined that it would be beneficial to you and your team to obtain a shielding kit in order to protect you, once you enter Colorado."

The Old Man watched the radio, thinking.

He held the mic in his trembling fingers, his weathered thumb as far away as possible from the transmit button.

"We have no idea…" General Watt paused, her voice tired. "I have no idea how bad things are above. But I wanted you to have some protection. Just in case. That's the reason I directed you to obtain the Radiation Shielding Kit."

"And was that also the reason you didn't tell us what we were going to find until we found it?"

You know the reason, my friend. You are angry at someone because they lied to you in order to save their life.

I am angry because…

Because of that, my friend. Because of that, and nothing more.

"Is there anything else you're not telling us, General?" asked the Old Man.

"No," replied General Watt. "There is nothing. I know very little beyond our limited access to a failing satellite network. In truth…"

Pause.

Static.

The Old Man saw the satellite in his mind, aging, drifting steadily out over the Pacific horizon once more.

"The truth, General."

"Call me Natalie."

"The truth, Natalie," said the Old Man softening his tone.

"The truth is, I don't even know if this plan will work. It is merely our last chance. I didn't want to tell you about the Radiation Shielding Kit because I estimated that you might not want to become involved if you knew there was a possibility of being exposed to high levels of radiation. Though I have no contact with those on the surface, I hypothesize that a fear of radiation poisoning has evolved into a healthy respect, if not outright avoidance policy, among postwar communities."

Sometimes she sounds so detached. As if the world is little more than mathematical chances and equations that must be solved so that an answer can be found.

And hoped for, my friend. After so many years of living underground, what else might she have except some numbers that give her hope?

And if I know she is lying to me, why are we continuing down this road?

Because you don't know if she is lying to you.

"All right, General," said the Old Man. "I'm sorry. Thank you for trying to protect us."

I should turn back now. We…

"Natalie."

"Natalie," agreed the Old Man.

Natalie.

"The shielding kit will protect you through most of southern Colorado. All you have to do is get close to the collapsed backdoor entrance and then aim the Laser Target Designator at the back of the mountain. We'll do the rest."

The rest.

Do I want to know what the rest is? Not today. There has been too much already for just today.

That is the love of letting things go for now.

The day that follows is hot and dusty.

They pass through the crumbling remains of eastern Southern California.

All day long they maneuver through scattered debris, time-frozen traffic jams, and long-collapsed overpasses while the Old Man scans the western horizon.

I was raised over there, beyond those mountains that stand in the way, near the sea. Like you, Santiago.

I have not thought of those places since the bombs. Which is not true.

In the days after, I thought of them all the time.

And then you married your wife and forgot them, my friend.

Yes. There was the work of salvage and you had to concentrate to dig out its story. There was no time for where I had come from. There was no time to think of where I could never go again. There was salvage. My wife. Our shack. My son. His family. My granddaughter. They were my salvage and they replaced all those burned-up places that were gone.

"Grandpa, how will we know where the 395 is?"

I thought only of them, my new family, in the days that followed the bombs.

"Roads lead to roads," he said. "If we follow this big road, we will find another road. In time we will find this little highway once called the 395."

The dull hum of the tank's communications system.

"Some always leads to more, right, Grandpa?"

"Right."

Some always leads to more.

That night they camp near the off-ramp at the intersection where the big highway spends itself into the untouchable west and the little ribbon of road the map names the 395 drops off into the lowest places of the earth. Death Valley.

They eat rations heated in the Old Man's blue percolator and sit around a campfire made of ancient wood pulled from the wreckage of a fallen house built long before the bombs and well before the science that would reveal their terribleness.

Yucca trees, spiky and dark, alien against the fading light, surround them and the silent tank.

The Old Man thinks of the fuel gauge and its needle just below the halfway point.

The drums atop the tank are empty.

If you think all night you will not sleep, my friend.

Natalie says there will be fuel, of a sort, in China Lake.

General Watt.

Natalie.

She sounds old. Like me.

"Grandpa, why do they call it the Death Valley?"

She has been quiet for most of the afternoon. Her questions have been few, as though the place that makes all her questions is overwhelmed by the road and our adventure upon it.

Maybe the world is bigger than she ever imagined, my friend.

"It was called Death Valley even before I was born."

"So not because of the bombs?"

"No. When people first crossed this country I guess they didn't like Death Valley, so they chose a bad name for it."

"Did everyone avoid it?"

The Old Man tries to remember.

Instead, he remembers other things.

Ice cream.

A place he worked at.

Steam.

The beach.

"No, I remember people went there on vacation. It was a place people needed to go and see what was there."

She watches the fire.

He can see each question forming deep within her.

I can almost snatch them out of the air above her head.

Tonight, when I sleep, I would like to really sleep. Only sleep, and no nightmares.

Especially the one nightmare.

Yes.

The one in which she is calling you as you die, as you abandon her.

As you fall.

As you leave, my friend.

Yes. That one.

No, Grandpa, I need you.

Yes.

"Will it be dangerous there?" she asks.

The Old Man searches the night for one of Natalie's satellites.

"No. No more than any other place we have been."

"I'm not afraid, Grandpa. Just the name, it's a little scary."

"Yes. Just a little."

She laughs.

I know what it is like to be afraid of a name and also a nameless thing. My sleeping nightmare is like Death Valley to her.

"Since we might be the first people to cross Death Valley in a long time, we could give it a new name. One that isn't so scary."

She stops chewing and he watches the machine inside her turn. The machine that makes an endless supply of questions. The gears and cogs that labor constantly so that she becomes who she will become in each moment and the next.

Sometimes she is so exact.

It might be against her rules to change the name.

To change the game.

No, Grandpa. I need you.

I would change that if I could.

"What could we call it?" she asks.

She is willing to rewrite history. Willing to make something new. Willing to change the rules of the game.

"I don't know. I guess… when we get there we could see what we think of it and then come up with a new name. What do you say about that?"

They both hear a bat crossing the lonely desert, flying up the desolate highway, beating its leathery wings in the twilight. Tomorrow we will follow him beyond those rocks and down into the desert at the bottom of the world.

"I would like that, Grandpa. Yes."

In the dark, the Old Man is falling into even darker depths.

I was falling.

No, Grandpa. I need you.

Yes.

The nightmare.

If only I could change it like we're going to change the name of Death Valley.

The Old Man drinks cold water from his canteen.

His granddaughter sleeps, her face peaceful.

No, Grandpa. I need you.

The Old Man lies back and considers the night above, though his mind is really thinking of, and trying to forget, the nightmare all at once.

I wish I were free of it.

I wish I could change the rules of its game.

If she called me by another name, then the nightmare wouldn't frighten me anymore. Then, I would remember in the dream that she calls me by another name and I could hold on to that.

And thinking of names, his eyes close and the sky above marches on and turns toward dawn.

CHAPTER 16

The morning sky is a clean, almost electric bright and burning blue. The desert is wide, stretching toward the east and the north. Small rocky hills loom alongside the road.

They have finished their breakfast and make ready to leave.

The Old Man starts the auxiliary power unit and a moment later, the tank. He watches the needles and gauges.

What could I do if there was a problem with any one of them?

Natalie might know something.

We should get as close to Death Valley as we can today. Then cross it tomorrow.

He watches his granddaughter lower herself into the driver's seat. She smiles and waves from underneath the oversize helmet and a moment later her high soprano voice is in his ear.

"Can I drive today, Grandpa?"

"Stay on the road and when we come to an obstacle, like a burned-up car or a truck that has flipped across the lanes, stop and I'll tell you which way to go around, okay?"

"Okay, Grandpa."

They cross onto the highway and she pivots the tank left and toward the north. She overcorrects and for a moment they are off-road.

"Sorry, Grandpa!"

"Don't worry. You're doing fine."

She gets them back on the road and the tank bumps forward with a sudden burst of acceleration as she adjusts her grip.

"Slow and steady," he reminds her.

"I know, Grandpa."

They drive for a while, crossing through a high desert town whose wounded windows gape dully out on the dry, brown landscape and prickly stunted yuccas as peeling paint seems to fall away in the sudden morning breeze of the passing tank.

"Are you excited about finding a new name for the valley we'll cross tomorrow?"

She doesn't reply for a moment as the tank skirts around a twisted tractor trailer flipped across the road long ago. Inside, the Old Man can see bleached and cracked bones within the driver's cab.

"Yes, I am."

The dull hum of the communications system fills the space between their words. Each time they speak, they sound suddenly close to each other.

"If you were going to give me a new name, what would it be?"

The dull hum.

Wheels turning.

"Why would I do that, Grandpa?"

Why would you indeed?

Because I am frightened that I might die and leave you abandoned out here, all alone.

Because a nightmare torments me and calls me by the same name you do.

Because I am trying to change the rules of the game. And.

Because I love you.

"Oh, I don't know," says the Old Man. "Sometimes 'Grandpa' makes me feel old."

"But that's who you are. You're Grandpa!"

Silence.

If we can change the name of a valley, can we change my name?

"I don't know," he hears her say. "You're not so old, Grandpa."

"I know."

"But I guess… I guess if you wanted to be something else, I could call you… Poppa, maybe?"

I like that.

If I were Poppa, then when I was stuck in the nightmare, I could remember my new name.

And then I would remember it is just a nightmare, and that all I need to do is wake up.

I don't ever want to be anything else but Poppa.

"I like Poppa. It sounds young. Like I'm full of beans."

Silence.

They start up the grade that climbs into rocky wastes beyond the fallen buildings of the little town that once was and is now no more.

Where did all the people go? To our west is the Central Valley, Bakersfield, and the Grapevine. I remember passing by those fields on long highways. Long drives are some of my first memories. We had family in Northern California.

Fried chicken.

Summer corn.

White gravy with pepper.

Sweet tea.

The Kern River.

There was a song about the Kern River. My father always sang it when he thought of home. When he found himself in places far away, places where the big jets he flew had taken him. Places not home.

"Poppa?"

The Old Man felt the heat of those long-gone kitchens and early Saturday evenings when the Sacramento Delta breeze came up through the screen doors. Evenings that promised such things would always remain so.

How did they promise?

The Old Man thought.

Because when you are young and in that moment of food and family and time, you cannot imagine things might ever be different.

Or even gone someday.

"Poppa!"

That's me. I'm Poppa now.

"Yes. What is it?"

"Just practicing. You need to practice too if you're going to be Poppa now."

"Okay. I'll be ready next time."

"Okay, Grandp — I mean… okay, Poppa."

Fried chicken.
Saturday dinners.
The heat of the oven.
The Kern River.
Poppa.

The day was at its brutal zenith when they saw the Boy crawling out of the cracked, parched hardpan toward the road. Their road. Dragging himself forward. Dragging himself through the wide stretch of dust and heat that swallowed the horizon.

"Poppa, what do we do?"

She has taken to Poppa. She's smarter and faster than anyone I ever knew.

"Poppa!"

I don't want to stop and help this roadside killer.

He thought of the drawings inside the warehouses.

He thought of what the world had become.

He thought of the Horde.

The Roadside Killer.

But you told her, 'The world has got to become a better place.'

"We'll stop and see what this person needs."

The Old Man grabbed his crowbar from its place inside the tank.

They stopped the tank and climbed down onto the hot road, feeling its heat melt through the soles of their shoes, new shoes from long ago that they had taken from the supplies Sergeant Major Preston had stocked. The Boy was young. Just a few years older than his granddaughter.

One side of him was rippled by thick, long muscles.

The other is thin, almost withered, like that other boy who chased me across the wasteland.

The Boy was mumbling to himself through lips that bled and peeled. His skin, though dark, was horribly burned, even blistering. On his back was an old and faded rucksack. He wore tired, beaten boots that must have once been maroon colored but were now little more than worn-through leather. He wore dusty torn pants and a faded and soft red flannel shirt. At his hip, a steel-forged tomahawk hung from an old belt. And in the Boy's long hair, attached to a leather thong, a gray-and-white feather, broken and bent along its spine, lay as if waiting for the merest wind to come and catch it up.

He is like that other boy who tried to murder me.

The Old Man looked down and saw his granddaughter's big dark eyes watching him. Watching to see what he would do next.

Inside them he saw worry.

And…

Inside them he saw mercy.

They knelt down beside the Boy.

The Old Man let the crowbar fall onto the road.

"Who is he, Poppa?"

"I don't know. But he needs our help. He's been out here far too long."

"I'll get some water, Poppa."

The Boy began to cry.

Shaking, he convulsed.

Crying, he wheezed, begging the world not to be made of stone, begging the world to give back what it had taken from him.

"Who am I? sobbed the Boy.

"I think he's asking, who is he, Poppa!" said his granddaughter as though it were all a game of guessing and she had just won.

The Old Man held the shaking, sobbing Boy and poured water onto his cracked and sunburned lips in the shadow of the rumbling tank.

"He doesn't know who he is, Poppa. Who is he?"

"He's just a boy," said the Old Man, his voice trembling.

"Who am I now?" sobbed the Boy.

The Old Man held the Boy close, willing life, precious life, back into the thin body.

"You're just a boy, that's all. Just a boy," soothed the Old Man, almost in tears.

The Old Man held the Boy tightly.

"You're just a boy," he repeated.

"Just a boy."

CHAPTER 17

The Boy lay on the floor of the tank atop the Old Man's sleeping bag.

When they'd lowered him through the wide hatch after helping him up from the hot crumble of the road, he'd mumbled, "M-One Abrams," and after that he had said nothing.

Now the Boy lay on the cool floor of the tank as the Old Man ran the air-conditioning system at full power. The Old Man wondered about fluids and their replacement and how much farther the tank could go without such vital substance.

They crossed broken landscapes and high rocky hills where the thin remains of fading white observatories still waited for someone to come and look at the stars.

The Old Man could feel unseen eyes watching them as they passed such forlorn places.

They drove through an intersection where large slabs of metal and iron, long ago fused into uselessness, lay behind a crumpled fence alongside the road.

There were once many power transformers here. During those hot days near the end, when the systems began to collapse as unchecked energy surged toward its maximum output, wild power must have flooded through the lines, overloading overridden breakers, and suddenly everything began to melt in volumes of hot white heat. That is the story of this place.

Its story of salvage.

They moved on, leaving the slag and molten-made shapes to write their questions in the desert sands.

The Boy continued to sleep and once, when the Old Man looked down from his place in the open hatch, he could see the Boy, eyes open, watching him. The Old Man leaned down and handed him his canteen, keeping his other hand out of sight, ready with the crowbar.

Is he like that other savage boy?

The other boy who chased me across the desert.

The boy who chased my flare out into the night and must still lie at the bottom of the pass.

You would tell me, Santiago, that it was nothing personal. You would tell me that so I am not bothered by the memory of it.

It was nothing personal, my friend.

The Boy drank, swallowed thickly, and laid his head back down on the sleeping bag, exhausted. A moment later, his eyes were closed and the Old Man wondered if the Boy was sleeping and what he dreamed of.

Twisting hills and rocky ravines wound through ancient islands of mining equipment rusting long before the bombs. Stone outlines blackened by fire showed where once a village might have done business by the side of the thin ribbon of road.

Such times are long gone now. Now there is only the wind and burnt stone lying amid the red dirt and whispering brush of dry brown stick.

"We'll stop here for the night," said the Old Man over the intercom. A moment later his granddaughter pivoted the tank sharply to the left and pulled into a vacant lot banked by the fire-blackened stones of what had once been two separate buildings.

The Old Man shut down the tank, climbed out and down onto the hard red dirt that glimmered with broken glass and quartzite, his granddaughter meeting him near the massive treads.

"How'd I do today, Grandpa… I mean, Poppa? How'd I do?"

"The best. Better than I could've ever done. Better than anybody ever."

"What'll we do with that boy, Poppa?" she whispered, concentrating hard on remembering the Old Man's new name.

"I don't know yet."

Silence.

"We can't just leave him, right?"

"No, we can't," said the Old Man after a short pause.

There was still a little daylight left and the Old Man turned to setting up their camp for the night. He built a circle of stones for a fire pit, gathered dry sticks with his granddaughter, and considered finding some snake for fresh meat. But in the end they simply heated more of their rations.

In the dark, as they watched the orange glow of the coals and a thin trickle of red flame that leapt upward, the Boy exited the tank, a dark shadow against the blue twilight of the coming night. He limped to the fire and took a seat on the hard ground.

The Old Man watched the Boy and then saw his granddaughter watching him also.

The Old Man took the plate of food he'd made for the Boy and handed it across the fire.

The Boy looked at it for a long moment, dipped his hand into it, and brought the food up to his cracked lips. He chewed slowly, painfully.

The Old Man watched the unused fork he'd given the Boy with the tin pie plate.

The Old Man sighed. He felt overwhelmed by all the questions he had for the Boy.

None seemed right.

None seemed appropriate.

That there was a great weight, a sadness even, that hung over the Boy who stared listlessly into the depths of the fire, that much was evident.

"Thank you," said the Boy. His voice hollow. Deep.

The Old Man smiled.

"You're welcome."

"Where'd you come from?" erupted from his granddaughter. The Old Man winced.

The Boy turned to her. He smiled sadly.

Did he shake his head?

"Everywhere," mumbled the Boy.

"Oh wow," she squealed. "We're just from…" She barely caught the look the Old Man briefly gave her. "We live in a village alongside the Old Highway. Have you been to the cities?"

Have you been to the cities? She must wonder what was in them. Imagine things about them as though they were a fantasy place. A palace of dreams, maybe.

Why wouldn't she?

The Boy nodded.

He continued to chew slowly, painfully.

"Which ones?" she asked.

She is like Big Pedro when he gambled. She cannot restrain herself.

The Boy turned his gaze back to the fire.

"Washington, D.C., Little Rock, Reno, Detroit, and…"

But he didn't finish.

He watched the fire.

But he is not watching the fire, my friend. He is there, wherever that city is that he cannot name.

"Here, drink a little; it will help you recover," said the Old Man when the pause had become both long and uncomfortable.

The Boy put his food down. He took the canteen with his good hand. The withered hand was heaved into position as he grasped the cap with the good hand and twisted. Then the canteen was transferred back to the good hand and the Boy took a long pull, his Adam's apple bobbing thickly in the firelight.

A night owl hooted, its call lonely and inviting.

When the Boy finished, he handed the canteen back to the Old Man. "Thank you."

Silence.

"When I was young," began the Old Man, "I lived in a city. At least I thought it was a city. It was really just a town on the outskirts of a big city. But that town was my whole world."

The Old Man placed a few more sticks on the fire.

"Sometimes I think back about those times. There used to be nights when the town was quiet, when I was young, and my friends and I would roam the streets in cars. We would eat fast food and play video games. We saw movies."

The Old Man looked at his granddaughter.

She loves these stories and I don't know why. I have explained fast food and video games and movies. But they are just words.

She will never know those places. Those things.

She will have to make do with mere words.

Still, she loves these stories, my friend.

"Do you know those things?" asked the Old Man of the Boy.

The Boy nodded.

Someone has told him of the things that once were.

"So," the Old Man continued, "these things were my world, and if you would've asked me at the time what the world was like, what its shape was, I guess I might have described it that way."

He nodded at both of them.

"Even when I was older, just a few years beyond both of you, I knew the world had many places in it and I had even traveled to some of those places expecting them to be different. But life in one place is much the same as another. Life is life, despite your street address."

The Old Man smiled at their blank faces.

You never told her about street addresses.

Didn't I?

No, maybe not, my friend.

"Well," said the Old Man, lost for a moment. "Life is life. All my nights and days would be with friends or in places that had water and rooms and pizza and video games. I thought I would always see movies. Probably until the day I died. Then the bombs fell."

The Old Man watched the fire.

"Since that time I have had many nights out in the desert. Out under the stars. Nights I never would've imagined when I was young like you and spent every night in the same room I had grown up in."

There were cars on the walls.

Yes.

And comic books.

Yes, also.

"Poppa?"

Pause.

I am not in that room anymore. Not for a long time and I wonder what became of it.

What do you think happened to it, my friend?

"Poppa!"

"Well, it is good to be here," said the Old Man, returning. "Under the stars tonight, with you." He looked at his granddaughter. "What I'm trying to say is that I never thought my life would lead here, and that I would be happy. Do you understand?"

She thought for a long moment.

Then…

"I just want to go everywhere, Poppa."

After a moment the Old Man nodded, concealing his fear that one day she might actually do that. Concealing his fear of those days and places and the people that must live there now in the "everywhere" of all the places she would go.

The Old Man turned to the Boy who watched the both of them.

He almost becomes invisible.

It's like he's barely there.

Like he's fading away.

"What are all those cities like? What is it like out there in the world?" asked the Old Man, waving his hand across the night sky as if to cover every known place.

As if to wipe away his sudden fear.

Pause.

"All gone," said the Boy. "There is nothing left. And the world…"

Pause.

The Boy looked into the eyes of the Old Man.

The Old Man saw none of the malice he'd seen in that other boy, that savage boy who'd chased him across the desert with a parking meter for a club.

Instead he saw an emptiness within the Boy's green eyes where a fire that once burned had gone out. Like an old campfire gone cold long ago. Or a wreck from Before, still lying on the highway waiting for someone to come and cry out with horror.

And grief.

Like this campfire will be after we leave tomorrow and for the years to come. Just tired ashes fading in the sun and disappearing with the wind.

"… the world," said the Boy. "Is gone."

CHAPTER 18

"General Watt? Natalie, are you there?" In the night the Old Man sits in the tank, feeling the cold metal against his sunburned skin.

The nightmare that awoke him, the one of falling and hearing his granddaughter say *No, Grandpa. I need you*, has come again. And even though he reminds himself that she calls him Poppa now and that the terror has no power over him, should have no power, that he has changed the rules of the game and changed his name so the devil cannot find him, still he lies awake.

He slips away from the camp to urinate on ancient blackened stones that were once someone's home, someone's business, who can know anymore? Then he drinks cold water made pleasant by the night's cool air.

I will think of tomorrow and the fuel we need to find at China Lake.

And when he cannot think of or envision what they might find there, he leaves his bedroll, knowing he will not return for the night and starts the APU on the tank.

He checks the radio frequency though he knows he has not touched it and can think of no reason why he should have.

"General Watt? Natalie? Come in."

The Old Man wonders if the white noise he hears as he waits for a response from the General, from Natalie, is always there, waiting even when no one is listening.

How many years are there between these few brief signals since the bombs?

"Yes. I'm here," says General Watt.

Natalie.

The Old Man finds an unexpected comfort in the woman's voice. Older, softer, yes. Tired even. But a comfort he did not expect to find.

And yet you must have known it was there, my friend, or why else would you be calling her in the middle of the night?

He watches the barely red coals and the sleeping forms of his unmoving granddaughter on one side of the fire near his empty bedroll, and the Boy, his good arm thrown over his face, his body twisted as if tormented even in sleep.

"We're not too far from China Lake, General… I mean, Natalie."

"Good. I have more information for you on where to locate a possible fuel source. I planned on waiting until morning to contact you. I was estimating that you might still be asleep."

"I can't sleep tonight."

"Why, are there problems? Is everything all right?"

"No. I mean… Yes. I mean… we picked up a passenger today. But now we're proceeding on to China Lake. I'd expected this trip to be much more difficult than it has been so far."

"Then why can't you sleep?"

"I guess… because I'm old."

"How old are you?"

"I was twenty-seven when the bombs fell. How long ago was that?"

"Forty years, six months, eight days, seventeen hours, and seven minutes since the nuclear detonation that occurred on Manhattan Island in New York City."

The Old Man moved numbers around in his head.

We had lost track of time back in the village.

There had been more important things to do in those days after the bombs than to keep track of meaningless days.

I am old now.

"How old are you?" he asked.

"I am one year older than you," replied Natalie.

Pause.

"Do you remember…?" asked the Old Man.

"Yes. I remember everything."

Pause.

"Does it… bother you… to remember what's gone?"

"No," said Natalie. General Watt.

"Why?"

Pause.

"Because I still have hope that things can get better."

The Old Man listened.

"I have hope that you will come and set us free from this place. I have hope that one day every good thing that was lost will return again. I have hope, and there is no room inside my hope for the past."

"Oh," said the Old Man and realized that his days, his story, this journey, were not just about him and his granddaughter who was his most precious and best friend. Or even the Boy they'd found alongside the road who seemed hollow and fading from a worn and thin world. This journey was about someone else. Someone who needed help. Someone who has only hope in the poverty of what remains.

"Every day is the chance that tomorrow might be better," said General Watt.

Natalie.

CHAPTER 19

Piles of volcanic rock rise to the height of small mountains as the tank crests the barren desert plateau. Below them, the entire world seems to slope downward to some unseen terminus that must surely await them.

Now we must fall to the bottom of the earth. This thin highway will pass through the military base once called China Lake and then we must follow that until we come to a small road the map has marked the 190.

And then… Death Valley.

The Boy liked to ride atop the tank, holding on to the main gun, watching the far horizon.

The wind catches his hair, pulling it, tossing it.

The gray-and-white feather with the broken spine flutters in the breeze.

The Old Man watched the Boy from the hatch as they bumped along the descent into the lowest parts of the desert.

That morning, as they'd loaded the tank, the Old Man had stopped the Boy, who seemed familiar with what must be done when breaking camp. Moving on.

He has probably done this every morning of his life.

"We're going far to the east."

He waited for the Boy to ask him why. When he didn't, the Old Man continued.

"I can't leave you here, there is too little to survive on and to salvage. But later today we should come to an old military base."

The Boy waited.

Whether this pleased or displeased the Boy, the Old Man could not tell.

"We can leave you there, if you like?"

The Boy nodded and returned to helping load their things back onto the tank.

The Boy tapped the spare fuel drums and all of them heard an empty *gong* that came from within each.

"Where will we get fuel today, Poppa?" his granddaughter asked.

"Ahead of us there's supposed to be an underground storage tank near a long runway. When we get there, I'm told we'll be able to load the tank up with rocket ship fuel."

Will we, my friend?

General Watt, Natalie, said so. Shuttle fuel. Left over from the last shuttle flights. Stored in case there might ever be a need for it again. Stored with fuel stabilizers in an underground, airtight storage tank where they had hidden the fuel once those shuttles had landed after circling the earth.

"Though shuttle fuel is not listed as a reliable fuel source for the M-1 Abrams Main Battle Tank," General Watt, Natalie, had told him last night, "reviewing its specifications and requirements, I fail to see why this fuel source will not suffice."

"If it is all we have, then it will have to do," said the Old Man during their deep-of-the-night conversation, when he could not sleep.

"Yes," agreed Natalie. "It may increase the engine temperature though, and that should be a concern worth noting."

"Runs a little hot, eh?" said the Old Man, laughing for no reason he could think of at the time.

Maybe I was relieved there would at least be something to use for fuel. If not, it would be a very long walk back home or even just to the bunker.

"Yes," Natalie had said.

Now, turning along a wide curve underneath dusty gray granite rock, the high desert town of China Lake lies buried beneath wild growth turned brown and yellow. Hints of collapsed buildings occasionally peek out from beneath the rampant tangle of wild desert shrub and thorn.

The base is on the far side of the town.

"Continue down this freeway," he told his granddaughter. "We should be able to see the control tower from the road. If we reach the remains of an overpass, we've gone too far."

"Okay, Poppa!"

The people came stumbling out of the tangle of undergrowth, some lumbering, some crawling, others dragging themselves free of the riot of briers, thorns, and wild cactus.

The Boy saw them first and pointed. The Old Man followed the gaze and finger.

They were misshapen.

Withered limbs.

Missing limbs.

They wore rags.

They held up their bony and scratched arms. If they had them.

Their mouths were open.

Some held up tiny, milky-eyed blind children, as if offering, as if pleading, as if begging.

The shape of their ribs was revealed through sagging skin above potbellies distended by starvation.

Tears ran down their cheeks.

The Old Man recoiled in horror.

The desert freaks fell away behind the slow progress of the tank, which easily outpaced their shambling and weakened lurch toward the machine.

The Old Man watched them fall to the ground in defeat.

They're starving.

There wasn't a weapon, a stick, or a rock among them.

Just hands, pleading. Claws begging.

The Old Man looked at the Boy.

"They're starving," he shouted above the engine's scream.

And after a moment the Boy nodded in agreement.

The Old Man watched one of the crazed and starving desert people, a thin and bony gaunt man, the front runner of them all, kneeling, pounding the dry ground in frustration with a tiny claw-hand as puffs of dry dust erupted in his face. A woman with a child knelt down beside the Gaunt Man. Comforting him. Comforting her broken man who'd tried his best to catch their tank that he might beg for help as the starving child wailed from her back.

They're just people.

They're just people, and they're starving to death.

"Stop the tank."

"What, Poppa?"

"Stop the tank. They're starving. We have food. We can give them some. What we have, we can give to them."

The people stood as the tank stopped.

Amazed.

The Old Man waved to them.

Come.

The Boy and his granddaughter began to bring their boxes of food out onto the turret.

The Desert People came forward. Fear and hope in large watery eyes. Disbelief as bony bodies stumbled and finally leaned into each other for support and comfort. A woman jabbered, shrieking hysterically. The oldest, spindly legged and skeletal, simply cried, heaving out great sobs that racked their concave chests. The rest, dirty and tired, opened their mouths, stunned into silence, saying nothing, unable to believe what was happening.

After a moment, the Boy began to speak to them in their jabber-patois.

He speaks their language.

The Old Man tore open an Army-gray package of spaghetti and meatballs. He handed it to the Gaunt Man whose wife struggled to help him hold up his too-bony and too-thin arms to receive the gift.

The starving man opened his mostly toothless mouth and the Old Man could see the drool of extreme hunger within.

'He'll devour the whole packet in one bite,' thought the Old Man.

The Gaunt Man reached two thin fingers into the gray packet, his huge dark eyes like ever-widening pools of water, and scooped out the meal within.

His mouth wide.

He turned to the woman beside him and fed her.

Her eyes closed and she chewed slowly.

The child on her back whimpered.

Even with her eyes closed the pure joy was evident as she chewed slowly, swallowing thickly.

'They're still human,' thought the Old Man. 'They still care for each other as best they can.'

The Desert People surged around the tank, dozens of them, holding out their arms weakly for as long as they could, waiting while the Old Man and his granddaughter held out the opened packets of food to them. Soon the Boy was helping too as the people of the high desert ate and wept, jabbering what the Boy told the Old Man was their way of saying, "Thank you, thank you, thank you."

The Desert People followed the tank as it slowly moved to the old airfield. When the tank stopped, the Desert People stopped.

The Old Man searched along the sides of the runway for the cover to the underground fuel storage. The cover that Natalie, General Watt, had told him he must find.

Storage Tank B.

When he found it, he waved for his granddaughter to bring the tank to him and soon they were drawing fuel from the deep, untouched reservoir that had opened with a pungent suck of long denied oxygen.

"They've had a hard year," said the Boy as the Old Man watched the fuel hose thump and shake, greedily drinking up the long untouched fuel.

"You speak their language."

"They speak a language that is like one I heard in another place."

"What happened to them?"

The Boy turned to look at the Desert People.

"They tell me they have lived here since before the bombs. They've been sick since. Their crops failed this year and because of their… condition… from the poison inside the bombs, they cannot hunt the goats and deer up in the rocks. The animals are too fast for them to get close to with their slings."

The Old Man turned from the hose, knowing he would see the Desert People watching him.

He watched the women gather about his granddaughter, making soft cooing noises, stroking her hair.

I have to take care of her also.

Yes.

But you know many tricks, my friend, and you are resourceful.

Yes, you would say that to me.

I did.

The Old Man climbed onto the tank and disappeared inside the turret.

When he came back out he carried the hunting rifle, the cleaning kit, and the two boxes of shells.

I am glad to be rid of this gun. I didn't like having it with us.

The Old Man beckoned the Gaunt Man, who seemed the healthiest among them.

He wobbled forward.

The Old Man loaded a bullet into the rifle, shot the bolt forward, shouldered the rifle, and aimed it at a small satellite dish attached to a building on the other side of the field.

He fired.

The small satellite dish bent and then, a moment later, fell onto the decaying pavement.

The shot echoed off the gray mountain rock all around them.

"Tell them to hunt with this."

The Boy watched the Old Man.

Then the Boy turned and began to speak to the Gaunt Man in their jabber.

"Tell them they will have to keep this gun clean, I'll show them how," said the Old Man.

"Tell them to use these bullets sparingly, only hunt what they need to get back on their feet. Get their strength back."

And…

"Tell them this is all we have."

It was time to go.

When the Old Man had shown them how to clean and care for their gun, it was time to go.

They brought their children forward to touch the Old Man and the women smelled his granddaughter's hair and the Boy jabbered their jabber and told them all goodbye.

When it was time to go.

The Old Man looked at the Boy.

"I want you to come with us. I think we will need your help where we are going."

The Boy watched the Desert People.

The tank.

Heard a voice he did not share with others.

A voice from long ago.

A voice that said, *Whatchu gonna do now, Boy?*

The Boy nodded and climbed onto the tank, standing in his place alongside the main gun.

The Old Man started the APU and donned his helmet.

He spoke to his granddaughter as the engine spooled up into its whine and then roared to life, sending waves of heat blasting out across the gravel and dust.

"Are you ready?"

"What will we do now, Poppa? They ate all our food."

The Old Man watched the Desert People.

What I have, I give to you.

Where did that come from, my friend?

I don't know.

"Let's head back to the highway," he told his granddaughter over the intercom. "Don't worry, we'll be fine."

CHAPTER 20

The Old Man looked at the temperature gauge again.

Already, the engine is too hot.

And still, it rises. Also, today the heat is merciless and I'm sure that will not help matters.

The tank cut through carved gashes within the burning, stony hills as they descended into wide iron-gray wastes.

All this must have once been under an ocean.

Long beaches of prehistoric sand fade for miles, falling away from rocky outcrops that were once islands. These islands of once-magma hover above the gray dust of the road and in time, even these fade into the red rock hills where stands of soft green feathery trees shelter among cracks in the earth.

Like the oasis the bee led me to.

Would I find water there in those stands of willowy green trees on this hottest of days?

Foxes for food.

Shade for rest.

Even a moment to think about what we're doing as this infernal day turns into a bread oven and the tank's engine heat rises like an overworked furnace.

How long can the engine run at this temperature?

"Natalie? General Watt?" The Old Man releases the push-to-talk button and waits for her reply.

"Natalie here."

"This spaceship fuel is making the engine run hotter than maybe it should."

Ahead the road opens out onto a steep grade that surely leads to the bottom of the desert, or so the Old Man thinks.

If the bottom is just ahead, then this has not been so bad.

"You can try," replies Natalie through the static, "to shut the tank down until dark. Then continue on to the final descent. I am watching you in real time on a satellite I've managed to change to a higher, slower orbit."

The final descent?

I thought this was the final descent. What will this other fall-to-the-bottom places of the desert seem like?

"I have bad news," says Natalie, her warm voice suddenly clear, as though right in his ear.

"Go ahead."

"The road that leads to the bottom of Death Valley might not prove serviceable. Once you pass a scenic overlook the road becomes impassable. You'll need to find a way down by going off-road to continue on to the bottom of the grade."

"Is that going to be a problem for you?" asks Natalie. General Watt.

"No. We'll be fine."

The Old Man wipes away the thin sweat that collects around his neck.

The road they must take, the one that leaves the 395, is mostly buried under drifting white sand. At the lonesome intersection they watch it carve away into the east, into red ridges and dark gullies.

According to the map, this must be our turn toward the valley. Toward the east.

"Poppa, I can see the road as it rises above the sand. That way." She leans out of the driver's hatch in front of him, pointing toward the red rock that cuts the horizon.

The Boy atop his perch near the main gun scans the bright sands, and the Old Man watches him nod.

"Try to follow it as best you can," the Old Man tells his granddaughter.

Soon the sun is falling toward the west, and with every moment the color of the red rock deepens into rust and blood.

The engine temperature is high, but it isn't in the red, not yet.

How hot will it be tomorrow, deep down in the oven at the bottom of Death Valley, off-road, crossing the baking rocks and hardpan?

The Old Man waits and does not hear an answer.

If we were in the boat together, Santiago, what would we do? Make a hat from the wet gunnysacks. How would we stay cool enough to get this tank across the bottom of the driest sea in the world, my friend?

The Old Man hears nothing and thinks only of the sound the waves might make as they slap against the side of their tiny boat. The sound he and his friend would listen to as they searched the silences in between for an answer.

They wind through the last of the low hills and in brief snatches they glimpse the basin far below.

It is so far below, I cannot imagine there could be a deeper part to this desert. It is like a giant hole in the earth. A hole we must fall into.

And…

It will be even hotter down there when the sun rises tomorrow.

At blue twilight they heave into a wide parking lot erupting in blacktop blisters.

Once the Old Man turns the engine off and shuts down the APU, he expects he will feel some relief from the relentless heat that has marked this day, but he doesn't.

The early evening is like a warm cup of water left out in the sun.

He watches the engine temperature gauge grudgingly withdraw.

As though it does not want to, my friend.

I hope I haven't ruined anything within the tank's engine.

But would that be so bad?

He hears his granddaughter calling him. Telling him to come and look before it's too late.

But still he watches the temperature gauge barely move toward its own bottom.

When he looks out the hatch of the turret he can see the Boy standing next to his granddaughter as she climbs up on the warped railing that guards the parking lot from the edge of the drop. She points at something far below.

The Boy is close to her and the Old Man knows, though he does not know why, that the Boy will not let her fall.

In the dark they camp far from the tank, lying against the warm sidewalk that encircles the parking lot. Stars beyond count begin their slow night dance above them. The moon, a fat crescent low above the hills, seems near and detailed as it shimmers above the ridges and rocks turned night-gray.

My biggest concern is the heat of the engine.

We'll need to cross the desert as fast as we can tomorrow.

But if we go too fast, the engine will become even hotter.

And then there is food.

If it is anything like the worst parts of the wasteland, what food there is down there will be hard to find.

It is good we are all so warm and exhausted. They didn't mention anything about eating tonight.

They also handed out the food, my friend, and they already know there is no food tonight. That is why they remain silent.

Are they asleep?

"Are you awake?" asks the Old Man in the night.

"Yes, Poppa. It's too hot to sleep."

After a moment the Boy whispers a tired, "I am awake," as though he has been and does not want to be.

"We have a problem."

"What is it, Poppa?"

The Boy says nothing.

"The fuel we pumped from beneath the runway is making the engine of the tank too warm. I don't remember much about engines but I do remember that if they are too hot for too long they might melt."

No one said anything.

"Tomorrow we will reach the valley floor. It will be even hotter down there."

After a moment his granddaughter asked, "So what do we do, Poppa?"

"I don't know," confessed the Old Man.

It seemed like the admission of ignorance, the surrender to helplessness. His statement lured him into a brief moment where he may have been asleep or falling toward it.

"Then we must go now," said the Boy quietly.

The Old Man sat up.

Natalie said the road we must take to the bottom is gone now. Off-road, in the darkness, feeling our way down the side of a cliff, that would be madness.

"It's a good moon to see by tonight," said the Boy as if reading the Old Man's thoughts. "Good for traveling. In an hour or so it will be very cold. The desert is like that."

CHAPTER 21

The tank is running.

The night is colder, and ever so slightly, the needle is a little lower than it was in the heat of the day.

The Old Man circles the running tank, then climbs onto the turret and into the hatch.

Inside, his granddaughter is buckled into the gunner's seat.

He shows the Boy how to use the seat belt in the loader's station.

"I can drive, Poppa, or at least be in the driver's seat up front."

The Old Man, sweating slightly and feeling weak, as if nauseated, climbs up into the hatch.

"I think it's better if we're all strapped in here, together. It might get pretty rough."

The Old Man takes hold of the control sticks Sergeant Major Preston had built to maneuver the tank from the commander's seat.

The Old Man looks down inside the tank and sees the Boy bathed in red light.

He is looking forward at nothing.

Nothing that exists anymore.

How do you know, my friend?

I just do.

The Old Man puts his hand on the switch that will activate the tank's high-beam light.

A moment later, everything in front of the tank is bathed in a wide arc of white light, throwing long shadows of deep darkness away from the blistered pavement and scattered rock.

For a few hundred yards they are able to follow the winding road, but almost immediately the road lies buried beneath a collapsed wall of red volcanic rock. The Old Man taps the throttle and listens to the two wide treads grind and crunch the porous rock as the tank climbs up onto the pile. On the other side, the final descent begins as the road rounds a curve, falling away out of sight.

So far, so good.

The Old Man smiles and adjusts his grip on the twin sticks, which are already slick with sweat.

On the other side of the curve, a fallen bridge sends only a strip of a railing across the gap.

The Old Man nudges the tank forward and looks into the empty space.

It's not deep, but it's steep. If we go down in there, we might get stuck.

To the right is a small plateau of crumbling rock that is little more than a wide ledge and a drop that disappears off into the night. To the left, a rock wall.

The Old Man maneuvers the tank out onto the wide ledge.

There is more than enough room.

Once the tank is back on the narrow two-lane road, the descent steepens and then halts.

The rock wall has shifted over the road. There is no ledge to turn onto and bypass the wall.

The Old Man waits, straining to see something in the arc of light that he has not yet seen.

He checks the temperature gauge.

Warmer.

But not as warm.

If we sit, if we wait, it will get warmer.

But I need time to think.

Right now you must be very rich to afford such a luxury, my friend.

The Old Man pulls back on both sticks and the tank shifts gears and begins to back up the road. When it's wide enough, which is just barely, he pivots the tank, mashing one stick forward and pulling back on the other, then he races back up to the ledge.

He climbs up out of the hatch and runs forward through the night across the warm rock.

Don't trip and break anything. A hand or a wrist, or even a leg.

Yes, that would be bad.

Below, the ledge falls steeply down a small hill onto a ridge that seems to cut back toward the road.

We could make it back to the road that way.

You might also get stuck.

Time.

Back in the tank, the Old Man starts the machine toward the ledge.

"Hang on," he mumbles over the intercom.

The near horizon is gray rock and long shadows in the brightness of the tank's lamp. The darkness of the night seems to devour the ground just beyond the light as the earth falls away and disappears.

Like the surface of an asteroid tumbling through the dark.

There is a moment when the tank is pointing straight toward the horizon, and a moment later it feels as though the gun barrel is aimed down into a black pit that lies just beyond the shattered rocks that dot the arc of light. All of them feel as if they are falling out of their seat belts and harnesses.

The tank picks up speed and the Old Man is leaning hard into the brakes as the tank slides forward into what must be an abyss.

The tank hovers halfway down the cliff and the Old Man can hear himself muttering.

"Poppa?" asks his granddaughter, breaking the dull hum of the intercom net.

The Old Man can see that the ridge ends abruptly and well before connecting with the broken road that winds off toward the unreachable north.

If I back up, the temperature will rise. It'll put too much strain on the engine.

The Old Man gives slightly on the brakes and the tank begins to ease forward, the gun barrel pointing even lower.

A hundred yards later, the tank is sliding down through rocks and dust, and the Old Man can only give and release on the brakes as the massive war machine slides faster and faster toward the unknown, unseen bottom.

Ahead, a large rock juts out of the dust that seems to chase and overtake the tank every time the Old Man jams his feet onto the brakes.

The Old Man engages the right tread and steers wide of the rock, clipping it at one edge and sending a spray of gravel off into the night.

"Wheeeeeee!" squeals his granddaughter over the intercom.

It feels like we are being bounced to death.

Like a roller coaster.

She has never known roller coasters. So this is her first roller coaster.

And though the Old Man is frightened, afraid he has chosen badly from the start and will soon be responsible for unnamed tragedies that lie in each moment beyond the high beam, he smiles.

I remember roller coasters…

Concentrate! You must pay attention now.

Still, I am glad she is having fun.

At the bottom of the steep and never-seeming-to-end slide, the tank lands and the Old Man yanks it sideways into a skid and finally a halt.

An avalanche of falling dust shrouds them for a moment.

The Old Man is shaking. Sweating.

"Poppa?"

When the Old Man speaks, he hears the fear in his own voice. The age too. "Yes?"

"That was fun! I hope there's more." And she is giggling and laughing and the Old Man laughs too, though he doesn't know what he is laughing at.

You are laughing at yourself.

No, not because of that. I am laughing, because for another moment, we are still alive, despite all my failures.

Yes.

And I am laughing also because of the sound of her laughter. My granddaughter's laughter is a good thing.

The best thing.

At dawn the Old Man saw the rubble of a wide and tall hacienda set within the crevice of a hill by a road leading up out of the far side of Death Valley.

It has been a long night.

Longer than the night you walked after the motel and the moon went down and you were all alone in the dark?

Yes, it feels longer than that one.

The journey down into the bowl of the deepest desert hadn't ended at that teetering ledge. For hours, the Old Man had coaxed the giant tank down through wadis and ravines and hills that may have been as steep as that first, terrifying, almost-drop.

She'd laughed all the way.

At the bottom, they'd gotten out to stretch their legs and feel the cool of the night drying the sweat on their bodies.

Even the temperature gauge was back to normal.

The road at the bottom disappeared underneath the drifting desert, and the Old Man thought, 'Surely this must be the bottom.'

But it wasn't.

No.

They'd crossed the valley and climbed a road that was mostly intact as it wound its way up through wicked formations of wind-carved rock.

Then down again.

By that time, his granddaughter and the Boy had been asleep.

Then it was just me. Alone in the night and crossing the desert.

Like before.

The tank rolled across the bottom of the ancient ocean.

In the night, the Old Man spied the skeletal remains of sunken RVs drowning amid the sand and rock.

The blackened frames of buildings clustered by the side of the road and the Old Man wondered what their story of salvage was.

Old habits die hard.

I think you should keep that habit. The fuel you'll need is more than what you have. You have a long way to go before this is done. Far beyond tonight, my friend.

Yes.

In time, the rolling motion of the tank and the Old Man's concentration on the mere rumors of road that lay buried beneath the mercurial sand lulled him into a thoughtlessness where even his constant memories could not find him.

I am too tired to remember.

When he came to the bottom of the desert, he found something in its center he had not expected to find. Clusters of feathery green trees, clutching at the lowest point of the desert, drifting like remembered seaweed in the moonlight. Moving slightly in some soft breeze that had wandered far and long to arrive here on this late night.

Like us.

In the center, at the bottom of Death Valley, next to a wide swath of dry alkali flats, there was life.

The Old Man shut down the tank and crossed the thin sands alone to feel the feathery branches and touch the soft white bark of the trees.

A strong breeze came up and the branches whispered all around him.

There was once an ocean here and this was its bottom.

I have seen its shores far up near where we obtained fuel from the old spaceship runway. Since then we have fallen and fallen into its dry depths.

As though sinking, my friend.

Yes, as though we were sinking.

'And underneath this tree,' the Old Man thought to himself, feeling its soft bark, 'is what remains of that long-ago ocean.'

Soon he is back aboard the tank and rolling on toward the east; his granddaughter and the Boy remained undisturbed by his stop in the night. By the last of the moon's light, the Old Man watched the white alkali flats spread away to the south.

What lost things lie within you?

What are your memories?

Blankness surrounded him and there was nothing but the road and the night long after the moon had crossed the sky and fallen into the shadows of spiky mountains on the far horizon.

Just before dawn, when the Old Man suspected there might be something, some structure within the rocks ahead, he rubbed his tired eyes and thought of oceans buried deep beneath the desert.

Those alien creatures that had lived within it and along its shores must have thought their world would never end. That the sea and their islands would always be there, long after even they had gone.

Just as we did before the bombs.

And…

One day, will we be just a few savages alongside a ravine at the bottom of our history, clutching at the remains of what once was?

Like those soft feathery trees in the moonlight at the bottom of a dead ocean.

Can we ever be forgiven for what we did?

In the gray light of first morning, the Old Man shut down the tank in the shadow of an ancient pile that rose up from the desert floor.

The hacienda had once been a hotel or a desert resort.

There might even be salvage within, but I am too tired to think about that right now.

He waited through the morning silence for his granddaughter and the Boy to finish their sleep. He watched the daylight rise and turn to gold, sweeping away the long night.

My life since the bombs has been like those trees at the bottom of the ancient ocean.

And yet, you are still here, my friend.

Yes.

CHAPTER 22

The Old Man awoke after noon. He raised a hand, shielding his eyes from the glare of the blinding sun.

He lay in the thin shadow of an ancient building.

He was alone.

He drank warm water and listened to the silence.

Far away, in the building above him he could hear his granddaughter's voice. She was talking to someone.

The Boy.

He listened to them as they explored the ruin.

In time they returned to him.

"Poppa!" She dropped a sack of treasures onto the pavement of the courtyard where he had been resting since they'd awoken that morning. "We found salvage."

The Boy appeared and the Old Man was comforted by the tomahawk the Boy kept at his belt and the dead snake in his hands.

I should have known better than to bring her. If the Boy had not been with her she might have gotten hurt.

I must be more careful.

But I was so tired.

On the ground lay a corkscrew, a feather duster that looked in good shape, and a bowling ball.

"What's this?" she asked holding up the corkscrew. A weapon?"

He must have killed the snake with his tomahawk. The young are always impressed by the accomplishments of weapons.

"No." The Old Man picked up the corkscrew and inspected it. A wooden handle from which the thin spiral of the metal corkscrew rose up. He spit on it and polished it. "But it could be if you needed it to be." He put the handle in his fist and let the corkscrew erupt through his middle and ring fingers. "You could punch with it like this." He showed her.

Eyes wide, she watched, and when he had given the corkscrew back to her she also made a weapon of it.

Should I have done that? Should I have shown her how to make a weapon out of something that isn't one?

The world is a dangerous place now, my friend.

A moment later she grabbed the feather duster.

"This, Poppa? What is it? What was it for?"

The Boy set to gathering thin strips of the darkish deadwood that lay scattered about. The Old Man's mouth watered at the thought of the cooked snake.

I like snake.

"That's…" But the Old Man could not think of what a feather duster was once called. He knew what it did. But its label remained lost and no matter how hard he tried, he could not dig out a name for the feather duster within the cemetery of his mind.

My mind is like a burial place for the forgotten dead.

He remembered the ancient tombstones he and Big Pedro had come across out in the southern reaches of the desert, far out beyond the village. Far out beyond any salvage spots anyone could remember, they'd found the little cemetery resisting the desert. Surrounded by sinking ironwork, the nameless graves waited, their markers shifting in the sand throughout the years.

"No good," Big Pedro had said all those years ago. *Malo*. Bad.

When I'd turned to face him he had seen a look in my eye.

I'd wanted to open those graves and search them.

I'd shamed him.

The Old Man picked up the feather duster.

"You cleaned things with it?" Then, "It made dust go away."

For a moment, the name leapt out of the bushes clustering at the adage of his thoughts and then ran off down the road.

Later they finished the snake, which there was a surprising amount of.

It was a big snake.

As they sat waiting out the heat of the day, the Old Man thought of Big Pedro.

He was a good man.

I was wrong to have even thought about disturbing those graves.

What could we have found?

That was not the point.

I had grown calloused. I had gotten used to searching the things of dead people because we needed to survive. Taking their things and making them mine. Ours.

It was survival.

It was wrong.

Like the corkscrew.

Yes, that felt wrong even in the moment I was showing her how to make it a weapon.

He waited.

Waited for the answer he must give himself.

But what lies ahead is very dangerous.

To think that everything will be as easy as it has been up to this point is childish. She might need a weapon.

Now she has one.

I wish the world were different.

The world is what it is, my friend. The world is what it always has been. A very dangerous place.

Feather duster.

CHAPTER 23

It was late in the day, after they'd eaten the snake seasoned with some pepper that had survived the Old Man's charity, when they began the climb up and out of the valley. The grade was gentle and the climb little more than a final sweep up onto the eastern desert plain.

There are maybe eight miles between here and the secret testing area.

You are trying to think of other things.

Yes.

The Old Man watched the Boy as he rode atop the turret, eyes constantly scanning the far horizon.

Yes, I am trying to think of other things than the right tread of this tank.

"What shall we call the valley now that we have seen it?" he asked his granddaughter over the intercom.

There was a pause and he knew she was thinking. He knew her face when it thought. The pressed lips, the eyes searching the sky. Thinking.

"It wasn't scary, Poppa."

"No, not so much."

Remember the fall to the bottom. That was scary to me when we drove in the dark and I could not tell where the edge was and what would happen next. It is even scarier to me now when I think back about it. That is how you know things were really very dangerous, when you think back and are still frightened about what might have happened. That is the fear of what-might-have-been.

"How about..." she said through the dull hum of the communications net.

The Bottom of an Ocean Valley.

The Roller-Coaster Valley.

The Valley of the Longest Night.

"How about the 'There Is Nothing to be Afraid of Here Valley,' Poppa?"

How about that?

Since that afternoon, after the long night of driving through the bottom of the once-ocean, the Old Man had felt the falseness in the right tread, and if he listened closely, a metallic *clank* that had not been there before. A *clank* he sometimes heard and other times, when he was sure he would hear it, not at all.

Maybe it is just an uncertainty and nothing more?

For now?

Yes, for now. And it could be these jury-rigged joysticks Sergeant Major Preston fixed up. That could be the problem.

Then you should ask your granddaughter to take over and guide the tank from the driver's compartment. See if she notices it also.

But the Old Man could not bring himself to ask her.

If it's true...

Then it is true.

Yes.

That night under desert skies turned western flames surrendering to the blue comfort of night, they sat and watched their fire.

I cannot stop thinking about the bad tread.

But what can you do about it?

"Where are we going?" asked the Boy.

The Old Man looked up to see both of them watching him.

"Tomorrow," he began, "at noon, I'll call the General and find out where we must go exactly. From what she has told me, we must find a device somewhere within this area. She tells me the device will help free her and those trapped within their bunker."

"What does this device do? Is it a weapon? asked the Boy.

"I don't know," mumbled the Old Man, feeding dry sticks into the fire.

But you should know.

Yes.

"Poppa?"

"Yes."

"I'm hungry."

And there is that too.

Just before noon the Boy raised his hand. The gesture was so sudden and the Boy so long unmoving, the Old Man felt electrified at its sudden movement and meaning. The Old Man stopped the tank. Below them, in a long valley amid the salt flats, lay the once-secret base, Area 51, where Natalie had directed them to find the Laser Target Designator.

The Boy scrambled across the tank and shouted above the engine's roar in the Old Man's face.

"There are goats, big ones, along that ridge." The Boy pointed toward a jumble of rocks that looked like some bygone battleship crossing the ocean of a wide desert. The Old Man could not see any goats.

But he is young and his eyes are good.

"I'll hunt one and bring it down into the base. It might take me a while."

The Old Man nodded and the Boy climbed down from the rumbling tank and loped off in his awkward manner toward the distant rocks.

Later, after the engine had faded from whine to silence, as the wind whispered through the ancient hangars, sweeping tumbleweeds along the dry runway, the Old Man watched the distant rocks and saw nothing of the Boy.

"Where is this laser machine, Poppa?"

The Old Man turned to the base.

There is no one here and there hasn't been for a long time.

The broken stalk of a control tower rose above the airfield. Debris remained scattered across the blistered tarmac.

"She said we would find it in there," said the Old Man, pointing toward the tower. "In the basement."

They began to cross the runway.

"What is this place, Poppa?"

I know.

I knew.

It was a myth. Even then.

"A place where they kept and made weapons."

"Do you think there will be salvage here, Poppa?"

"It seems like a good place for salvage."

It was a place they made weapons we should have never needed. I can say that. I have seen what happens if you make a weapon. If you hide it somewhere secret and even pretend that you will never use it. Pretend that it doesn't even exist. Someday, you will use it.

And others must live with the consequences.

Yes.

CHAPTER 24

The work of the day began in earnest once they'd located the entrance to the tower. It was hard work. Crowbar work. At one point they'd needed to use the tank and a tow chain to remove a section of concrete blocking the entrance.

Later, when the door was revealed and they'd stopped to rest, the Old Man, sweating thickly and drinking warm water, watched his granddaughter wander among the twisted and burnt remains of bat-winged bombers, gray with dust, sinking beneath the white salt and sand that swept in off the dry lake.

The Old Man was thinking of water.

How much is left?

And.

Where will we find more?

He turned to the aircraft scattered across the horizon.

There was a time when I would have wondered at the story of this place and those aircraft. But only because there was salvage here. Not because of the story of what happened on that last, long-lost day.

Not because of that, my friend?

No. There is too much to think of. There is water. There is this device we must find. There is food. Will the Boy be able to catch us a goat?

Goat would be nice with the pepper that remains.

And salt?

I do not think we can eat this salt.

Still, salt would be nice.

Yes.

And the tread that is going bad.

And fuel too. Do not forget fuel. You must think of fuel.

How could I not?

The Old Man took a drink of warm water from his canteen and sighed. A small breeze skittered across the desert and cooled the sweat on his neck and face.

He thought of the meal that the Boy in the book would bring Santiago. Rice and bananas.

I always like to imagine that there were bits of fried pork in it.

And don't forget the coffee with milk and sugar, my friend. That was the best part.

Yes.

This place. Its story. I'll tell you. They were caught by surprise. No bombs. No nuclear bombs. No, an enemy attacked this place. There were reports of the Chinese offshore in those last weeks, but after the first EMP, the news was thin and, really, I can say this now to myself since there is no one left to contradict me, the news we hung on then was of little value. I remember though the rumors of Chinese air strikes in the morning hours. The names of bridges and oil refineries I must have known at the time going up in the early morning darkness. We saw the smoke at dawn. That was when we began to flee.

It was Los Angeles.

Yes. That was it.

I bet Natalie knows.

One day these bombers we trusted in will sink beneath the salt and the sand and who will know what happened to them? To us. Or who will even be interested?

There is always someone.

But what if there isn't?

The Old Man watched his granddaughter return from her explorations. She was holding a jacket.

"I found this in a bag behind the seat in one of the planes, Poppa!"

She held it up triumphantly. It was green and shiny on the outside, almost brand-new. And on the inside it was orange.

A flight jacket.

And what if there isn't anyone left?

The Old Man watched her smile.

He nodded.

There must be.

At dusk the Boy returned, limping across the sands, the dressed goat slung over his shoulders.

When the Old Man saw the shadow of the Boy, he turned from the rubble they'd been clearing in the stairwell that led to the collapsed rooms beneath the tower. The Old Man dropped his crowbar weakly and set to gathering what little wood he could find.

It was full dark and the stars were overhead when the goat finally began to roast. In the hours that followed, the three of them drank lightly from their canteens as their mouths watered and they watched the goat.

Close to midnight, the Old Man cut a slice off the goat and tasted it. He handed it to his granddaughter and she began to chew and hum, which was her way.

"It's ready, Poppa."

They fell to the goat with their knives, eating in the firelight, their jaws aching as grease ran down their chins.

We were hungrier than we thought.

Yes.

CHAPTER 25

The Boy found the black case underneath a desk beneath the collapsed roof of the basement he'd crawled through under the tower.

"I found it!" he shouted back through the dust and the thin light their weak flashlights tried to throw across the rubble.

"Are there words written on the side of the case?" the Old Man called through the dark.

I must remember what Natalie told me to look for. The words she said we would find. What were they?

Pause.

Maybe he doesn't know how to read. Who could have taught him?

"Project Einstein," shouted the Boy.

Who taught him how to read?

"That's it. Bring it out."

Later, in the last of the daylight beneath the broken tower, they looked at the dusty case. On its side were military codes and numbers. But the words Natalie, General Watt, had told him to look for, the words were there.

Project Einstein.

I should be…

Excited? Happy? Hopeful?

But I'm not. It means we must go on now. It means we must go all the way.

Yes.

"Halt!"

The voice came from behind them. It was strong yet distant, as if muffled.

"Raise your hands above your heads!"

"Poppa," whispered his granddaughter.

"Do it," he whispered back. He noticed the Boy struggle to raise his left arm as quickly as the strong right one. Even then the left failed to straighten or fully rise.

Behind them, the Old Man heard boot steps grinding sand against the cracked tarmac of the runway.

If there is just one, we might have a chance.

The Old Man looked to see if the Boy's tomahawk was on his belt. It was.

"Grayson! Trash! Move in and cover them."

Movement, steps. Gear jingling and clanking together.

The voice stepped into view, circling wide to stand between the Old Man, his granddaughter, and the Boy and the broken tower.

He carried a gun. A rifle.

An assault rifle, remembered the Old Man.

His face was covered by a black rubber gas mask.

Beneath a long coat lay dusty and cracked black plastic armor.

'Riot gear,' thought the Old Man. Just like in the days before the bombs.

On top of his head was the matte-scratched helmet of a soldier.

At his hip, a wicked steel machete forged from some long-ago-salvaged car part lay strapped.

His boots were wrapped in rags.

Within his long coat, lying against the black plastic chest armor, a slender rectangle of dented and polished silver hung.

A harmonica.

The Old Man snatched a glance at the Project Einstein case on the ground.

"What the hell are you doing out here?" said the man in the dusty black riot armor as he raised his helmet and removed the rubber gas mask from his face. The man with the harmonica about his neck.

"And more importantly, where'd you get that tank?"

He was a few days unshaven.

He was young.

He's just a man.

Like me.

But he's young.

Like I once was.

So maybe it ends here. Like the dream I have done my best to avoid. It ends with these scavengers murdering me as my granddaughter watches.

It cannot end that way.

"What're you doing out here?" repeated the Harmonica Man.

If I can get to my crowbar maybe the Boy will use his axe... Maybe.

"Listen," said the Harmonica Man. "You need to tell me what you're doing out here at the old base, right now!"

"They're not with them," said either Trash or Grayson from behind their masks.

"We don't know that," said the Harmonica Man. "And hell, they've got a tank."

There is a moment in between.

A moment when things might go one way or the other.

A moment when those who are prone to caution, hesitate.

And those who are prone to action, act.

"We're on a rescue mission," said the Boy.

Silence.

Maybe the guns just dropped a bit.

Maybe the masked gunmen have softened their stance.

Maybe there are other good people.

Maybe, my friend. Just maybe.

"Who?" asked the Harmonica Man.

"I don't know. He does." The Boy points to the Old Man.

Everyone turns to him.

The Old Man nods.

"All right," says the man. "We'll lower our guns and you'll tell us all about it. Then, we'll see what happens next."

The Old Man lowers his hands.

Should I?

What choice do you have? None that I can see now, my friend.

"There are some people," begins the Old Man. "They're trapped inside a bunker to the east. A place once called Colorado Springs. They need this device to get free."

"What does it do?"

"I don't know."

"Are you with King Charlie?" asked the Harmonica Man.

"No. We don't know any King Charlie."

"How'd you get this tank?"

"I found it."

The Harmonica Man thought about this, watching all of them.

The Old Man could see his granddaughter. Her mouth formed into a small "o."

"Where will you go if we let you leave?"

If?

"We will go east and try to help those people."

Silence.

"Why?"

Why?

Yes. Why, my friend?

"Because they need help."

Harmonica Man lowered his gun and leaned it against his hip.

"We have food. Do you have any water?"

"Yes," said the Old Man. "Some."

"It'll be night soon. Let's eat and I'll tell you why you might want to turn back."

CHAPTER 26

Around the fire, sharing the goat and some wheat cakes the strangers have brought out from their patchwork rucksacks, they see the faces behind the black rubber gas masks.

Grayson is a young man. Not much older than the Boy. He is quiet and smiles with dark eyes. The Old Man knows he's shy and that women find him handsome.

Trash is a girl, a woman really. Maybe in her midtwenties. Her race is mixed. Maybe some Asian. Some black. Blond dirty hair. Her tight jaw and clenched teeth show she is older than the other two, but not by much. She does not speak.

'She reminds me,' thinks the Old Man, 'of a wounded bird, or a good dog that was once mistreated.'

Harmonica Man's real name is Kyle.

He is ruddy faced and swarthy and the Old Man knows that he is the kind of young man who would fight the whole world if he had a good reason to.

Names from Before.

Names.

"If you keep going east," said Kyle as he chewed some goat meat, "there is only one island of sanity between here and Flagstaff. That's the Dam, where we come from. Beyond that, I've heard there's electricity in ABQ but that might just be something the Apache made up, 'cause they're crazy. I don't put much in what they say, especially these days."

They eat around a fire next to the tank in the shadow of the broken tower. Night falls. Only Kyle talks. There is goat, dry wheat cakes, and warm water.

"Then there's the bad news. Between you and that island of sanity is a small army of crazy. Even worse, something big is going on to the east and we don't have much information other than what the Apache let slip when they come in to trade. The real truth is, I don't know what's going down out east. What we've heard is there's a big, organized group, almost like an army come up outta Texas. They seem to follow some guy who calls himself King Charlie and what he's all about doesn't sound good. Slaves. Torture. Voodoo. Bad stuff. It was six months since we'd heard from Flagstaff when our bunch got sent out here, and that was a little over a year ago. But whatever's going down out that way ain't so good. The Apache, on a good day, are hard to deal with. But whatever's going on beyond their lands is makin' em even crazier than usual. So there's that. Which still ain't your biggest problem."

The Old Man chewed some of the springier goat meat, letting the newcomers enjoy the tender goat they'd seasoned with the last of their pepper.

"Your biggest problem," continued Kyle, inspecting the rib he'd been gnawing on to make sure it was indeed devoid of meat and fat. "Your biggest problem is that small army between here and the Dam. You make it to the Dam, you can go forward. But we've been stuck out here for a year. They've got Vegas all booby-trapped up, never mind the radiation. Hell, we had a tank just like yours. I mean, maybe not the same, but old Art, he kept her running. We had some motorized flatbeds we got together and we'd run 'em up to the old air base at Creech and do some salvage. Well, that little army came in and cut us off a year ago. Now things are weird. We can't get back to the Dam. They can't get to this old place, which we think they want to real badly. They can't attack the Dam 'cause they'd never make it to the front door. But word is, they've got a bigger army somewhere out to the east. If that's actually the case, then that's a game changer as the old say. In the end, there just ain't no way through that madhouse for you and your tank."

There were no more ribs.

Kyle stared into the fire.

"Where is this 'Island of Sanity'?" asked the Old Man.

Kyle sighed.

"Home. Our home. The Dam east of Vegas."

"And so if we can make it there… to the Dam, then we might find some fuel if you had vehicles once."

"Yeah, we gin up a little fuel that's probably not the best, but it'll get this hunk o' metal a little farther down the road for you. Problem is, mister, you're not makin' the connection. We can't get into the Dam. There's an army between us and it. King Charlie's got an advance force all dug in like a hornets' nest."

The Old Man looked at the tank waiting in the shadowy darkness beyond the firelight.

"Did you hear me, old man, when I said we also had a tank? How d'ya think we lost it? It's in a ditch out in North Vegas. They knew we had vehicles so they booby-trapped the whole place. You try to go through Vegas, north or south, and you'll lose your ride. Plain as day, there just ain't no way through!"

Silence followed and the Old Man listened to the dry sticks within the fire crackle and pop. He watched the night wind carry sparks up and away from them.

"I don't mean to be hard on you, mister," said Kyle softly. "But you can't make it. At least not that way. You'll need to go off-road way out into the desert. If your ride's in good shape, that won't be a problem. Unless you get really stuck and then yer out in the sticks with their patrols."

Silence.

Overhead, a comet streaked through the atmosphere and burned up in almost the same second it had appeared.

Life.

And death.

"We need to stick to the roads," said the Old Man, thinking of the bad right tread.

"Well, you can't," whispered Kyle in disgust. Or fatigue. Or both.

The Old Man watched them all.

The girl, Trash, seemed somewhere else.

Grayson looked off into the night.

Kyle stared into the fire.

The Boy appeared to watch the night but the Old Man knew, or felt was more like it, that he was somewhere else, far from this fire and this night.

His granddaughter watched everyone.

And yet we must.

"We can make a way." It was Grayson.

Grayson stared hard at Kyle who refused to return the look.

"We can make a way," Grayson repeated. "Straight through, and it's all on-road."

Silence.

"Yeah, I figured you was gonna say that," mumbled Kyle after an interval full of something electric. "I figured that already."

Grayson looked at the Old Man and began to speak softly.

"We could go straight down the Strip where their lines are thinnest. Right where the bomb went off. The radiation's not too bad. They say it was just a dirty bomb but I don't know what that really means. The important thing is the road is mostly clear of booby traps between the old casinos because of the radiation. We can go that way. We can guide you. We can make a way through."

"We," said Kyle softly. "We," he thundered at Grayson and began to laugh. "We." He snorted finally. "There just ain't no way of gettin' through!"

No one spoke and the mad laughter of Kyle died away on the night's breeze.

"Kyle?" said Grayson.

"Yeah," mumbled Kyle.

"We."

"Yeah. I figured that already."

The morning light shows an orange desert floor and a day turning into a forever blue. Hanging from the tank, riding in seats, or sitting atop the turret, they all depart the once-secret base.

There are still secrets buried in these sands.

Then let them stay buried, my friend. Let them stay buried forever.

Yes.

They travel south heading toward Vegas. The buckled road keeps straight, passing beneath toothy hills that guard a wide valley. An airfield rests in the center of it and buildings straddle the highway. Beyond and to the south lies a sea of rusting vehicles that stretch away to the indeterminate horizon.

Our Great Wreck seems small in comparison.

Yes.

"What happened here?" asks the Old Man leaning into Kyle's ear as he shouts above the noise of the tank.

"Before my time," yells Kyle above the wind and roar of the tank. "But they say that when the bomb went off, everyone in Vegas fled in two directions. Up here if you happened to be on the north side of town. If you were on the south side, then you might have gone out into Apache lands. My dad and mom were at the Dam on a 'field trip' when it happened. But most thought the Dam would be hit next so they just kept on moving. We never knew what really happened up here until we started coming to salvage parts years later." He stopped, and then added, "It was like this when we got here. There hasn't been anyone here for a long time."

They drove down into the valley, passing the airfield where planes lay fallen and scattered. There were visible bullet holes in the walls of the buildings.

Later, in the large fields between the small mountains that bracketed the valley, they passed RVs formed into squares that had burned down to their axles and frames. Cars torn to pieces. Not in accidents, but methodically. All the tires on every vehicle were missing. They saw shreds of tent still hanging from poles, still flapping in the breeze of their passing. Ancient blue tarps lay dustily strung between the wrecks. Every imaginable possession seemed strewn about in the dirt and dust, some forever entrenched in the ancient mud of past rains.

I know the story of this place.

If I were going to salvage here, I could tell you their story.

But it would be a bad story.

And so, what is their story, my friend?

Somewhere, there will be a pit. Somewhere within all that wreckage, all those vehicles turned to shelters, there will be a pit. A pit of bones forty years gone.

Yes.

This bomb goes off in Las Vegas. Right in downtown. I must have heard the news of it then, but I have forgotten since. But it happened in those first early days. The bomb goes off and those who are not killed outright run.

As we ran.

As I ran.

Yes.

There is nothing but a desert to run into. The nearest cities are hundreds of miles away. And what good is it to go to those places, those cities? They too are targets. So the survivors stop here and begin to wait for help.

But there won't be any.

They wait for food and medical attention.

But there won't be any of that either.

The skies were dark within weeks.

Then there was winter.

For two years.

That is why there are no tires.

And the bullet holes?

When there is only a little left and there are many, then there are bullet holes.

And the pit?

If you wandered this maze of rusting and frozen vehicles and walked through the burned-down ruins of makeshift fortresses hustled together by a frightened few against a terrified many, on this hot desert day that will soon turn to dry afternoon, you will feel alone and a sadness you can't name as you listen to the accidental wind chimes of wreckage and bone. You will ask yourself, where did they all go?

And soon after that, you will find the pit.

Because there was sickness.

The flu, some virus, a horrible infection racing and unchecked consuming the weak, the tired, the burnt, the hungry, the desperate. The survivors.

Because there was a sickness, there will be a pit.

The Old Man stoped the tank. Ahead of them, tractor trailer trucks and ancient military vehicles long stripped of their tires and things that might burn for the simple luxury of heat have blocked the road.

This was their checkpoint.

Their attempt to control what was inevitable.

The Old Man looked for a way around the wreck.

Easing the tank down off the highway, they skirted the ancient wall of vehicles, riding rough over the hard-packed dirt.

Ahead, the Old Man spied a deflated soccer ball half sunk in the calcified mud.

The Old Man avoided it jerkily.

Why, my friend?

I don't know. But it seemed wrong to run over it.

They were back on the road and headed south.

The wind and the sun feel good and the opposite of that place, that cemetery.

Why? Why did you avoid the soccer ball? You must answer, my friend. You always have. Now, don't be afraid.

Because…

He drove on.

Why?

Because it is the opposite of all those secrets buried in the desert. All those weapons. All those burned tires and open pits. It is the opposite of those things.

How so?

It just is.

CHAPTER 27

At dusk, a wan sky diffused with eastern dust storms roiled across the horizon, covering the melting ruins of Vegas.

They unpacked and unfolded the Radiation Shielding Kit, which was little more than a fitted blanket of coarse nylon that smelled of charcoal. They began to drape and then secure it across the tank as Kyle, Grayson, and Trash cleaned their weapons and adjusted their gear.

'We'll go ahead of you on foot and carry torches to guide you through the tight spots," said Kyle. "The two outside torches will show you how wide the path we've found is. Keep the person carrying two torches, one in each hand, in the center."

"What if you need to tell us something important?" asked the Old Man.

"I don't know… we could shout through the hatch maybe?"

"There's a telephone on the back of the tank inside this little cupboard," said his granddaughter. "You could use it to talk to each other."

How did she find that?

"Have you gone this way before?" asked the Old Man.

"No. No one has. But we've all been to parts of it even though we weren't s'posed to. Besides the lions that sometimes pass through, and the radiation from the wrecked airplane in the center of the Strip, the old casinos aren't too safe and seem more likely to fall down on you as much as stand up. So we were never allowed in there. But you know how it is when yer a kid."

I want to say to him that he is, they are, still kids. That it should be me out there in the dark tonight carrying the torches and them, these children, safe behind however much this blanket will protect those inside the tank. But I can't. They know the way, and I don't.

The Old Man drank some of the warm water that remained.

"If we…" Kyle started to say, then stopped.

He's under too much pressure. He doesn't know it, but there's a twitch just beneath his eye.

Either that or he just needs some water, my friend.

"Drink this. Drink the rest. We'll have enough water for the night. In the morning, when we reach your Dam, is there water?"

Kyle took the water and drank.

The Old Man watched the tremble in the hand of the too-young man. His Adam's apple bobbed jerkily.

"Yes," gasped Kyle. "Lots."

He's afraid.

Wouldn't you be?

Yes.

"If we don't make it," said Kyle, wiping his mouth with the back of a calloused hand, "just stay on the Strip until you get to the end. Head east when you get there and pick up the big highway that's still in good shape except for the overpasses. We made little roads around the debris. Take that highway on out to the Dam. Tell them…"

Kyle paused.

He doesn't know what to say. The thing he's afraid of, he cannot name. As if this moment he's lived in fear of for so long, cut off out here in the desert, is finally going to happen.

The Old Man rested his hand on Kyle's shoulder. He could feel the uneasiness there. The anxiety.

"Everything will be okay," said the Old Man.

Do you believe that, my friend?

But the Old Man had no response.

"Who will hold the two torches we must follow?"

"I will," said Kyle quickly.

"And the others, they will guide us through the tight places?"

"Yes. Grayson and Trash know what to do. Our armor should protect us from the radiation if we don't stick around for too long."

"That doesn't sound so bad. Then it's just a little walk in the night."

And slowly the twitching muscles in Kyle's shoulder beneath the Old Man's gnarled hand stopped.

The boy soldier, the Harmonica Man, Kyle, began to breathe again.

"Maybe the dust storm will cover us?" he said and smiled.

The Old Man nodded.

"Why do you call her Trash? She's very beautiful. I know I'm old but 'Trash' doesn't mean…"

Kyle picked up his chest armor and began to examine it.

"No," he said almost to himself. "It means the same for us too."

"Then why such an awful name?"

Kyle put down the armor, bent to take up another piece, and seemed to let go of the idea halfway through. He straightened and stared at the Old Man.

"She won't respond to anything else."

The Old Man said nothing, his blue eyes searching for meaning.

"She and a trader we did business with for years came out of the North. We knew the trader long before she came with him. She didn't say anything ever. We thought she was just shy. The trader just referred to her as his girl. Maybe a daughter we thought. One night the trader got a little drunk, which was his way, and he told us how he'd rescued her from a bunch of hillbillies up in the mountains. They, the hillbillies, they'd called her Trash. They'd also removed her tongue. Treated her pretty badly, I guess."

Kyle looked toward Trash. She worked intently with dirty blackened rags cleaning her gun.

"We kept trying to give her new names. Normal ones like from Before. Jenny. Susie. The trader said he'd even made ones up that he thought she might like from words that used to be beautiful before the bombs. But she wouldn't have any of it. She wouldn't respond. Not unless he called her Trash. He explained to her it wasn't such a good name for good people. But she wouldn't have it. He said one day they were high up on a pass and the snow was coming down. He started building their shelter, said it was like to turn a blizzard more than not. He decides he's gonna call her this name he thinks is real pretty whether she likes it or not. Aria. Weird name if I ever heard one. Aria. So he starts using it and she just won't help. It's getting cold and their mules are freezing but she just stands there in the snow. The trader's still callin' her by that weird name and it's gettin' dark and the snow is fallin' sideways. But she stands there in the snow. Won't do nuthin'. Night falls. She won't even come in to his little tent. Finally he said he just laughed to himself and gave up for good. Trash it was. I remember I thought that was the end of his story. People got up and left the cantina. Saul, the guy who runs the place, he turned the lanterns down. He always did that when it was time for all of us to go home."

Kyle fell silent for just a moment, and in that moment there were memories and thoughts of good things from home. Lanterns. Cantina. Home.

"That trader stands up. He was a big man. Big like a bear almost. We'd been drinkin', and he says to me, 'You know what the name Trash means to me?' I didn't say nothin', just listened. He says, 'It means valuable. Like somethin' so valuable, there's no piece of salvage or skin or meat you'd trade for it. 'Cause if you did the world just wouldn't seem right anymore. When I say that word I see her. And that's a good thing to me. It's one good thing that's still left in this burned-up old world. Maybe the last piece of good we all got left.' About a year later she came back alone. We don't know what happened to the trader, but it wasn't good. So we took her in."

The Old Man watched her. She was cleaning her gun. Cleaning it as though it was the most important work left to her in a burned-up old world.

Trash.

CHAPTER 28

The tank followed the three dark figures through the dust storm. Ahead, the ruins of Las Vegas hovered in and out of the skirling grit that sent sheets of brown and gray across the dark sky and swept the crumbling highway.

There should be a good moon out tonight but the dust is too thick to find it.

Ahead, the superhighway that once cut through the desert and the city had long ago collapsed into rubble. The Old Man could see the oil drums filled with fire and belching black smoke from atop piles of fortified concrete. Stakes and spears and tattered banners jutted and flapped madly in the storm.

Who are these people? This Army of Crazy. King Charlie's advance force Kyle called them.

They're different from the Horde. More organized. More dangerous. They've made traps and they have flags and lines of defense. They've come to rule, not like those I faced at Picacho Peak. They were little more than locusts. These are like wolves.

Yes.

Ahead of the tank, the three figures lit their four torches. Grayson on the right. Trash on the left. Kyle holding two in the center.

The Old Man checked the case again, making sure it still rested on the floor of the tank.

The Boy sat in the loader's seat, watching the Old Man.

His granddaughter was in the driver's seat, forward and buttoned up.

"Are you all right up there?" he said to her over the intercom.

"Yes, Poppa. Can I drive now?"

"No. Not yet. Maybe on the other side."

The bobbing torches descended off the freeway, following an off-ramp down into the ruins of the ancient gambling palaces.

Crumbling casinos like canyon walls rose up dirty and dusty on both sides. Debris skittered wildly down the side streets. Ahead, the Old Man could see the broad thoroughfare they must traverse.

Kyle's father and mother and all the old ones of the Dam had told of the day when the airliner, taking off from the airport south of the city, had been crashed directly onto the Strip.

Terrorists.

It wasn't until hours later that the authorities, and then everyone else, realized the plane had also been carrying a dirty bomb. A low-yield nuclear dirty bomb. That was when the panic started. When everyone fled.

Like you did in Los Angeles.

Yes, like we all did.

Kyle said the plane and its dirty bomb were why they'd been told to avoid the main road through the casinos. Because of the dirty bomb. Only the bravest kids claimed to have seen the actual wreckage of the plane, lying halfway up the Strip in the middle of the street.

That must have been a bad day.

There were a lot of bad days back then, my friend.

The Old Man turned to wondering if the Radiation Shielding Kit would indeed protect them.

He looked at the radio.

Concentrate on the path through the rubble. If you get stuck in this city, you've made things worse for everyone, and for no reason at all.

Yes.

He followed the jumping torches onto the main street.

Fractured monuments fell away into the dusky gloom behind them. Alongside the road, a million darkened and shattered windows looked down upon them. Crumbling walkways crossing the street resembled strands of moss draped over swampy water. The torches guttered in the blasting wind, their oily fuel barely illuminating the ground beneath the feet of their guides as the flames fought desperately against the storm.

Those torches won't last long.

Frozen buses lay on their sides, thrown across the road, while petrified cars littered the streets in haphazard directions. A clear reason why they'd stopped on that last, long-ago day seemed just out of reach, and in the end, unknowable.

Their procession of torches and armored tank began to weave through the wrecks, occasionally crushing a smaller vehicle, its rusty destruction blossoming for an instant like a sickly rose, suddenly carried off by the storm.

Ahead, a cluster of dust-caked and ashy gray emergency vehicles, fire engines and ambulances from that long-ago lost day of an air disaster turned terrorist attack, walled off the street ahead.

On that day, those firefighters must have thought the downed aircraft was the biggest tragedy they'd ever seen, were likely to ever see.

And then someone told them about the radiation.

The Old Man looked at the dosimeter.

It's very high here.

Kyle knows I am worried about the right tread. I hope he doesn't ask me to drive over those fire engines. Besides, we must be getting near Ground Zero, and it should be time to go around the actual bomb site.

Ground Zero.

I have not used those words… since I cannot remember when.

The Old Man marveled at the thought.

Those words were once a common part of my vocabulary. Of all our vocabularies. I remember entire conversations, courses of action, fears that were based on those two simple little words. Ground Zero.

As if listening in on the Old Man's thoughts, the four torches veered to the left, heading into the gray and dusty ruins of a darkened casino. It loomed high above the tiny tank and the three figures like some scavenger bird of the wasteland. The wings of the two towers almost enveloped the street and all within it like a hunched and greedy eater of carrion.

We've passed the unmanned defenses of this Army of Crazy. If they're anywhere, they'll be hunkered down from this storm, inside one of these old places. Waiting for us.

And…

I don't want to go in there. I don't want anyone, any of these children, to have to go into that dilapidated and evil pile of ruin.

But we must, my friend. There is no other way through this city. No other way to stay on the road and keep the tank from throwing a tread, which we could never fix. If we take our chances on the side streets we could end up caught in one of their traps. Trust these children, my friend.

But why would they help us like this?

And the Old Man thought of his own journey and General Watt. Natalie.

When the Old Man didn't follow immediately, Kyle, masked and armored, turned back in the thundering wind and waved both torches toward the tank and then back toward himself.

Are you sure?

He must be.

The Old Man pivoted the tank, once again feeling the weakness in the right tread, wondering if it wasn't the control mechanisms that were responsible for his suspicions.

They attacked at that moment.

They came gushing out of the casino's open mouth.

The Old Man watched through the hazy green optics of night vision as wild figures surged downward upon the three torchbearers.

At once, bright flashes erupted from the rifles of Grayson and Trash.

A bare-chested man waving an iron pipe studded with spikes was flung backward onto the rotting shreds of carpet that once dressed the steps of the palace.

A one-armed giant hurled a heavy stone, nearly crushing Grayson who batted it away with his arm. The Old Man saw the arm go limp, but Grayson continued to fire into the onslaught with the other.

Lumbering men in armor that shimmered in small points of white fuzz by the green light of night vision raced forward, leaping over downed comrades, waving machetes and nail-studded clubs. They wore turbans that wrapped their faces.

With her machine gun, Trash stitched a bright line of death across their charge, flinging some sideways as others stumbled forward waving their blades halfheartedly while blood pumped out darkly onto the dusty steps and shredded carpet. They fell before they reached her.

Now she was reloading, and the Old Man could see that the shimmering armor of the crazies was made up of coins. Coins that had been hole punched and stitched together into coats of mail.

Their coin-mail armor must be good against hand weapons but guns are another story.

He felt the Boy at his side.

"Sit down in there." He pointed toward the gunner's seat. "Look through this and you'll see what's going on."

The Boy slithered past him.

When the Old Man looked into the night-vision scope, he saw Kyle moving forward, while Grayson covered him holding his rifle with his good arm. Trash seemed to be intent on fixing her battered rifle while still walking forward.

Her weapon is jammed.

The attackers were retreating now, disappearing into the dark gray of the casino halls beyond the once-grand entrance of marble and arch.

Kyle mounted the steps, waving his torches forward over his shoulders, indicating the tank should follow them in.

The Old Man gently pushed forward on the sticks and the tank began to mount the steps.

The attackers were all gone now.

Trash turned and waved at him with her torch, showing him how much room he had to thread the opening into the casino.

The Old Man gave it more gas, hearing the top of the archway leading to the casino scrape against the turret and then give way in a stony crumble of dust and metal that bounced off the armor above their heads.

Inside, a large dust-covered marble lobby vaulted toward a high domed ceiling of broken glass and blackened ironwork. Kyle waved both torches into an X and laid them on the debris-littered marble floor. He ran to the back of the tank, out of sight, and the Old Man knew he would hear from him on the small telephone attached to the rear of the tank.

"We can't make it any farther down the street," yelled Kyle over the internal hum of the communications system and the howling wind outside. "Follow us through this casino. On the other side of the machines there's another entrance back onto the street on the far side of Ground Zero."

"Okay," said the Old Man.

"Oh," said Kyle almost as an afterthought. "Does this thing have any ammo for its gun? Ours did a long time ago but we used that up."

"There are eleven rounds left."

"Don't fire in here! It's too dangerous. These buildings are barely standing up."

The line went dead, and shortly after, Kyle reappeared in the fuzzy gray optics, picking up his torches and waving them forward over his shoulders in bright white blurs of light and shadowy smoke toward a long hallway that stretched off into the depths of the casino.

When it became so dark inside the long hallway that the Old Man could see nothing but gray, green, and ash, he switched on the tank's high beams and turned off the night vision.

They followed a wide way of rotting red carpet and dust-covered advertising. Signs that had once held meaning remained embedded in graffiti-gouged wood paneling. Beautiful girls, faded and long dead, promised wealth untold. Thrilling spectacles dully offered entertainments that were sure to dazzle. There were even peeling pictures of unending amounts of food.

Lobster.

I had forgotten about lobster!

Concentrate, Old Man!

They entered a massive room of slot machines and overturned gaming tables. Silvery coins lay heaped in piles. Large torches guttered from makeshift holders along the walls. Campfires burned intermittently among the arranged stockades of slot machines.

The Old Man could see the three guides talking among themselves as they moved slowly forward.

They're worried. They didn't expect this.

We've walked into a hornets' nest.

Sudden dark shadows arched through the upper atmosphere of the room and began to fall among the tank and the three guides.

They're firing arrows at us!

The Old Man could hear their impact distantly on the outer hull of the tank. The three guides retreated to the far side of the vehicle, using it for cover. Coins used as sling bullets began to ricochet like metallic rain upon the tank.

"Move forward toward that arch at the far end of this hall." It was Kyle on the tank's phone. "We should be able to get back out to the street if we go that way."

The Old Man gunned the tank's engine, hoping the three of them were clear, unable to know for sure if they were.

"Poppa, are they going to be okay?"

"Yes. I would prefer if maybe you just closed your eyes until I say it's good to look again, okay?"

There was no immediate reply and he suspected she would disobey him.

Beyond the arch, the tank's headlamp illuminated another long hallway. The ceiling sagged the length of it. Rich wood paneling that must have once assured the gambling audiences this was indeed the finest of places to lose all their money and homes had long since been pried loose in wide patches.

For firewood, I imagine.

At the end of the hall, they turned onto an arcade of shops long gutted. Fixtures spilled out onto a marble palazzo or hung like the bones of criminals from the ceiling.

The Old Man swiveled the gun sight, searching the optics for his three guides. He found them behind the tank, covering their retreat from the hall as dark figures swarmed beyond the light of the tank's headlamp. Far down the hall he could see more of the coin-mailed warriors advancing behind crude shields.

The Old Man backed the tank out and onto the main thoroughfare of the arcade pointing it toward where he hoped the exit might be.

I'm lost in here.

Grayson ran forward and waved at the Old Man to follow him.

Their torches are lost or gone out now.

The Old Man maneuvered the tank after the armored and masked Grayson who ran forward weaving into and out of the destruction and litter that had once been a grand passage of fine shops and luxuries. What the Old Man could not steer around he crushed beneath the tank's treads, hoping each time the right tread would not suddenly break and strand them all.

He checked the dosimeter.

The radiation is higher here. Maybe we are getting closer to the street again.

It's better than being trapped in here with these lunatics, my friend.

"Can I look now, Poppa?"

She listened to me.

And…

She is good that way.

"Not yet, just a little farther."

It was hot inside the tank and the Old Man wiped at the thick, stinging sweat on his forehead.

Maybe I am still sick.

Concentrate!

The explosions went off behind them.

The Old Man felt the tank lift up slightly and then shudder as it settled back down onto the palazzo. When he swiveled the gun sight to see what had happened behind them, all was a blossom of powdery white dust in the tank's optics. He could see nothing through its sudden storm.

He switched off the lights and activated the night vision.

Everything was still gray and floating dust.

No good, my friend.

He switched the headlight back on and returned to normal optics.

They've brought the ceiling down upon us. They must have explosives.

He searched for Kyle and Trash within the swirling dust and settling debris.

Trash stumbled forward, bleeding and waving at them to push on.

Where is Kyle?

There is no time, Old Man! Move forward or you and your granddaughter and the Boy will be trapped in here too.

The Old Man gassed the engine and swiveled the gun sight forward in time to avoid Grayson's crawling body. Large arrows jutted out of his back and chest and arm. He rose stiffly, firing his rifle wildly with one hand into a darkened arch to their left. A moment later, another massive iron spike shot from the darkness and went straight through his chest.

The Old Man could hear his granddaughter screaming.

Ahead of the tank, dust clouds, thick and ashy, swirled through a jumble of broken debris. Where the path through the casino lay the Old Man could not see.

There is no clear way forward!

Trash appeared and waved wildly, passionately for him to follow her now.

She is all alone out there.

And…

She is very brave.

And…

They all were.

Everywhere, the Old Man could see moving shadows and sudden figures leaping as Trash walked forward, firing at unseen foes. When they neared the far end of the arcade, a massive dirty marble fountain rose up. Above it, bodies dangled from a dome of smashed glass and skeletal ironwork directly over the darkly stained marble sculptures within the dry fountain.

Trash went wide to the left, her gun hammering bullets into walls and doors where unseen oppressors lurked in the darkness. Suddenly her gunfire stopped and she slung the rifle back onto her shoulder, drawing out a large knife with her other hand. A man with tiny rat teeth rose up from within the fountain behind her and pulled her down onto the marble floor. Coin-mailed men rushed from the darkness and dragged her across the dusty litter, back toward the blackness behind a broken-down double door. They were already greedily clutching at her armor, ripping away her mask, revealing her horrified and angry face.

She's gone now.

There's nothing I can do to save her.

The Old Man had to release his sweating hands from the controls for fear of breaking them.

Think!

There is nothing I can do to help her.

You can't save her. But you can help her, my friend.

The Old Man swiveled the main gun toward the broken-down doors, pointing the barrel into the darkness beyond where they had dragged her. He reached over to the fire control switch.

The Boy slid past him, opening the emergency hatch in the deck plate.

How did he know that was there?

The Boy looked at the Old Man.

"Just get back to the street," he said, his voice hoarse and dry. "I'll find her. Then I'll find you."

And he was gone, closing the hatch behind him.

The Old Man waited, unsure of how long it would take the Boy to crawl out from between the treads. A moment later he appeared, steel tomahawk out, limping toward the broken-down door and the darkness beyond.

Go now!

The Old Man gunned the engine and circled the fountain. On the other side he found a large arch, once grand and opulent, now fading in neglect and damage, leading to another long hallway. Along its length, torches revealed a hall of horrors as beheaded mannequins held their arms upward. The long hall narrowed to an opening impossible for the tank to clear and the Old Man pressed the engine to full power, closed his eyes, and smashed the tank straight into it.

On the other side he slammed on the brakes and the tank skidded across marble, careening into a lone desk that must have once greeted arriving guests. The Old Man swiveled the turret and found a wide entrance leading back out onto the street. He pivoted the tank and throttled the engine to full as it tore through the last remnants of broken glass and bent steel, surging out onto the wide steps and a driveway that led off toward the main road. The tank bumped its way down the steps, crushed an ancient taxi, and charged up the driveway and out onto casino row.

All around him, radiation-rotted towers and palaces rose up in only the color of burnt ash. Dry white grass and burnt earth lay beneath a constant snowfall of settling radioactive debris. In the middle of the street lay an airliner in two distinct parts, its center section long gone, the tail rising up at an odd angle in the background, the cockpit smiling sickly at some bad joke played forty years ago. Its sweptback wings akimbo, as though in some confession of final helplessness.

The dust storm had stopped.

The moon was out.

Fading flakes of ash drifted like snow on a winter's night.

Everything that was not burnt black or tired gray remained bone white.

The Old Man checked the "outside" dosimeter. It was pegged to the red line. The "inside" counter was high, but still within the green.

It works.

Our little blanket works.

The Old Man maneuvered the tank onto the main road.

A path of frozen destruction lay carved from when the airliner had come down onto the street moments after takeoff and left a clear path through the forty years since. The Old Man settled the tank into the ditch of scarred asphalt and followed it east through the last of the collapsing palaces.

At dawn, in the shadows among the pink light of first morning, the Old Man watched the ancient city refuse to illuminate in color. He had the tank backed up against a wall in a vacant lot beyond the casinos, watching the leaning towers and fallen arcades, waiting for the Boy.

There isn't much fuel left.

I'll give him until noon and then we must leave.

His granddaughter was asleep.

He'd had to explain a lot of what had happened. What she had seen. What she should've never seen.

And there was much he could not explain.

So he told her about ice cream.

She'd never had ice cream.

"One day we'll find an ice cream maker, one with a hand crank. All we need is some milk, maybe we can get some from our goats, and then we only need to find some salt. Then we can have ice cream. You will love it."

Sugar. You will need sugar, my friend.

There is the sugar from the date palms. We could use that.

"I know I will, Poppa. I just know I'll love it."

"There are even flavors." And the Old Man began to name as many as he could remember.

Soon she was asleep.

I hope she dreams only of ice cream.

Ice cream dreams.

You were wrong to bring her with you, my friend.

I know that now.

In time, he saw the Boy limping across an abandoned lot of glittering broken glass, crossing a gray and dusty road, and cutting through a fallen mesh fence. Heading for the tank.

He was alone.

CHAPTER 29

As the morning sun began to bake the quiet destruction between the empty spaces and cracked parking lots of Vegas, the Old Man climbed down from the tank and handed the last of a half-filled canteen to the Boy.

The Boy began to drink, holding the canteen with his powerful right hand. The Old Man looked at the dried blood covering the Boy's arms, still staining the tomahawk.

There is no need to ask him what happened in there.

He left the Boy to drink water alone in the silence of the place.

Inside the tank, he started the APU and radioed General Watt. Natalie.

"We're on the other side of Las Vegas now."

"Good." Her voice was warm and clear. Like she'd just had a cup of morning coffee. Like there might be a cup waiting for him, wherever she was.

As if such good things exist anymore.

As if there are such moments left in this world.

"It's a good thing you got us to that Radiation Shielding Kit," he said. Then he told her what he could of the night. He told her about the three. How they'd made a way when there seemed none. And how each had died in doing so. He could not tell the one without the other. When he told General Watt of the bomb crater they'd come upon, she asked about the shielding kit. "We needed it to cross through a bomb crater."

"You've used it already?"

There wasn't exactly alarm in her voice. Not exactly. But something.

Concern?

"Yes." Then, "Is that going to be a problem?" asked the Old Man, hearing the sudden worry in his own voice. "Should we… is there something else ahead…"

Pause.

"It won't be a problem," said Natalie, her voice gentle and calm. "We'll find a way to keep you safe. If you had to use it to survive, then it had to be used."

"I hope we didn't… I hope that was all right," stammered the Old Man. "I hope…"

"It's all right."

Her voice is like the voice of someone who knows that eventually everything is going to be just fine, no matter how bad it looks right now. No matter what you've done to mess things up.

You need that, my friend, so take it because it is being given away for free and also because you are too poor to disagree.

Yes.

"There is nothing to worry about at this present time," said General Watt. Natalie. "It'll be all right. We will find a way to get you here."

But the Old Man knew that it wasn't all right. That some change had taken place in the wind and weather, the current and tide, and finally as it must, the last port at journey's end.

And.

There is always a price to pay for such things.

Yes.

Always.

And someone will have to pay for it.

Someone will.

In the hatch, beneath the sun, the Old Man felt cold.

The road up and out of southern Las Vegas climbed through tired rocks and vast crumbling urban sprawls of falling houses and collapsed roadways. A barely readable sign indicated the way to Lake Mead.

In time Las Vegas disappeared behind them, fading into the heat of a day that chased them with its memories of the night. The road led alongside the outlines of buildings once standing and now long gone. The land opened up onto a massive downslope of red earth and gray rock. At the bottom lay the glittering blue of a wide lake stretching out and away from them.

The road began a series of twists through rock formations that seemed foreign and somehow of another world. Another world the Old Man dimly remembered from the covers of science fiction books about strange and alien planets. A crumbling tower rose up from the red rocks alongside the lake and the road. Its tenure seemed thin and merely a matter of time.

The road that led to the Dam cut across the face of this reddish-brown rock above a steep drop into canyons below. Beyond all this, the Dam climbed skyward and their eyes saw what man had once made.

"We made this, Poppa?"

"Yes," was all the Old Man could say, his voice unexpectedly choking with pride.

I did not think it would affect me this way.

And…

I had no idea.

The Boy lay sleeping. The Old Man stopped the tank and shook him.

He should see this too.

He should know we weren't all bad.

They climbed out from their hatches, his granddaughter in her new flight jacket, the Boy still covered in blood. The Old Man shielded his eyes against the blaze of noon with his wrinkled and calloused hand. The massive Dam stretched high above them.

Yes.

We built this.

And…

We were not all bad.

The people who came out from the Dam wore the same shreds of armor and carried the same rifles as Kyle, Grayson, and Trash.

A large man walked out in front of them. There was a smile on his face. He wore faded denim and an old Stetson hat, sun-bleached and torn.

"You can't be with King Charlie if you've gotten out of your tank," he bellowed, his voice bombastic, echoing off the canyon walls and the Dam.

"We aren't," said the Old Man, sounding thin and dry, his voice a small croak.

When did my voice start to sound like that of an old person?

The people behind the Big Man began to clap. Someone whooped with excitement. They patted each other. There was even weeping.

These people are in need of good news.

Yes, my friend, and they seem to think you are it.

The people of the Dam approached the tank, surrounding it at once. Feeling it. Touching it. Marveling.

These are Kyle's people. Grayson's.

And Trash's too.

We took her in.

That's what Kyle had said.

We took her in.

There were questions all at once and each one different.

Who are you?

Where'd you get the tank?

How'd you make it through?

Where are you going?

Do you need fuel?

Have you seen…?

The Old Man grew confused in his rush to answer each question. Starting an answer and then being pulled away by another. Until he saw the Big Man staring at him. Still smiling. Waiting. And even though there was a smile, a big smile, there was also worry. Worry in the eyes. There was a question about the three and the Old Man could tell it was waiting for him and that the Big Man would never ask it. He would never ask it because maybe in the long days since its first being asked, he had answered it for himself. In his mind Kyle, Grayson, and

Trash and all the others who had been trapped beyond Vegas had perished long ago. They must've.

But there are nights. Nights when one wonders what might still be possible despite all the evidence to the contrary. Nights when you rise alone for just a drink of water, and in the silence you sigh and think of unanswered questions.

You think of loved ones and where they might be.

And even…

If, they might be.

And when there are no answers in the night, you sigh and think…

What am I going to do now?

"Do you know Kyle?" asked the Old Man.

The Big Man nodded, his eyes changing to hope and belief and then disbelief all at once. Speaking as he nods. Speaking words as if he cannot believe these words he has said so many times in the night might actually be real words.

"He's alive? My son is…" the Big Man's voice faltered, unwilling to form that last word again.

Alive.

His son. All this time he has imagined him dead and hated himself for it.

"He…" tries the Old Man and stops.

Tell them, my friend.

I'm afraid to. How?

Just tell them. In time it will be a mercy to them, though they will not know it today.

No.

No, today will be for grief. Which is also, sometimes, a mercy.

Other names are quickly shouted out. Names that are not Kyle or Grayson.

There were others before it was only just the three of them.

An older couple. She is already clinging to a man turning white with shock, holding on to her as much as she is holding on to him.

Holding on to each other.

The Old Man sees his own son.

And wonders…

What is he doing right now?

And…

How do I tell them?

The truth, my friend. The truth. In the end it is what we must have. There is nothing else.

All eyes watched him.

He shook his head slowly.

"They made a way for us," said the Old Man. "Where there wasn't one."

The Old Man wanted to lower his eyes. He wanted to look away as they stared at him for meaning, for answers, for some shred of long denied truth.

But it would be wrong to look away. Cowardly.

And then someone asked, as if it wasn't already known to all. Someone asked, "Did they make it?"

The Old Man remembered weeping and feeling he had no right to. The three were theirs, not his.

But he wept for them all the same and they did not stop him.

Grayson's mother cried out her son's name.

The Old Man saw her husband pulling her into him, holding on to her. He was like a man being swept away by a river.

CHAPTER 30

The Old Man sat in the cantina drinking clear, cold water and listening to the old pipes above his head creak and gurgle within the Dam. Only a frail lantern illuminated the small dark room.

This is where they gather when the day is done.

Like when the boy would bring you the papers, Santiago, that were a few days, or even a week old, and you would read them together and talk about baseball.

And like your village, my friend, in the late afternoon, when the first of the evening brought out the scent of the desert sage, heavy and thick.

We did not have papers with baseball scores, though. But yes, this place is where they come at the end of the day or when they have something to celebrate like a birthday. Just like we did back in the village, in the old mining hall outside the kitchen. So I know this place, and I know these people.

The Big Man came in.

Kyle's dad.

He went to the cooler that held the cold spring water and poured some into a porcelain mug. He drank, filled it again, then drank again, each time emitting a tired but satisfied, "Ahhh."

"You have a good spring for your water," said the Old Man.

The Big Man turned, surprised.

He must have thought he was all alone. He was expecting the solitude, the moment apart. The moment apart from their collective grief. He must be their leader. He must have wanted time for his own, personal grief.

For his son.

"We've always had that to be thankful for," said the Big Man. "Good water. A good safe place. Good people."

The Big Man sat down.

"Normally we'd have been celebrating your arrival… but… I guess not." The Big Man looked down into his mug of water. "We thought, that is, some of us did, we thought we'd buried those who didn't make it back, a while ago. Others kept holding out. Hoping there might be a chance some of 'em would make it back, someday."

You. You were holding out.

And.

I would too.

"I'm sorry," said the Old Man.

"Ain't your fault."

"Tomorrow," began the Big Man, "we'll be back to our old selves, fightin' and crabbin' at one or the other. Maybe we'll kill one of the cows and have a 'Q' up top. That'd be real nice."

"The showers were enough," said the Old Man. "More than enough. We'll move on tomorrow if you can spare some of your fuel."

"Fuel? You can have all the fuel you want; we've done lost all our vehicles trying to keep the roads open. All our rides are either out there in pieces, torn to shreds by King Charlie's crazies, or they're broke down in the garage below."

"What will we find in the east?"

"East," said the Big Man and rubbed his chin. "East is Kingman and Flagstaff and then you're in Apache lands. The Apaches told us there was some people out in ABQ who were makin' a pretty good go of it."

The Old Man waited. The Big Man looked like he had more to say.

"Truth is, I couldn't tell you what you'll find beyond a thousand meters out in front of this Dam. These raiders come down from the North a year and a half ago and ruined our plans to get a network of roads and outposts open and connected. They went wide of Apache lands but they came down hard on Kingman and straight into Vegas. We caught a few. That was how we found out they were lookin' for old Area 51. We didn't know what they were up to but we figured we needed to keep them out of there. Tried to get 'em to focus on the Dam but they wouldn't have it. They dug in all around Vegas and kept us out of our salvage up in Creech. That was how you met my boy. Kyle."

Silence.

"He was a good leader," said the Old Man.

In the dark of the cantina, in the shadows thrown by the dim lantern, the Old Man heard the Big Man sob once and so suddenly that a moment later he wondered if he'd even heard it at all.

"I know," mumbled the Big Man. "I know that about my son."

Later, the Old Man found the Boy near the tank, sitting against its dusty treads. The Old Man sat down next to him.

It's time I try to talk to him.

"Are you hungry?"

The Boy shook his head.

"When you went back… did you find her?"

The Boy looked at the Old Man sharply.

He's confused.

There's another "her" besides the girl Trash.

When the look of bewilderment passed from the Boy's face and he understood who the Old Man was talking about, he said, "I did."

The Old Man waited.

It'll come. Whatever his story is, it'll come.

Just wait. Be patient.

Inside the Boy's eyes, the Old Man found a story he didn't know how to read just yet.

Just like salvage. There's always a story. Even in the eyes of a man. Or a boy.

He's all alone.

The Old Man groaned as he got to his knees.

He rested his hand briefly on the Boy's muscled shoulder, and after it jumped and settled at his touch, he squeezed it firmly.

I'm here.

And…

You are too.

That's important these days.

The Old Man stood and walked back toward the doorway that led from the garage within the Dam, back to the small rooms they'd made available for them.

The Boy spoke.

Just before the Old Man reached the door.

"We take everything with us."

The Old Man turned, searching the dark and finding the shadow of the Boy.

"They never leave." The Boy's voice was husky and deep. "Even if you want them to."

Silence.

"Then maybe we really don't want them to go just yet," said the Old Man and turned back to the door and was gone.

Deep in the night, the Old Man awoke, sweating.

I was drowning, but not in water. In darkness.

His granddaughter is asleep on her cot.

The Boy's is empty.

The Old Man lay back down, breathing slowly, willing his racing heart to settle.

The Boy is still disturbed by what he's had to do within the casino. Maybe he is forever damaged just like his weak side. Maybe I should just leave him here.

Stop. It's the middle of the night and it's dark, my friend. The worst time to try to make plans or important decisions.

And the Old Man thought of how his friend Santiago had followed the fish all through the night, all alone, being pulled deeper and deeper into the gulf.

CHAPTER 31

Night fell across the western horizon, and atop the Dam the first ribs of meat were handed out to those who had waited throughout that long, hot, dusty afternoon.

The ribs were meaty and full of juice.

The Old Man ate one sitting next to his granddaughter, surrounded by the people of the Dam, telling them of Tucson. Telling them about a city that was lost and now found. Telling them of lemon trees and salvage.

"We were trying to open the roads and keep the lines of communication up between the settlements," said one of them after the Old Man had finished telling all there was to tell of Tucson. "Maybe we could still do that with Tucson."

Everybody quietly agreed this might be a good idea.

Despite the lack of vehicles.

The Army of Crazy in Vegas.

The rumors of the East.

The tragedy of the three still hangs over them.

What could I offer that would make it better for them?

Nothing, my friend. Nothing.

"Poppa, where is he?" she said referencing the Boy.

The Old Man looked down into her big brown eyes.

Has she already fallen for him? I thought she was still too young for that.

Who can know the heart, my friend?

I thought I did.

And…

You were wrong.

I'm almost convinced now that we must leave the Boy. He's wounded. Damaged and what if he fails when we need him most. Or what if he turns on us.

If you were to ask yourself, my friend, can you trust him? What would your answer be?

I don't know.

"He's missing everything, Poppa!" she said looking up from her plate. Worried.

"I'll go look for him. I'll find him. Watch my plate."

"Okay, Poppa."

The Old Man found the Boy near the tank down in the garage. Securing their gear. He had rearranged the drums into a better configuration for drawing fuel.

When he saw the Old Man watching him, he stopped.

"It will be better this way," he seemed to apologize.

The Old Man walked across the silent and dark garage.

Tell him he'll have to stay behind. That he can't go on with you.

You mean, tell him I don't trust him.

"It will be better that way," said the Old Man. "You've done good. Thank you."

The Boy smiled.

In the days since he has been with us I don't think I've actually seen him smile. Inside of him there is still something that wants to though. Something that "done" things and a life on the road hasn't managed to burn up yet.

"Come. There's meat. Good ribs from a steer. There might even be one left for you."

The Boy hopped down from the tank awkwardly and limped toward the Old Man, the memory of his smile refusing to let go.

Sometimes he is so able and strong, you forget half his body is withered.

They turned and the Old Man patted the Boy once more on the shoulder, feeling the powerful warmth of his strong right side, remembering the sudden smile.

And he thought, 'I won't leave you.' And, 'Maybe you just need to be salvaged.'

The Old Man did not sleep much.

Maybe I slept a little.

But not enough to be of measure, to count. To be worth it.

He was up before anyone.

Close to dawn.

He went to the tank.

The tank and drums were full of the home-brewed fuel.

Also, we have all the water we can carry.

They would have rice and beans, cooked already, and flour tortillas they could heat on the warmth of the engine.

There are over two hundred and fifty miles to Flagstaff. They tell me there might be fuel there. So maybe…

I am tired of worrying about fuel. It will either be there or it won't. But I am tired of worrying about it. I am anxious to be on the road and to be done with this errand.

You are not worried, my friend?

I am that too.

At dawn, the Big Man and the others arrived. In time the storage cases full of rice, beans, and tortillas were loaded on board the tank. The Boy came carrying their things. The Old Man's granddaughter, fresh from the showers, wrapped in her shiny green bomber jacket against the cold that lay deep within the Dam, carried just her sleeping bag.

The Old Man started the APU and fired the main engine. Smoke erupted across the garage and the people raced to raise the big door.

The Big Man climbed up on the turret as the Old Man throttled the engine back and forth, hoping the cause of the thick smoke was just moisture in the fuel.

"Never mind that," yelled the Big Man over the whispering roar of the engine. "Our home brew is a little watery, burns rough, but it works!" He smiled broadly. "Tell Reynolds at Kingman that Conklin sent you and to give ya any fuel, if he's got it. Reynolds is good people."

The Old Man shook the Big Man's hand and made ready to go.

Once everyone was clear, he pivoted the tank toward the entrance and gassed it until they were out in the morning sun followed by a cloud of blue smoke.

The right tread may or may not be going bad and we make more smoke than we should. So there is that to worry about.

You complain too much, my friend.

Yes, I know.

Beyond the Dam, a long valley slid away toward the southeast and a timeworn highway ran through it. The Old Man checked his map.

We'll link up with the 40 in Kingman. We can follow that all the way into Albuquerque.

Long-gone fires had consumed much of the land in the years after the long winter. Wild growth covered what lay in the flatlands between the two mountain ranges that defined the valley.

It reminds me of the highway alongside our village, except it's lonelier.

Hours later the Old Man spied the first riders high atop the cut-rock mesas as the highway twisted through red rock, closing in on Kingman. Who they were and what they wore was unknowable at distance. They were mere shadows high up on the broken rocks. They rode horses and carried long spears from which dark feathers dangled in the breeze. But that they knew of the tank and its passage was sure to be counted on.

CHAPTER 32

The Boy looked back at him and the Old Man nodded.

We have both seen the riders.

The Old Man was driving, following the bumping, uneven road that wound toward Kingman.

"Just keep on the road and try to stay near the center," his granddaughter told him. "It looks to be in better shape there than on the edges, Poppa."

"Okay."

Now she is giving me advice on how to drive this thing. Hoping that maybe I will let her take over.

The Old Man switched from the intercom to radio and spoke.

"Natalie?"

After a moment the General was there.

"We're beyond the Dam and headed toward Kingman. Supposedly there are settlements along Interstate 40 and we've been told there might be some warlord called King Charlie causing a lot of trouble. I just wanted to let you know about that and our progress."

White noise popped and crackled.

"I've reviewed the satellite imagery from our archives." Now the General's voice was loud and clear.

"And I do find activity along your route when I use a time-lapse algorithm to detect signs of human activity. Do you have any idea who this King Charlie is and where he might be headquartered?"

'That was fast,' thought the Old Man. 'Unless she'd already been looking at these places.'

But how could she have known?

"I don't know much about him. Just that they call him King Charlie. Does he have anything to do with your situation?"

"The truth is, I don't know. We can't actually leave our bunker and find out who is trying to enter the complex. The radiation outside is incredibly high and would be lethal for even a short duration of time. Other than vague low-res satellite images of a large group of people trying to break down our front door, we know very little. Our engineers tell us the main door won't hold much longer."

"How long?"

Silence.

"A week."

The Old Man looked at the case on the deck of the tank.

Project Einstein.

What does it do?

Ask her now.

Maybe I don't want to know just yet.

"So we must hurry then?"

"I would advise so, yes, for our sakes."

"If we can find fuel, then it shouldn't be a problem."

There is fuel.

There is also King Charlie.

There is also all that end-of-the-world between here and there. All that destruction caused by nuclear warheads and two-year-long winters and after that, the forty years of neglect and craziness that followed. But yes, if we can find fuel then we can show up with this device and free you from your prison. By whatever means the device uses.

I must ask her what the device does.

Yes, my friend. You should.

"Please hurry," said Natalie. General Watt.

"We will."

The riders had disappeared. The Old Man leaned out of the hatch and tapped the Boy who slithered back inside the turret, out of the wind and heat so they could talk.

"Who are they?" asked the Old Man.

The Boy shook his head.

"I don't know. Some sort of tribe. They don't seem to be like the people back at the Dam."

"So maybe they're not from Kingman. We're close to there."

The Boy thought for a long moment.

"No, I do not think they're from Kingman. Perhaps they are the Apache the people at the Dam talked about. Maybe that's who we see up in the rocks."

"Maybe."

"Poppa!" shouted his granddaughter over the intercom.

"Is everything okay?" the Old Man asked.

"Poppa! Everything is great! I think it's a circus! Look at it!"

They had come suddenly upon the stockade settlement at Kingman. From the highway overpass they could see the remains of an L-shaped strip mall centered around an old chain grocery store as the eastern and southern walls of the settlement. Claptrap towers had been thrown up from the roof. The parking lot had been walled off to the north and west with stacked cars and other precarious towers. The driveway into the shopping center was now a junk-welded gate thrown wide open.

In the middle of the road that led underneath the highway and alongside the gate and walls of the stockade, there was indeed a circus.

Colorful patchwork tents rose up drunkenly into the vivid orange daylight. Banners and flags whipped frantically in the sudden breeze. An elephant bellowed loudly as activity and movement ground to a halt.

From the street of the carnival all eyes looked up toward the overpass and the rumbling tank.

Above cups held to open mouths, the glossy eyes of the Stockaders watched the Old Man. And among the Stockaders, fire-breathers, contortionists, and strong men also watched, their eyes quick and darting, deep and dark.

Wide-eyed children played in the dirt and merriment.

Adults with overly large freak eyes in heads misshapen and deformed held ladles within punch tubs.

In the center of it all stood one small figure. Huge dark eyes set in a narrow head, adorned by lanky hair and a woven crown above punch-stained lips, gazed up at the Old Man knowingly. A scrawny neck and a gangling body ending in too-large feet, all dressed in foolery, hands tensed as claw-like fingers rhythmically opened and closed.

"Is it a circus, Poppa? There's tents and colors and punch and games just like you told me about. Is it?"

Yes, the circus is in town.

CHAPTER 33

The Old Man, still holding his map, climbed down from the tank. His granddaughter was already dancing around, doing cartwheels along the overpass.

"What's that big animal, Poppa?"

"An elephant."

"An elephant!" she screamed.

A delegation of Stockaders seasoned with circus performers climbed the dusty embankment toward the tank. The Old Man checked the Boy who stood atop the turret.

"Be ready."

The Boy nodded softly.

It's good he came with us.

A paunchy Stockader came forward, his face bright red and burning beneath a bushy mustache. His fat lips were punch stained, his eyes glossy from drink.

"What a day of miracles! First the circus and now this! I'm Reynolds." He held out a beefy hand and the Old Man shook it, feeling thick viscous sweat on it.

"We're just passing by," mumbled the Old Man.

"Oh come now, ya gotta see this thing!" bellowed Reynolds too loudly.

"Oh, Poppa, the ele — the elemant… the… what's its name, Poppa?"

"Elephant."

"The elephant!" she cried.

Everyone cheered.

And the Fool was there.

He beamed at the Old Man.

"We need fuel," said the Old Man. "The people at the Dam said you might have some. Then we really must go."

The Old Man felt his hand suddenly taken between the Fool's long claws.

"But we've come all this way and we have so much to give you!" begged the Fool. "Oh please, come see the elephant!"

"The elephant!" shrieked his granddaughter again.

Everyone cheered and even the elephant bellowed distantly.

"You're going to love this, Nuncle," assured the Fool as he dragged the Old Man forward, down the off-ramp and into the circus. "Things that were lost are coming back. Amazing things. Free things. The whole world will be ours again!"

His granddaughter raced forward toward the throng surrounding the elephant. The Old Man turned his head back to look over the heads of the pushers who pushed him forward into the circus outside the gates. The Boy stood atop the tank, his strong right arm dangling just above the haft of his tomahawk.

A tin cup is pressed into the Old Man's hand and he drinks knowing he should be careful, but all eyes and even the eyes of the Fool, are watching him.

Pleading.

Begging.

"Huzzah!" shout all the Players when the Old Man takes a thirsty drink.

His granddaughter is hoisted by three Strong Men aboard the elephant who immediately stands on its hind legs, raises its trunk, and bellows again.

The Old Man breaks out into a cold sweat sensing the sudden uncomfortable fear and helplessness one feels as he watches his granddaughter atop this gigantic and wild beast.

Reynolds, close and breathy, whispers hotly, "Ain't it a trick?"

Conklin!

"Conklin says hello."

For a whisker Reynolds seems bewildered. Then he slaps his head, spilling punch across his vest and bushy mustache.

"There's a fellow!" roars Reynolds. "Knew'd him ever since the first days after. How is McKenna?"

"I don't know McKenna. But Conklin told me to ask you for fuel if you still have any."

His granddaughter screamed with delight, her face merely an open mouth, her head thrown back as her hair sprang wildly out into the blue sky.

This is wrong. What is something horrible happens to her? What if the giant beast throws her and then tramples her? What if anything goes wrong?

The Old Man feels cold sweat beginning to run down his back as he imagines the worst.

"Fuel? Got all the fuel you can take on," says Reynolds. "We'll see about it tomorrow, all right?"

The Old Man starts to protest but Reynolds is off through the crowd roaring and backslapping, calling for more of the circus-brewed punch.

The day is hot.

Too hot.

When the Old Man looks down, his tin cup is drained and his mouth feels sugary.

"Where'd ya get that machine, Nuncle?"

The Fool stares smilingly up at the Old Man, his thin body posed into a slant, as though leaning backward over a cliff.

The Old Man doesn't answer, wants to answer, but cannot.

I am tired and I feel my body relaxing into all this.

Let go and enjoy it. The only one ruining it is you and your fears.

And I feel so good.

Like…?

Like?

Like the motel, my friend?

Oh…!

"You look like you've just swallowed a rotten bug, Nuncle." The Fool is ladling more punch into the Old Man's tin cup.

I feel rooted to the earth.

I can hear my granddaughter. High above and far away.

You never should have brought her with you.

Then I would've had to come all this way alone.

And die alone.

"Great things are coming again, Nuncle," simpered the Fool. "Medicine and well-being. Food for all. Oh,

Nuncle, here is the best part. There'll be a work. A work to rebuild it all just as it once was but better and completely new. Even different. Isn't that amazing, Nuncle?"

The Fool seems confused. The Old Man stares at him as though he is looking at a picture on a wall.

He is merely a drawing.

A photograph even.

Pictures were once so common you deleted them if they weren't exactly what you wanted.

"Nuncle, you must stop swallowing these bugs. Perhaps you'd like to lie down. I'll sing you a song or recite a poem. The Fool threw his head back and put one long claw-like hand across his chest. "The Twenty-Dollar Burger for just a Quarter! At FattyBurger you'll think your stomach's been hit by a mortar. FattyBurger, All Meat, No Veggies, All Night."

The Fool beamed and threw his claws wide and open, accepting applause.

"I bet you remember that one from Before, Nuncle. I bet you remember when it was shown on the telly-screen? Those times were grand, those times were fun, those times are coming back I tell you all and one. What we lost is coming back the same and different. And the difference is better. Difference is always better. Change is always good. Right, Nuncle?"

His granddaughter is at his side. She is clutching him and showing him a streamer on a stick someone has given her.

"Poppa! Look!" She waves it across his vision and it seems a dragon crossing the desert sky full of flame and smoke.

We must…

"We must go," he mumbles.

All around the Old Man the cries and shrieks of the crowd mixed with some awkward and distorted off-tone music have been playing and growing in his ears. But beneath that, the Old Man hears the guttural growl of a small but vicious animal.

He looks deep into his granddaughter's eyes.

We are surrounded and there is no way out.

The world begins to tilt. First one way, and then another.

The Fool is growling.

"It's your turn to drive," says the Old Man.

"Okay, Poppa!" she explodes.

"You can have mine," he mumbles to himself as she grabs him by the hand.

She is dragging him back to the tank, pulling him forward in fact.

"Oh, thank you, thank you, thank you, Poppa!"

He feels claws pulling at his other arm and he shakes it stiffly as though controlling it from very far away. The Fool cartwheels in the dirt and an instant later is up in a wide-legged stance. His too-long arms hang down and low, the claws opening and closing.

He is growling.

The Old Man closes his eyes at the foot of the embankment as his granddaughter scrambles up and away toward the tank at the top.

The tank she gets to drive again.

"C'mon, Poppa!" She beckons, leaving him behind.

"What about yer fuel, mister?" Reynolds's face looms comically into the Old Man's narrow field of red dirt and rock and sudden blue sky.

The Old Man is grabbed heavily from behind.

The Boy is dragging him, one-armed, up the hill with little effort and much force.

The Fool at the foot of the hill seems no longer friendly. In fact, he seems given completely over to a purple anger none of the other revelers notice. The Fool stares hatefully upward at the retreating Old Man and the Boy.

Teeth gritted.

Jaw clenched.

A fire burns in the darkness behind his too-large puppet face and coal-black eyes.

The tank's engine whispers into its roar.

The Old Man is dragged upward across the hot armor and rests, catching his breath and holding on to the turret, while the Boy pours water over his burning old head.

Thank you, he thinks he says aloud but is not sure if he has.

The circus before the Stockade races away behind them and even though the Old Man can only see the colors and pennants in the distance, he can feel those hateful eyes of the Fool still on him.

Watching them.

Following them.

Chasing after them.

CHAPTER 34

The Old Man is sleeping on the deck of the tank, inside the turret. When he awakes, he feels the rumbling engine and the grinding treads shuddering through the frame all about him. He looks up and sees the Boy in the hatch. It is still daylight in the hints of sky he can see beyond the Boy.

I feel like I've been drinking.

You were.

Yes, but more than I actually did.

The Old Man rubs his face, feelings saliva along his cheek.

I was really sleeping.

He sits up and feels dull and faraway and thirsty. The Boy sees that the Old Man is awake and climbs out onto the turret and the Old Man rises into the hatch. They are headed north. It is late afternoon.

I've been asleep most of the day.

The old highway winds through a ponderosa of wide dry fields and clusters of stunted oak. Stubby fortresses of rock erupt suddenly throughout the landscape.

It feels quieter here. I can tell, even above all the noise of the tank. It feels like we are climbing upward now. Climbing to the top of the world.

Later when they shut down the tank alongside the road and the noise of the engine has faded, the Old Man hears the quiet he'd suspected might be there and it envelops their resting place for the night.

We are heading up onto the high plateau now.

There is no sound of bird or beast. The smell of dust and grass are heavy in the early evening. His granddaughter sits on her haunches, watching the fire the Boy had built, the two of them waiting for the beans and rice to heat.

They would be just fine without me.

The Old Man watches the dry slope of the land and red rock and the stubby trees packed tightly together.

It feels like no one has been here for some time.

So where did the circus come from?

The thought of the Fool sends a cold shiver through his thin muscles and chest.

The whole thing felt wrong.

Maybe you just overreacted, my friend?

No. No, I don't think I did. There was something wrong about the whole…

When you were young, you noticed that older people were always afraid. Afraid of kidnappers and telemarketers. Afraid of the new. Afraid of the unknown. Maybe you are old now and afraid of new things, my friend?

Maybe the old of my youth were just cautious. And I am old.

He walked back to their small fire, smelling the smoke and the food and the heavy scent of sagebrush thick in the first of the evening cool.

"Poppa, tell me all about elephants," she said.

The Old Man looked at the Boy. The Boy watched him.

Is he nodding? Does he want to know about elephants also?

Remember he too is young. To the young the world is exciting and not frightening. The world is elephants and not… fools or clowns?

Psychopaths.

Evil.

"What do you want to know about them? he asked as she handed him his plate. In the first bite he knew he was starving.

I am hungry like I was when I was young. So maybe I am not old.

You are old, my friend. Like me.

"Where'd they come from? What do they eat? Can they do other tricks? Was that the biggest one you've ever seen? You know, Poppa, tell us everything.

Chewing quickly, shoveling another bite into his still-moving mouth, he looked at the Boy.

The Boy nodded.

And so the Old Man told them all about elephants. All about Africa. All about lions and things he'd read in books and been taught in school when he was young.

Later, when the fire was low and he could hear them both sleeping, he lay still and watched the stars above.

I did not think I knew so much about elephants.

CHAPTER 35

The road wound higher and higher into the forests that surrounded Flagstaff. For a while the going was slow as the tank maneuvered around lone eruptions of pine that shot through the lanes of the old highway.

In time, the crumbling remains of buildings poked through the unchecked growth, and when the Old Man went to consult the map as to how much farther they might go that day, he could not find it.

When did I…

When the Fool shook your hand.

The Old Man replayed the moment in the miles to come, as his granddaughter called out her intentions each time they needed to maneuver off-road.

"Okay, Poppa, we're going around this crazy tree."

I was pretty out of it yesterday. I could have dropped it in the dust perhaps.

"Poppa, we'll go to the right of this collapsed bridge, okay?"

Or anyone in the circus or the town could have snatched it from me.

"Poppa, how do you think that truck managed to flip itself across all the lanes? What a bad driver he must've been!"

Or it is somewhere here with us and I have simply misplaced it.

They passed the fire-blackened remains of a vehicle, the likes of which the Old Man had never seen before. Three blackened skeletons lay next to its massive wheels, still twisting in agony.

Or laughing.

In the end, when we are all skeletons, who will be able to tell if we were crying or laughing at what has happened to us?

No one, my friend.

And…

It won't be important anymore.

"What kind of car was that, Poppa?"

"I don't know. I've never seen its like before and maybe the fire made it unrecognizable."

"Why do you think they just sat there and let it burn, Poppa?"

He didn't answer.

"Why, Poppa?"

"Because there was nothing they could do about it."

"That doesn't make any sense."

No, it doesn't.

The Stockade at Flagstaff was a collection of fallen pine logs that had once formed a wall for defense and since had been dragged away from a hotel that overlooked the old highway.

The Old Man let the tank idle outside in the parking lot of the hotel. They watched, waiting for somebody to come out and greet them.

The Boy's strong hand rested against the tomahawk.

There are leaves and debris here. No one has been here in quite a while.

Yes. No one.

The Old Man turned off the tank and listened. He could hear a crow calling out stridently.

I have a very bad feeling about this place.

What kind of bad feeling?

The kind that says I do not want to know what I might find in there. That kind of feeling. The feeling of knowing that whatever you find, you won't like it.

The Old Man dismounted and the Boy followed.

As his granddaughter began to climb out of the driver's hatch, he motioned for her to stay. Her look of displeasure was instantaneous.

"It's your turn to guard the tank," he called back to her.

She sat down, dangling her feet over the side.

The Old Man heard the crunch of gravel beneath his boots as he and the Boy crossed the tired parking lot.

In the lobby they found nothing. No one.

The old furniture was gone. Instead there were desks.

As though someone had set up some kind of headquarters here.

And where are they now?

And where will we find fuel?

"What do you think happened here?" asked the Boy.

There is a story of salvage here. But what it is, I don't know.

"I can't tell. They had walls. They had shelter. If they were attacked, there should at least be bodies."

The Boy limped through the dusty light to the back of the lobby.

He's heading to the bar. There was always a bar back that way in these kinds of places. How does he know that?

Maybe he knows more of these places alongside the road than I do. Maybe he was born and raised in these places. Maybe they are as familiar to him as my shed would be to me.

You don't live there anymore, my friend.

It's hard to think that I live or lived in any other place, ever. My shed will always be home for me.

After a moment, when he could see only the dim outline of the Boy, he called out, "Did you find anything back there?"

The Boy returned, holding a coffee mug.

He held it out to the Old Man.

Inside, the remains of a punch-red syrup had dried into a shell at the bottom of the mug.

The Old Man smelled it. He smelled the heat and the straw and the sugar and the Fool.

The Circus had come to town.

They had driven through the remains of the town and now the heat faded as the summer day bled away. In the afternoon, a cool pine breeze came up and dried the sweat on the Old Man's back.

North of town, a massive rock the size of a small mountain loomed high into the darkening sky. Flagstaff, falling into disrepair, surrendering to time, settled as night birds and small animals began their first forays into the early evening.

Above him, the pines that were reclaiming the town, growing up through roads and sidewalks and buildings, whispered together making a soft white noise.

They parked the tank underneath an overpass, and as they began to make the night's meal, the Old Man wandered through the remains of a nearby gas station.

There is nothing left here.

How could there be after forty years?

All those years of living and salvaging in the village, I thought that much of the world was the same as Yuma, or Los Angeles or the cities I had seen on TV. Destroyed. I felt as though our little village was the only place in all the world that had survived.

Remained.

Then you found Tucson and all these places. The Dam. The outpost. All the other places that seemed to have had their own stories since the bombs.

Yes, they were not all "nuked" or touched by war as we had imagined.

But everything is touched by our downfall.

Yes.

Everyone in those days ran for cover. Into the hills. Into the wilderness. Wherever they could, thinking only of escape. Unprepared for what it takes to live in such places…

Of wilderness.

Of desert.

Of wasteland.

The Old Man found a cash box underneath the counter inside the gas station, hidden on a small ledge out of sight.

He pulled it out onto the countertop where once lottery tickets and quick snacks must have waited for purchase. Now there was nothing.

How did they miss this?

The Old Man opened it and found a stack of brittle paper money lying within.

When you are coming for food you take what you can find. You've been living in the wilderness and all you've brought is long gone. Days turn to months. Months turn to years. So you go into town. Hoping that somewhere in it is a bag of stale chips or even a can of soup or stew that might still be good. Your mouth waters at the thought of such once-common delicacies.

You no longer think of lobster.

Or even money. What good is it when you're starving?

There was a kind of canned stew I loved in college. But I grew tired of it. I remember I didn't even buy any of it that last year.

What was it called?

The Old Man thought about all the times he had shopped for it, prepared it, eaten it.

And now I can't even remember its name.

He returned to the tank in the blue twilight of evening.

The Boy and his granddaughter had already eaten and when he approached through the darkness he could hear his granddaughter laughing.

The Boy must have said something, which is strange because he never talks unless he is spoken to.

He sat down to his plate of beans and rice. His granddaughter handed him a few fire-warmed tortillas.

This is like camping. When I was young we went camping a few times. It was like this.

You are thinking too much about the past and not about the present. You need fuel and to find a map so you know where you are going.

I remember the map mostly. All the way to Albuquerque, turn left, go north.

You cannot afford to make a mistake, my friend. Your fuel tanks won't suffer a wrong turn.

"Have either of you seen my map?"

The fire popped.

His granddaughter and the Boy each shook their heads.

The Old Man sighed to himself.

"I think I may have lost it."

Or the Fool took it, my friend.

I don't want to say that. I don't want to make him seem more frightening than he already is.

Why?

Because it will worry them.

No, why are you afraid of him?

Because there is reason to be afraid of him. Of that, I am very sure.

"Do you think it is lost for good?" asked the Boy.

The Old Man set his plate down, rubbing his fingers together because it had gotten hot as it lay next to the fire. He picked up the plate again. He sighed.

"Yes," he confessed.

It is best to admit the truth, even when you don't want to. Even if it makes you look old and foolish. We have too little fuel to afford my pride.

Yes.

The Boy stood up and disappeared into the darkness. The Old Man could hear him rustling through his pack. Then he was back by the fire, standing above them.

The Boy held out a folded map that glistened in the firelight.

The Old Man took it and began to unfold it.

It was larger than his map.

The entire United States.

Roads crossing the entire continent.

And…

Notes like "Plague" and "Destroyed" and "Gone."

Has he been to all these places?

The Boy sat down and stared into the firelight.

He is somewhere else. Somewhere else with someone else.

On the back of the map were names and words and identifiers that hinted at the details of an untold story.

CPT DANFORTH, KIA CHINESE SNIPER IN SACRAMENTO

SFC HAN, KIA CHINESE SNIPER IN SACRAMENTO

CPL MALICK, KIA RENO

SPC TWOOMEY, KIA RENO

PFC UNGER, MIA RENO

PFC CHO, MIA RENO

PV2 WILLIAMS, KIA RENO

And…

Lola.

Lola.

And who was Lola?

When the Old Man looked up at the Boy again he'd meant to ask him how and why and even, where, but the Boy was staring at something high up. Something on the massive rock that loomed above Flagstaff. The Old Man followed the Boy's gaze.

High up the rock burned a small campfire, and above it the stars wheeled like broken glass moving in time to some unheard waltz.

CHAPTER 36

The Boy sat by the fire sharpening his tomahawk.

"What're you going to do?" asked the Old Man.

"I will go up there. Near there, and see who it is. Maybe they know where we can find the fuel that's supposed to be here."

The Old Man started the tank and backed it out from under the overpass. When he came back to the fire he said, "We can watch you through the night vision. If you get in trouble maybe you can signal us from up there. We could try to come up and help you."

The Boy nodded as he finished lacing up his old boots. He stood, stretching the weak part of himself, twisting back and forth. The Old Man watched his granddaughter watch the Boy.

What does she see?

What do you think she sees, my friend? She is young and so is he.

When the Boy was ready to go he turned and said, "I'll try to be back before dawn."

Then he was gone into the darkness. For a moment they heard his steps and then nothing. As if he had been swallowed by the night.

The Old Man sat down next to the fire.

His granddaughter watched the dark shape of the massive rock. It blocked out its section of the night like a piece of black velvet hung to blot out the stars. Or an empty place in the universe.

"Will he be okay, Poppa?"

The Old Man wanted to think about that question, but he knew he mustn't. He knew he must give her an answer quickly. And when he responded, he knew he should've been faster. He knew when he saw the worry and doubt in her eyes.

"I think he will. He seems to know the ways one needs to survive. I think he has been alone for much of his life."

"Na-ah, Poppa. He was raised by a soldier."

How does she know that? When have they talked about it?

"He was?" asked the Old Man.

"Yes, Poppa. I had to ask him what a soldier was and he told me. Do you know what a soldier is, Poppa?"

I do.

But maybe his meaning is different from the one I know. I must listen more than I speak.

Yes.

"What did he say a soldier was?"

"He said it was someone who never gives up, Poppa."

The Old Man thought of Sergeant Major Preston. The tank and all that the soldier had prepared for the Old Man's village to come and find one day.

I think cancer got me… God bless America.

Yes. That is what he wrote in the journal I found. I had not said that word "America" in a very long time before I read it in his journal.

And if I'm completely honest with myself, I had forgotten it.

What good was a word in the years of sun and sand and salvage that followed the winter that came after the day of the bombs? What good was "America" now?

It only reminded me of all that was gone.

The Old Man watched the fire.

But Sergeant Major Preston of the Black Horse Cavalry hadn't forgotten about America.

And neither had the soldier who'd raised the Boy. Whoever he was.

They didn't forget.

They didn't give up.

"Yes," he said to his granddaughter. "That is what a soldier is."

She was silent. She pressed her lips together, which was her way when she had more to say or was very excited about something she wanted to do but had to be patient until she could do it.

Young girls are hungry for all the good they think life holds. That is their innocence.

"Poppa?"

"Yes."

"He also had a wife."

"Oh."

"She's dead but he didn't tell me how."

"He seems young for that."

She was silent. And then, "Does he, Poppa?"

"Maybe not to you, but to me he is very young."

"Well, that's because you're old now, Poppa." She laughed and snorted.

The Old Man nodded.

"It's true. But it means I did something right, doesn't it? It means I was good at living. That's what getting old means. It means you're successful at living."

She laughed.

I love her laugh.

I wish I knew all the secret words that would make her laugh anytime I wanted to hear it. Anytime I needed to hear it. If there is anyone in control of this crazy life, that is my bargain I'll make with you. You can have anything you want. Just give me her laugh. Let me take it wherever I have to go after this.

Deal?

Silence.

And…

Please?

"He was in battles, Poppa. And he's crossed the whole country. The whole United States, Poppa."

Her eyes shine when she talks about him.

Her eyes remind me of my wife's, her grandmother. When she was young.

She is always young to me.

"He has done a lot for such a young man," said the Old Man.

"What is that, Poppa?"

"What is what?"

"The United States?"

I guess we never talked about that. We talked of salvage and ice cream and jet airplanes like my dad once flew across the world. Many things. But not the United States.

"It was our country."

She said nothing. Thinking.

Then…

"Is it still our country?"

In the night, when the moon was falling to the far horizon, long after the Old Man had tried to explain the concept of "States" and then tried to remember as many of their names as he could, which was not many, he flipped the switch on the optics. He scanned the giant rock. He could not see the Boy.

She'd only wanted to talk about him. Even though I was telling her all about California and the other states I had been to, she only really wanted to talk about him.

Yes, my friend. That is the way of the young when they discover something. They are like Christopher Columbus discovering the "new" world.

Yes. Sergeant Major Preston wrote that in the sewer.

They think everything is new and they are the first and they ignore us Indians who've been here all along.

In the past, if I taught her everything I knew about how a small engine once worked or what telephones were, she couldn't get enough of such things. The questions about those lost things would follow me for days. But not today. She only looked as though she were listening to me as I told her about states.

But she wasn't.

No.

That is the way of the young, my friend. You cannot help who you fall in love with the first time. You just do.

When you get up in the morning you don't say to yourself, *Today I am going to fall in love*. You just do.

He is very handsome. Strong too. That is a good thing for these days. But she is still young.

But there must always be a first time for love.

He looked down into the tank and saw her face. She was deep in sleep, still wrapped in her bomber jacket.

I will take just her laugh with me to wherever I must go next. Please? Is it a deal? Just the memory of her laugh. Can I have that?

Silence.

In the night, the Old Man thought he heard a horse galloping down the highway above his head.

I am dreaming.

Maybe the horse is on the bridge.

Maybe the horse is part of the dream.

The Old Man fell back to sleep.

CHAPTER 37

The Old Man woke with a start.

I was falling.

Yes.

She was calling for me?

No, Poppa. I need you.

I think so.

I smell bacon.

He opened the hatch. The Boy and a Stranger watched the campfire and a cast-iron skillet between them in which the Old Man could see splattering grease leaping in the waves of heat that came up from the flames.

The Stranger wore clothing made of tanned hide. A necklace of bones. His hair fell in curls around a circle of baldness that had consumed the back of the top of his head. Large sad brown eyes turned to the Old Man and gazed upon him.

The Old Man dismounted the tank, feeling the stiffness of his sleeping position in each handhold and footfall that brought him jarringly to the ground.

The Boy stood and hobbled toward the Old Man.

The Stranger looked exhausted. It had been a long night for him also.

"I found him up there on top of the large rock," said the Boy. The Stranger had turned back to the fire and the skillet.

"Was he alone?" asked the Old Man.

"Yes. He's harmless. I don't think we'll get much out of him, though." The Boy waited until the Stranger bent to inspect something within the skillet. Then the Boy raised his index finger to his temple and twirled it.

The Boy lay down near where he'd left his worn rucksack. He patted it once and then laid his head on it and closed his eyes. A moment later the Boy was asleep.

The Old Man retrieved a percolator from the tank and some tea, the last remaining packets in their supplies, and went to the fire. He set the percolator to boil on the coals and sat down across from the Stranger.

"Good morning," he said to the Stranger.

The Stranger raised his clasped hands to his mouth, squeezed his eyes shut, and began to rock back and forth.

This went on for a while and the Old Man was content to wait for the water to boil and for the tea to steep. He set out mugs on stones near the fire and poured the tea.

The day was still cool, though soon the heat would be up. In the blue shadows beneath the bridge, the Old Man watched the pork sizzle in the cast-iron pan and sipped his hot tea.

Like camping.

The Stranger produced a large meat fork and skewered a piece of sizzling pork, holding it out toward the Old Man.

"Thank you."

The Old Man chewed.

Should I be worried about the quality of this meat?

Life has already made several attempts to kill you my friend. This pork is probably the least of your worries today.

It's good.

The Stranger ate none of the pork.

He watched the Old Man, nodding slightly with approval.

He's not as old as me, but he is old enough to have lived through the bombs. Maybe he was young and never learned to speak. Maybe no one survived with him. Maybe he has been alone all this time.

"Your country is desolate," said the Stranger in a high voice.

As if his heart was breaking.

As if he were on the verge of tears.

"Your cities are burned with fire: your land, strangers devour it in your presence."

The Old Man nodded respectfully, chewing the pork. He picked up his tea and sipped.

"What's your name?" he asked through another mouthful of pork.

The Stranger looked as if he were about to go on, as if the Old Man had interrupted him in the middle of his speech.

"Your new moons and your appointed feasts my soul hates," continued the Stranger, almost pleading with the Old Man. "They are a trouble unto me: I am weary to bear them. And when you spread forth your hands, I will hide my eye from you." The Stranger covered his brown liquid-filled eyes with the palms of his hands. Then he looked up and, putting his hands over his ears, he whispered in horror, "Yes, when you make many prayers, I will not hear: your hands are full of blood."

Okay.

The Old Man's granddaughter emerged from the tank, rubbing sleepy eyes. He saw her look about for the Boy. She saw her grandfather watching her when her gaze had finally fallen upon his sleeping form. She climbed down from the tank, eyes still half closed, and settled next to the fire. The Stranger held out pork for her from within the skillet.

She chewed.

Just like camping.

Okay, I will try once more. But I already know I will be sorry.

"Do you have a name, sir?" asked the Old Man.

The Stranger nodded emphatically.

Then stopped.

"Wash you, make you clean: put away the evil of your doings from before mine eyes: cease to do evil."

"We are not doing evil. We are on a journey to rescue some people who are trapped in a bunker to the east. In what was once Colorado," said the Old Man reaching exasperation. "Do you know Colorado?"

"Learn to do well, seek judgment, relieve the oppressed, judge the fatherless, and plead for the widow," continued the Stranger.

"That's what we're doing!" said the Old Man, surprised with himself that he was already upset.

Usually I am much more patient.

The Stranger stopped. He leaned forward. There was hope in his voice when he spoke again.

"Come now, and let us reason together, says the Lord: though your sins be as scarlet, they shall be as white as snow; though they be red like crimson, they shall be wool."

"Crimson is red?" interrupted his granddaughter.

The Stranger nodded emphatically and continued.

"They shall be as wool. If you are willing and obedient, you shall eat the good of the land."

The Old Man stood. He was shaking.

I am angry and I do not know why!

You are angry at this man, my friend, because he will not answer a simple question.

Yes, that is why I am angry.

"What is your name, sir?"

When the Stranger did not immediately answer, the Old Man began to turn and walk away. A few steps and he heard the Stranger say, "Isaiah, Ezekiel, Jeremiah. I am as one crying in the wilderness."

When the Old Man turned back there were tears streaming down the Stranger's sunburned cheeks.

Don't be angry with him. He can't help…

He's crazy.

The Old Man sat down next to the fire again.

If you'd watched civilization go up in flames. If you'd watched what came after and had to survive any way you could through all those years alone. How could you not be crazy, my friend?

I did. I watched. I survived. I'm not crazy.

But you had the village. Your wife. Your son. Your grandchildren. Maybe he had no one.

The Old Man sighed and sipped his tea again. He had another piece of bacon.

"I think you understand me," he said to the Stranger.

The Stranger nodded.

"But for some reason you speak in riddles and I don't know why. So I will tell you that we are headed east to find some people who have asked for our help. We need fuel. Were you part of the people who lived up here?" The Old Man pointed toward the abandoned hotel that had been the center of the outpost.

The Stranger shook his head in the negative.

"Did you know them?"

The Stranger nodded.

"We need their fuel. Do you know where it is? Is there any left?"

The Stranger nodded again.

CHAPTER 38

"And they shall be desolate in the midst of the countries that are desolate, and her cities shall be in the midst of the cities that are wasted."

The Old Man watched the Stranger as he worked at pulling up the grating that covered what must have once been a pool inside the skeletal remains of a gym.

That is his answer to what lies east?

Yes, my friend. That is his answer.

When the metal cover was pushed back, the hint of kerosene bloomed in full. Inside the empty pool, salvage-fashioned fuel tanks lay along the bottom.

My eyes are burning from the fumes.

The Old Man waved the others back and dropped down into the shallow end of the dry pool. He tapped his scarred knuckles against a tank and heard the hollow echo of a half-filled volume.

Will it be enough?

It will have to be.

They brought the tank in through the shattered remains of the floor-to-ceiling windows. It crushed ancient fitness machines beneath its treads. Above them a barn owl screeched incessantly, refusing to flee into the daylight.

He has been here for some time.

If he waits, we will go away. But he must wait until we have taken all their fuel.

When they had maneuvered the tank as close to the pool as they could, they stretched out the pump hose until it barely reached the farthermost tank.

The fumes could ignite in a moment so we must be very careful.

"Go out and look for some salvage," he told his granddaughter. "See if there is anything we can use."

"Food would be good, Poppa."

"Yes, food would be good."

When she was gone he breathed a little easier.

If we explode she will at least be safe.

She will be all alone.

Yes, but she won't be dead.

The Boy took charge of the fueling once the Old Man had shown him how it was performed. Now they waited in the silence of the ancient pool area, the APU droning like the pumps of the pool must have once done.

The Old Man turned to the Stranger.

His words are church words.

As though he will only speak what he has seen or read. As though it is his punishment or his penance. But he understands. I know he does. How has he made it all this time? What is his story of salvage?

"What is your… what is your story?"

The Stranger who had been watching the fueling process with both amazement and amusement turned back to the Old Man with laughing, mirthful eyes.

The Stranger seemed to want to say something. Then stopped himself and simply shook his head. When the Old Man seemed to accept this, the Stranger turned back to watch the fueling.

The map.

The Old Man climbed up into the tank and retrieved Sergeant Presley's map, though he thought of it only as the Boy's.

Again he was amazed at the information contained in its markings.

It's the story of someone's life.

Is that not true of all maps, my friend?

True. And also, our stories are the maps of our lives.

The Old Man stopped.

Our stories are the maps of our lives.

Yes, my friend.

He spread the map out on the ragged rubber floor of the gym, in a space between crushed pieces of fitness equipment.

"Excuse me?" He spoke loudly trying to get the Stranger's attention.

The Stranger turned.

He saw the map. If the look in his eyes when he'd watched the tank drink up all the fuel had been one of amazement, the look in his eyes when he saw the map was one of awe.

He fell to his knees and a moment later his short thick fingers were tracing the roads. Tracing them back east. Tracing them to New York. Landing on Brooklyn.

And he wept.

His shoulders shaking.

Sobs gushing forth in tremendous heaves.

"By the rivers of Babylon," sobbed the Stranger. "There we sat down, yea we wept, when we remembered Zion. We hanged our harps upon the willows in the midst thereof. For there they that carried us away captive required of us a song; and they that wasted us required of us mirth, saying sing us one of the songs of Zion."

The Stranger hung his head and tears splashed down onto the map. The Old Man stood, frozen.

The Stranger raised his head, looking up to the Old Man. Asking him.

"How shall we sing the Lord's song in a strange land? If I forget thee, O Jerusalem, let my right hand forget her cunning. If I do not remember thee, let my tongue cleave to the roof of my mouth, if I refer not Jerusalem above my chief joy."

Through watery, joy-filled eyes, he spread his small hands outward, upward, and expanded them across the map.

He means, 'Where are we?,' my friend.

The Old Man looked at the map and laid his finger over Flagstaff.

The Stranger placed one finger on Brooklyn and then stretched another finger on his other hand over Flagstaff.

For a long time he stared at the map.

Stared at the distance between the two points.

Stared at all the stories of his wandering.

Some making a little more sense now.

Some coming to the surface after so many years on the road.

"Do you know of this 'King Charlie'?" asked the Old Man.

The Stranger looked up from the map.

There was fear in his eyes.

He looked back to the map and studying it, drew his finger away from the west, following the map east. Following the once great Interstate 40. Then, at Albuquerque he went north, and after making a wide circle that reached all the way down into Texas he spoke.

"Hell from beneath is moved for thee to meet thee at thy coming: it stirreth up the dead for thee, even all the chief ones of the earth; it hath raised up from their thrones all the kings of the nations. All they shall speak and say unto thee, Art thou also become weak as we? Art thou become like unto us? Thy pomp is brought down to the grave, and the noise of thy viols: the worm is spread under thee, and the worms cover thee. How art thou fallen from heaven, O Lucifer, son of the morning! How art thou cut down to the ground, which didst weaken the nations! For thou hast said in thine heart, I will ascend into heaven, I will exalt my throne above the stars of God: I will sit also upon the mount of the congregation, in the sides of the north: I will ascend above the heights of the clouds; I will be like the most High. Yet thou shalt be brought down to hell, to the sides of the pit. They that see thee shall narrowly look upon thee, and consider thee, saying, Is this the man that made the earth to tremble, that did shake kingdoms; that made the world as a wilderness, and destroyed the cities thereof; that opened not the house of his prisoners? All the kings of the nations, even all of them, lie in glory, every one in his own house. But thou art cast out of thy grave like an abominable branch, and as the raiment of those that are slain, thrust through with a sword, that go down to the stones of the pit; as a carcass trodden under feet. Thou shalt not be joined with them in burial, because thou hast destroyed thy land, and slain thy people: the seed of evildoers shall never be renowned."

The Stranger looked at the Old Man and nodded slowly, placing his index finger over Colorado Springs.

Bad news for us, my friend.

Yes.

I think he is saying that King Charlie is the devil. And that the devil is in Colorado Springs.

Where I need to go.

"It would have to be that way," muttered the Old Man to himself.

The Stranger took hold of the Old Man's hand. His touch was warm and soft. He moved the hand down to Albuquerque and whispered, "Ted."

"Ted?"

The Stranger nodded.

"Who is Ted?"

But the Stranger only smiled and nodded in the affirmative.

Whoever Ted is, he's good. Or at least he has been to the Stranger.

And he thinks Ted will also be good to us.

Didn't Conklin of the Dam say they'd heard there was someone who'd set up an outpost in ABQ as he called it? That they even had electricity?

Ted.

When the fueling was complete, the Old Man backed the tank out of the rickety framework of the ruin that had once been a gym and left the tank idling in the hot afternoon heat.

The Boy brought out an old weight bar he'd found in the shadows and dark of the gym.

"I can make this into a weapon," he said as he passed the Old Man.

The Stranger motioned for the map once more. When it was opened and spread out on the hot pavement, the Stranger pointed toward the land that lay between Flagstaff and Albuquerque.

"They shall lay hold on bow and spear; they are cruel, and have no mercy; their voice roareth like the sea; and they ride upon horses, set in array as men for war against thee, O daughter of Zion."

Then he pointed toward the sun overhead and shook his head. Making a fist, he pulled it down.

"You're saying don't cross this area in the daytime?"

The Stranger nodded.

Then held up one finger.

"In one night! You're saying cross all this in one night? That's a long journey, over bad roads!"

The Stranger nodded again.

"Who are these people?" asked the Old Man.

The Stranger looked about, leaned close, and then whispered, "Apache."

Later, under the bridge, waiting for nightfall, the Old Man walked up the street. Toward the outpost that had been.

How can these Apache stop a tank?

Who knows? But this fellow thinks they're dangerous enough to try. Or at least try and get you stuck, then wait you out.

Go in one night as quick as you can and it might prevent them from bringing their resources to bear. Surprise them.

But we could get stuck on the road in the night.

At the top of the hill, in the gritty crumbling parking lot of the hotel, the Old Man saw words written on the wall in a sickly green neon slop-paint.

Those words weren't there yesterday.

Someone has passed through in the night and left a message for me.

Someone on a horse.

"*Up is down, left is right. King Charlie brings you Peace through Might.*"

The Old Man wondered if this was the Fool thundering through the darkness on a horse too big for his gangling body, even now ahead of them, knowing where they are going, holding the stolen map in his claws.

And below that, as if addressed specifically to the Old Man, written in slop-paint strokes, was the word "*Nuncle.*"

CHAPTER 39

At dusk they drove out from underneath the bridge and into the twilight. The dry leaves and fallen pine needles crunched under the dirt-clogged treads of the tank in the warm, early evening.

The Stranger watched them, waving slowly, his sad brown eyes sorry to see them go.

And…

Sorry for all that had happened to the world.

The Old Man looked down into the turret and saw the Boy who'd returned to staring into nothingness. He tapped his leg, motioning for the Boy to put on his helmet. When this was done the Old Man switched on the intercom.

"What do you think of him?" asked the Old Man, referring to the Stranger. "About his information? Did you ever pass through the areas he warned us about?"

"We did not."

Who does he mean when he says "we"?

The soldier.

"Maybe he was just crazy?" said the Old Man.

The Boy said nothing for so long the Old Man wondered if maybe there wouldn't be a comment. But then the Boy spoke.

"I do not think he is touched in the head. Sergeant Presley would say… well, it does not matter, but, no, I don't think he is crazy. There was truth in his riddles."

"So what do you think he meant by all those riddles?" asked the Old Man.

Flagstaff fell behind them, and ahead, the long straight road cut through the high rolling plains.

It feels like we're still heading upward.

Still heading to the top of the world.

In the far west, fading blue light still shone distantly. Ahead the land lay covered in soft mist and darkness.

"There are people who act crazy," started the Boy out of the silent hum of the intercom. "I think it's some kind of defense. A way of keeping them safe on the road. Most villages treat such people with respect. They give them food and send them on their way. They're superstitious about such people."

"Are there many villages out there?"

The Old Man looked into the distant east and saw only the rising night.

"Some," said the Boy.

For a long time the Old Man kept the tank on the road. But when the road became impassable, they would deviate around broken chunks of highway and scattered concrete pylons and even the wild-haired rebar jutting from the remains of bridges.

Far out into the plains, miles off-road, they would see the skeletal remains of recreational vehicles rocking in a wind that blasted across the rolling landscape, causing the grass to bend in great waves like the tides of an ocean.

The Old Man switched on the night-vision optics and saw no one among the lonely outposts of wreckage.

People must have come here in the days of the bombs, forming up into small settlements. They would've driven here in those RVs and made alliances once they'd arrived.

Or murdered each other for what few supplies could be had.

How long did they last?

Not long. How could they? They only had what they'd brought. There are no places to salvage up here. No major towns or industry. What could they have found where there was little or nothing?

Later, the road disintegrated into little more than swallowed chunks of concrete through which tufts of yellow grass sprang upward. The tank moved slower along the broken highway, the Old Man not wanting to chance the fragile right tread.

You must go all the way, tread. You cannot give up tonight or even when we get there. After this is all done, we still have to get back home.

The last part sounded like an empty promise to the Old Man.

He began to think of the other dark possibilities that existed besides returning home.

But he cut himself off and would not think of such things.

Tonight I must concentrate. I cannot think of what will go wrong tomorrow or even the day after. Those things are for another day.

In the darkness there seemed to be no one out there. All the rumors of Apache might just simply be rumors. All the talk of Apache nothing more than the talk of ghosts. Boogeymen to frighten misbehaving children.

He drove on and watched the road, seeing nothing but scattered pockets of rusting and beaten destruction from long ago.

He saw the bridge far ahead as the road began a series of descents and rises through rolling hills. It should have been a bridge like any other overpass crossing. But it wasn't.

The bridge still stretched across the two hills that had been both its on-ramps and off-ramps for east and west traffic. But beneath the overpass, where the highway ran, lay a collection of vehicles tilted upright, their hoods pointed into the sky as if they had been suddenly forced upward.

Tacked across the front of each rusting hood was a human skeleton with a dog's head.

The Old Man switched on the high beam of the tank as they approached.

It's a message.

"They don't want us to come this way?" said the Boy over the intercom.

Or anyone for that matter.

"Is your hatch closed?" he asked his granddaughter.

"Yes, Poppa."

"Lock it now."

The Old Man maneuvered the tank up the overpass to the road that crossed atop the bridge. Against the bright moon, he could clearly see the pennants made of rags and oily crow feathers flapping madly in the windy darkness.

We are in their land now.

If we tell them what we're going to do, maybe they will let us pass.

And if they don't, my friend?

The Old Man started down the on-ramp on the far side and re-entered the old highway.

A few miles farther along, and the highway descended into a series of curves that entered a long and narrow ravine, which soon widened into a valley that cut through low, flat-topped mesas.

A small gas station town lay alongside the road and the Old Man could see greasy firelight behind some of the windows.

For a while the road paralleled a river. Weeping willows hung gloomily along the banks in the night. Later, in the deep of the valley, the road disappeared under a wash of sand where the river must have once overflowed.

Probably in the days after the long winter.

Yes.

The Old Man drove the tank down onto the sand bed, letting the high beam stay on, watching for places where the tank might get stuck. Ahead he could see the single remaining pylon of a bridge that must have once crossed over the wide river that ran through the canyon.

As they entered the dry riverbed, they dropped suddenly and the Old Man banged his head sharply on the side of the hatch.

His first thought was that the ground had suddenly given way underneath them.

Soft sand.

But he could see crumpled tin and splintered wood in the optics and a wall of sandy dirt beyond.

We've fallen into a trap!

"Are you all right?" he asked his granddaughter over the intercom as he reached up and shut the turret hatch.

"What happened, Poppa?"

"I think we fell in a hole."

The Boy, bathed in the red of the interior emergency lights, gripped his chair.

Rain began to fall against the sides of the tank.

Not rain.

Arrows.

The Old Man dogged the hatch.

Remember, be gentle with the right tread. We can get out of this like I did when I was stuck in the sand at Picacho Peak. But if you break the tread, we really will be stuck.

The Old Man switched on the night vision.

All around them, wild figures like white blobs against green and gray ran forward as torches flared too brightly in the night vision. The Old Man tried the left tread and the tank pulled forward. He could hear the snap of wood and rending metal above the whine of the engine. When the tank was almost at the top of the trap, the Old Man pushed the right tread forward and the tank popped nose upward as he gave it full throttle.

"Hold on!" warned the Old Man.

The tank slammed down hard into the sand and sped off, careening through a crumbling pylon that jutted from the riverbed.

The Old Man scanned the optics.

The figures were running back into the night, their torches burning angrily on the ground.

Did I just see the Fool?

Standing atop a small sandy hill, the gangly figure appeared for a moment, his wild fool's crown springing in all directions, his claw waving a torch frantically forward at the retreating figures, urging them to turn back and attack the tank.

It's him!

The Old Man backed away from the viewfinder in shock.

Don't be afraid of him, my friend.

When the Old Man looked again the Fool was gone. He drove the tank to the other side of the wash and surged up onto the road at full speed.

Now the road entered a tight series of turns that wound through the hills where the Old Man saw an ambush in every bend, or at the tops of the small hills that loomed above them alongside the road. The gibbous moon had turned a sickly red from some distant dust storm. It rose through spindly barren trees above the desert plateau. It shifted wildly across the sky as the Old Man fought to keep track of the twisting road in the night.

It must be after midnight.

The Old Man felt himself sweating heavily, his shoulders tensed like iron bands as he drove the tank forward into the night.

The road twisted into a series of long curves that reversed themselves into still more curves and the red misshapen moon swung even more frantically across the sky.

It's making me dizzy.

The clutching fingers of a dead orchard rose up all around them as they passed through the rubble of a town. Ahead, great piles of concrete had toppled onto the highway. Above them, the sides of cutoff mountains rose up into the darkness.

Are they forcing me off the road and into the town? Or are they forcing me to take the narrow opening ahead? Where is their trap?

The Fool is forcing you, my friend. It is the Fool who forces you into his trap.

I only thought I saw him. Maybe it was just a mistake or a trick of the light.

This must have once been a state checkpoint. The path looks too narrow for the tank to pass.

But if you get off the highway you could get lost in that abandoned town, and its streets are probably very narrow. A good place for a trap. There is no guarantee that there is a way around this obstacle or that the roads in the town are even any better.

No, there isn't.

"Are you ready to drive?" said the Old Man over the intercom to his granddaughter.

"I'm on it, Poppa!" she almost shouted.

The Old Man tapped the Boy and motioned for the hatch.

"We'll guide you through the rubble and make sure the path is wide enough," he said to his granddaughter. "Don't run over us, okay?"

"Okay, Poppa, I'll try not to."

Yes, please try not to run over me with the tank.

The Old Man took the left and the Boy the right and they walked into the dusty maze of rubble, waving the tank forward slowly. They crossed under a wide overpass and the Old Man spotted, with the moving beam of his flashlight, the words the Fool had left for him to read.

They were written all the way to the end of the tunnel.

REPEAT A LIE AND IT BECOMES THE TRUTH.

POINTING OUT WHAT'S "WRONG" IS THE SICK HABIT OF DELUSIONAL PERVERTS.

RIGHT AND WRONG IS WHERE WE WENT WRONG.

REPEAT A LIE AND IT BECOMES THE TRUTH.

COMPROMISE MEANS SEEING THINGS OUR WAY.

WHAT OTHERS CALL INSANE, I CALL PERSISTENCE.

REPEAT A LIE AND IT BECOMES THE TRUTH.

WE WILL MURDER THOSE WHO REJECT PEACE.

WANT WHAT OTHERS HAVE. THE MANY SERVE THE FEW, THE TRICK IS MAKING THEM THINK IT'S THE OTHER WAY AROUND.

REPEAT A LIE AND IT BECOMES THE TRUTH.

IF YOU SAY YOU'RE GOD, WHO'S TO SAY YOU'RE WRONG?

MAKE FRIENDS OF YOUR ENEMIES AND USE THEM TO DESTROY YOUR FRIENDS.

REPEAT A LIE AND IT BECOMES THE TRUTH.

WHEN YOU ARE NO LONGER BURDENED BY INTEGRITY, THE POSSIBILITIES ARE BOTTOMLESS.

CONVINCE YOUR ENEMIES THE BATTLE IS SOMEWHERE ELSE.

CONVINCE YOUR ENEMIES THEY'RE JUST LIKE YOU.

CONVINCE YOUR ENEMIES.

HEAVEN, HELL… REALLY?

REPEAT THE TRUTH.

And at the final yawning exit lying on the open and blistered highway beyond lay neon-green-colored sheets of paper scattered about, as if debris from a bomb revealed in the pale moonlight above the eastern dust storm. The Old Man picked up a sheet and found crude printing and wet ink that smeared at his touch. He read.

Everything be Ok
We mean it.
So loot and murder to your heart's content
Just make sure you got the strength to Take and Do before anyone else does to you

Everything be getting better
Don't believe the eyes
Or your stomachs holla
Or your lies,
Lies can be told about anything
Including the truth

THE ROAD IS A RIVER

There's been a lotta bad done in the name of good.
So we're done with that noise.
Religion and morals be all the same and only different
'bout who was right and wrong on everything.

So here's how it be
Man be man alone
And the man be
King Charlie.
King Charlie be not wrong or right.
He just be.
After King Charlie be nothing.
Heaven = Hell, only the unlucky die and the dead like to
tell some truth when they say nothing.
If there be a heaven, King Charlie imagine you'll get there
no matter what you do
unless you're the Hitler or Stalin who gave everyone the
aids.

We come so that all might live in prosperity.
And only the strong survive.
Get it?

We are an accident
Created by an accident,
And so the Apocalypse must be our promise
Of a better tomorrow

When we hear-ed that doomsday bell
The gunfire a Ratta-tat-tating,
Your screams for mercy
The blast that blew everything away that was,

*And when we saw the light of bombs bursting in air
Someone said ' 'Twas but the sound of man worshipping his maker,'*

So…

*Siege!
Lone Gunman!
Horde rapes outpost!
Nuclear Bomb Disintegrates London!
It's just be the sounds of man
worshipping his maker.*

At the bottom of the piece of paper, as if separate and a command, the Old Man read, **ALL HAIL KING CHARLIE!**

The Old Man let the screed fall to the ground. He motioned for the Boy to get back into the tank, and as he climbed once more into the hatch, his eyes fell to the final words that had been slop-painted onto the highway before the tank.

**ONCE YOU'RE FREE OF SHAME YOU'RE FREE TO ACT SHAMELESSLY.
GIVE UP, NUNCLE, YOU'VE GOT NO CHANCE!**

On the other side of the tunnel the night seemed cooler, the air fresher. The moon turned everything slightly blue with its glaring yellow light now that it had risen above the distant dust storm.

In the hours that followed, there were other tight spots and places where the road seemed impassable. They threaded each of these places carefully, waiting for an attack that did not come.

The road improved and soon they were making good time across the high desert with dawn just a few hours away. The Boy, whose chin had fallen to his chest, lay deep in sleep bathed by the red light of the tank, fastened into his seat. When the Old Man tried the intercom, his granddaughter only murmured and he knew she too was sleeping now.

Alone, he drove through what remained of the night and soon the eastern sky began to turn a pale blue.

Another day.

They topped the rise that looked down on Albuquerque in the soft light of first morning.

The city is still there.

Ted.

On the eastern side of town, the Old Man could see thin strings of electric light still burning distantly like twinkling gems in the pink of morning.

CHAPTER 40

They crossed gray concrete roads and empty sun-bleached buildings falling to rubble in the blaze of morning. The Old Man aimed the tank toward the strings of light still twinkling in the bright daylight below the foothills on the eastern edge of town.

Those lights should be off by now. Who would leave them on during the day?

But the lights remained on and when the Old Man found the settlement, a walled-off neighborhood below the easternmost foothills, the Old Man did not wonder why no one had turned out the lights. They were greeted by a soft dry breeze and the silence of abandonment.

The settlement was a large tract housing development lying alongside the highway leading north. A massive adobe brick wall, built before the bombs, surrounded the entire development.

Why was this place spared, like Tucson?

At the entrance they found a makeshift gate fashioned from the metal one might find at the gates of industrial warehouses. Two watchtowers that had risen from behind the wall had been pulled down, their frames sprayed outward like so many spilled matchsticks. The patchwork gate was wide open.

Why?

The Fool, the Horde, King Charlie. Does it matter? Someone.

Maybe they fled? Maybe they're hiding?

But the pulled-down watchtowers told another story.

Inside, the three of them found the town.

Streets.

Houses.

A humming generator in the distance.

Doors wide open.

Empty mugs and glasses whose insides were still stained with punch-red syrup.

The Boy went back to the tank and the gate once the Old Man had called out "hello" and received no response.

"What happened here, Poppa?"

"Nothing good."

"It seems bad."

"Don't worry. We'll leave soon."

But the fuel, my friend, there is only a little left.

"I'm not worried, Poppa."

"I know."

"Are you worried, Poppa?"

The Old Man did not answer her and instead continued to search the town as she trailed after him.

They wandered through a few houses, and what they found within told them nothing other than that one moment of life lived ordinarily had frozen, and that time had refused to move forward.

Beds unmade.

Wash hanging.

Each house smelling of dust and wood.

Tools, usable salvage, merely left for anyone to take.

In one house they found a spilled glass of milk.

The milk was warm and spoiled.

We should find the generator. Maybe it runs on fuel.

As if on cue, while the Old Man stood over the spilled milk and heard at the same time the distant hum of power, the generator died.

Outside, stepping over the front lawns turned to dying gardens, the strings of light above had ceased to twinkle.

The Old Man followed the darkened lights to thick rubber electrical cables that snaked through the streets and led to a house on the far edge of the settlement. Inside, the Old Man found hundreds of generators set up in every room. A central fuel bladder occupied the upper story. In the backyard they found a fuel truck that started cranking. Its tank was almost empty.

This was their power plant.

But the fuel is somewhere else.

Yes.

At the front entrance, waiting in the shade of the tank and drinking from a canteen, the Boy watched the land to the north of them.

"They were chained up over there," said the Boy and pointed toward the median. "There're drops of blood all over the dirt. The slavers must have put fishhooks in their noses or mouths and linked them to chains. Then they went north. I've seen it done before."

"Can you tell how many days ago that might have been?" asked the Old Man.

"A week. Maybe more."

The explosion shook the city.

It was distant. A boom, and then a crack that seemed to follow seconds after, echoed far out across the city and into the hills above them.

Back toward the center of the city, flames shot skyward as a black plume of smoke belched into the tired blue sky.

"Is it one of the bombs from before, Poppa?"

"No. Just an explosion."

She has no idea how big those bombs were. She has heard me and the other survivors who lived through those days talk of them and all that they took away, but she really has no idea how massive they were.

"Are you sure, Poppa?" she said, the worry evident.

"I am sure."

But he could see her face. Her wide eyes. The lips pressed together.

"Those bombs destroyed entire cities," said the Boy. "We would be dead if it had been one."

After a moment she seemed to accept the Boy's words. Relaxing.

She has lived in fear of those bombs her whole life. They are her boogeyman.

Yes. And this Boy said the words that comforted her, my friend.

Yes. There is that also.

They drove as close to the flames and smoke as they could. They could smell the thick scent of burning fuel.

It was an industrial district.

Narrow streets.

Concrete warehouse.

In green slop-paint the words "How now Nuncle Brown Cow?" were splashed across the smooth side of an old warehouse.

The Fool did this.

It would seem so, my friend.

This Ted must have been brewing their fuel here. He seems a very smart man. Our village could have used him.

The world could have used him.

Yes.

Black smoke erupted through windows and through the roof of a large warehouse as orange flames consumed the entire structure.

All their fuel must have been inside there, inside a big tank.

With no one to fight it, this fire will burn the city down in a few days.

And…

"What are we gonna do now, Poppa?"

We have, maybe, ten miles of fuel left.

So there is that also, my friend.

Yes.

CHAPTER 41

The tank limped through the fence at the far end of the international airport. Ahead, dirty and ancient jetliners waited forever at their gates for passengers on that last and long-ago day. Doomsday.

The needle in the gas gauge rested firmly on Empty.

I will not give up.

As if you could fuel this tank with your words?

I will not give up.

As if you can make it all the way to Colorado Springs?

We have made it this far. I will not give up.

And do you think the fuel in these jets is still any good?

It has to be, and if it isn't, we will find another way. I will not give up.

Why?

The Old Man did not answer himself.

Why? Why won't you give up?

Silence as he maneuvered the tank under the wing of one of the biggest jets.

A 747 I think.

Why don't you give up?

Stop!

Why?

Because in that moment when I saw the painted words of the Fool, I wanted to. Because this thing is bigger than an old man like me. Because this is too much, and seeing all that fuel we could've had, if we'd just gotten there earlier, go up in flames, crushed…

Crushed?

Silence.

Yes. It crushed me.

But you have been through worse, my friend.

Have I?

Yes.

"Will there be fuel here, Poppa?" she said over the intercom.

"Let us hope so."

Outside and climbing onto the hot metal of the wing, burning his knees and the palms of his hands, he searched for the opening to the fuel tank.

I can't find it.

Think. There is something you're forgetting.

It's underneath the wing, my friend.

Will the fuel still be good after all these years?

I will not give up.

It's underneath the wing.

"I found it!" he called out to them.

The Boy dragged the fueling hose away from the tank.

Think. There is something…

"Wait!"

He opened the cover to the wing fueling nozzle.

There will be water in the bottom of the fuel reservoir after all these years.

Water is heavier than fuel.

The Old Man found the lever that drained the fuel tank.

"Stand back!"

He pushed the lever and fuel gushed out onto the ground.

How will I know when it isn't water?

He waited.

Did it change color?

It smells more like kerosene now.

"Okay, bring me the hose," he said, slamming the fuel release lever back into the closed position.

Hopefully the fuel will not have as much water in it now. Now there will be a better chance that it will burn.

The tank drank up all the fuel it could from the insides of the old plane. Afterward, they topped off the two reserve drums still strapped to the turret.

In his mind the Old Man saw the map.

This is enough to make it there.

But what about getting back?

They let the spilled fuel dry. Over a fire of discarded luggage, they spitted and roasted some rabbit the Boy had taken near the settlement. They drank water in the shadows of the old terminal. Broken glass guarded the shadowy interior of the place, and they could only catch glimpses of suitcases and curtains near the daylight, high up on the concourses above.

There must have been panic that day.

I remember.

The Old Man made them stand far away and then went to the tank.

Off in the distance the fire in the center of town seemed to grow, its oily top like an anvil of smoke or an evil bird looming high over the city.

If the aircraft fuel explodes when I start the tank, would they be safe?

Would he protect her? Would he take her back to Tucson?

What other choice do you have, my friend?

The Old Man started the APU, waited a few seconds, and then fired the turbine. He watched the Boy and his granddaughter struggling with a manhole cover they'd managed to pry up from the tarmac as he listened for trouble within the noise of the tank's engine.

It sounds rougher and this time there is gray smoke instead of black.

Is that better? Is gray better than black?

I don't know, my friend.

The Old Man backed the tank out from underneath the jumbo jet. He drove down the runway once and then back.

If the fuel wasn't any good then it should be out of fuel or dying now, right, Santiago? The temperature gauge is also a cause for concern.

Yes, but it runs, my friend, and for now, that is enough.

In the distance, the black plumes above the fire had grown as smoke drifted east over the dead city.

The Old Man looked around at the terminal.

I wonder if my dad ever came here in the jets he flew.

In a few days the fire will come and it will all be gone. Maybe by tonight even.

Yes.

The ancient jets, immobile and waiting, seemed to him as if all they needed were pilots, pilots like his dad, and once again they might leap away from the earth.

I remember being pressed into my seat as we raced down the runway.

I remember that my feet did not reach the floor.

I remember that my dad was up front, at the controls of the plane.

I was very proud to be his son.

CHAPTER 42

They pushed north as the flames consuming Albuquerque climbed toward the old highway on the eastern edge of town. For miles they could see the billowing black smoke reaching high into the iron blue of noonday.

The old highway was sun-bleached and rent by gaping cracks as the tank pushed upward through a ponderosa of rocks and stunted twisting pines.

There is only Santa Fe between us and Colorado Springs now. It is the last major city.

When he showed the Boy the map and pointed toward Santa Fe, asking if the Boy knew anything about what they might find there, the Boy only shook his head.

In the late afternoon they arrived in Santa Fe.

The Old Man turned off the tank and watched the pink rocks in the last of the hot day.

There is nothing here.

The Old Man looked hard into the dense tangle of weed bracken and cactus that spread west of the highway across a wide rise that ended in a chalky ridge and tired rocky hills beyond.

If there was a city here it is gone now.

Were they nuked?

The Old Man checked the dosimeter.

There is radiation.

On the sudden and very light afternoon breeze that began to sweep the place, the Old Man could hear bone chimes rattling against each other, hidden but there all the same.

So what is their story of salvage?

The Old Man watched as purple shadows began to lengthen and as the sun sank into the western sands. Within the brush he could see the frames and structures of rotting buildings signaling their surrender to the landscape.

The land turned to red and what was not red was purple and cool.

The buildings are like victims tied to a stake, signaling through the flames that they were here. Trying to communicate their last message.

What do you know of such things, my friend?

They drove on until the dosimeter was back down to an acceptable level.

High. But not too high.

There will always be radiation now. With the amount of bombs we used, there must be.

I never fired one.

Yes. But it was your generation that can never be forgiven.

Silence.

In the dark, beside the tank, watching their fire turn and leap as it consumed the sweet-scented local pine, the Boy spoke.

"I know where you are going. But where did you come from?"

His granddaughter watched him, her eyes wide.

I am surprised she has not told him already.

She still listens to you.

"A city," said the Old Man.

The Boy continued to watch the fire, its flames within his green eyes.

"Ain't nothin' left of cities, Boy," said the Boy.

"What do you mean?"

The Boy shook his head.

"Just something someone used to tell me."

The soldier.

I wish we'd more of that rabbit than we did. Tomorrow we should hunt for a while.

"It's true," said his granddaughter. "Isn't it, Poppa?"

The Old Man nodded still thinking of rabbit.

"Poppa found it. We used to live in a tiny village but Poppa went out into the wasteland and found Tucson."

The Old Man shot a quick look at her and then the Boy.

"Sorry, Poppa."

The Old Man got up and went to get some water.

When he came back he said, "I'm sorry." He nodded at the Boy. "I didn't know if we could trust you. When we found you… well… you'd had a tough time. That was obvious."

The Boy only seems to listen to me now. But really, he is somewhere else. Maybe in his past, before we found him.

How do you know, my friend?

Whatever happened before we met him scarred him, changed him. Left its mark on him. He is there even now and I doubt he wholly ever leaves that place.

Yes.

"We don't need to know about your past," said the Old Man. "You've proven yourself to us. In fact, I don't know what we'd have done without you. When we finish with this business, you could come and live in the city with us, if you wanted to."

"You'd like it there!" said his granddaughter. "There's lots of salvage."

After a moment the Boy whispered a barely audible "thank you" and nothing more.

In the night, the others were asleep and the Old Man lay awake again, watching the night and the stars.

I would give anything to sleep like I used to. Like they do.

You're not thinking about rabbit even though you've been trying to.

Yes.

So what are you really thinking about?

Everything.

That's a lot to think about, my friend.

Yes.

A lot for one person.

Yes.

The story of Santa Fe? The story you would need to know if you were going to go and salvage there?

A little of that, although it is easy to understand what happened there, but mostly of other things.

Then what happened there?

A dirty bomb would be my guess. That is why we got the higher reading on the dosimeter. A dirty bomb parked in the downtown district.

Or the art district. Or even the historic.

Did they have such things?

Wherever it was, it went off and destroyed less than a block. The fire engines and police arrived. If it was the first bomb, or one of the first in those early days before we truly understood what was going on, they hadn't even thought of checking their dosimeters that day. But in the days that followed, before the EMP that knocked out the networks, an exploding van in any kind of populated area would have had them checking. In a moment they would've known.

Known what?

That the city was poisoned.

That everyone must flee.

Why?

Because what can you do now? The bomb has gone off. You can't put out radiation like a fire. Or clean it up like a flood. Or pack it into an ambulance and take it to the hospital. No. It is just there, somewhere under all that brush.

And that is what happened. In a matter of hours, by evening no doubt, because I remember the bombs always seemed to go off during the morning rush hour… they are all gone into the desert and the city is dead for all practical intents and purposes.

The bombs always went off at morning rush hour.

I have not thought about that in a long time. Funny, what comes back to you across the years. What surfaces in the little pond we call our mind.

Or sails across the ocean and back again.

Yes. That is an even better way to think of it.

By evening the city is dead. And in the silent years that follow, the brush grows. It covers everything. It pulls everything down into the dirt for someone to find at some far later date when we who lived through those days aren't even a memory in the mind of the oldest of them. Then they will find what we left behind.

If humanity survives, my friend.

Yes, there is that also.

If a fire happens, then everything is so much faster.

And the bone chimes?

Unseen people who live near here or pass by. They have put those chimes up as some sort of marker to warn others away from what has been poisoned.

Stay away.

Bones.

Death.

Soft notes in a gentle breeze.

The Old Man watched for satellites beneath the stars above.

He thought of Natalie.

General Watt.

I wonder what her story of salvage is.

CHAPTER 43

In the badlands, they crossed alongside pink canyons of stacked rock and through stunted forests twisting away beyond Santa Fe.

They began to find the bodies.

The first was a woman, her corpse bloated and lying in a ditch alongside the road.

The Boy exited the tank and searched the road and its sides.

When he returned he said, "Hard to tell, but less than a week. There was a fishhook in her lip but she didn't die from that."

He pointed to the center of the road.

"They were all chained together up there. She must have died along the march. Then they unhooked her and threw her over there."

"Should we bury her, Poppa?"

You know we will find more of them as we go, my friend.

"No. We have to hurry now."

To what? To overtake the slavers, and then what? Or do you mean the bunker and again, then what, my friend?

Project Einstein, whatever it does.
Whatever it does, indeed.

There were more bodies rotting in the merciless sun. They passed them and the Old Man wondered if any one of them was Ted.

The canyons and forest gave way to a wide plain of rolling grass and slight hills that swept away toward the hazy north.

When they stopped in the middle of the plain, the Old Man could hear insects buzzing in the long grass. In every direction, the tall grass ran off toward the horizon, its undefinable edges disappearing into a screen of summer haze and thick humidity. As if the wide plain simply fell off the edges of the earth.

At noonday, they rested in the small ledge of shade alongside the tank, drinking warm water and not eating. The Old Man asked the Boy if there was something they might hunt to eat.

The Boy stood and scanned the indeterminate horizon.

'We have no idea what's out there, any of us,' thought the Old Man. 'No idea.'

"It looks like horse country," said the Old Man hopefully.

Whether it was horse country or not, the Boy didn't bother to respond.

In time they mounted the tank and continued along the road as it cut like a straight line into the hazy north.

I cannot believe we've come this far. It feels like we're in a strange land at the top of the world. A land I never knew existed. Or maybe it is like an ocean. Like a sea of grass so high up.

That's because you spent so many years in the desert, my friend. You thought the whole world had become desert.

I thought often of the sea. Every time I read the book, I thought of the sea and the big fish.

Later, they passed more bodies.

At dusk, they pulled off to the side of the road. All around them, the plain continued to stretch off into a hazy pink nothingness where there was no mountain, or forest, or city, or even an end to things. An unseen orchestra of bugs clicked and buzzed heavily through their symphony well into the twilight and falling dark.

Down the road, dark barns crumbled beside a lazy stream about which oaks clustered greedily along the banks. The occasional wooden post showed where fences must have once claimed the place.

The Boy wandered off in the dusk and the Old Man hoped he would come back with something for them to eat.

His granddaughter gathered sticks for their fire.

She must be hungry too, but she has said nothing. She is good that way.

I am grateful to have them both. I would be too tired to hunt and make a fire after driving the tank all day.

The Old Man lay on the ground and closed his eyes.

In the dream he is slipping.

The voice, the familiar voice keeps asking him the same question. That same question it has always been asking.

Can you let go?

He is in the gravel pit south of the village this time.

The forbidden pit.

The gravel pit where Big Pedro died.

The Old Man climbs across the shifting gravel hill to reach Big Pedro, which is really how it happened. How Big Pedro died.

But I am dreaming. So it cannot happen again.

Yet the Old Man can taste the long untouched dust of the pile shifting beneath him, threatening to slide him right down to the bottom. And at the bottom of the pile is the pit's edge. And below the edge is the fall into the pool of dirty water where Big Pedro will fall and die because the fall is very great and the pool is shallow.

Which is how it happened.

But this is a dream.

So you say.

But you taste the dust and it is very hot like it was that day when you had been trying to salvage the material off the conveyor belt and part of it had given way and Big Pedro went down onto the gravel pile that had not been touched in so many years. Now it is shifting, and as Big Pedro tries to climb out it shifts, pulling him each time closer to the pit's edge.

Toward the fall.

Toward the shallow pool of dirty water.

Just as it happened.

'But this is a dream,' thinks the Old Man and hears the uncertainty in his own voice.

Then why are you trying to save him?

Because he is Big Pedro. Because he is my friend. Because I must.

And the Old Man feels the gravel shifting beneath his belly as he tries to get a little closer to Big Pedro. That way he can grab his hand and they can climb back up the rope that the Old Man has secured about his waist and to the conveyor belt.

The rope is not there.

Big Pedro smiles.

But this is a dream, right?

"Yes, of course, my friend," says Big Pedro in his high Mexican tenor.

You screamed when you went over the side.

"Yes."

And I heard that scream for years.

Yes, but this is a dream.

If you say so.

And Big Pedro falls and does not scream.

In fact, he smiles, and nods, and encourages the Old Man, just as he did when he taught the Old Man who was then a young man, a survivor of the Day After, all the skills one needs to live and survive in the very dangerous Sonoran Desert.

Traps for rodents.

Traps for Serpiente.

Traps for foxes.

"Can you let go?" asks the familiar voice.

Can you let go?

And the Old Man is sliding fast down the gravel, toward the pit, toward where Big Pedro has gone and the pool at the end of the drop where they will meet again. The pool that waits for us all.

Can you let go?

Yes. Yes I can.

And the Old Man lets himself think for a moment that he is tired. He thinks that his dusty and bleeding fingers could merely splay outward and he would glide down this pile and over the edge.

Yes. Yes, I can let go, if you will let me. If I don't hear my granddaughter. If she doesn't… then yes, I can finally let go.

Poppa, I need you.

And the Old Man is on his back and tumbling down the pile, and though he doesn't see her he hears her calling for him, crying, *Poppa, I need you.*

Which is the worst.

Which is what makes the Old Man try and grab the shifting sand to save his falling life.

I must because the edge is so near.

And…

Because she needs me.

Why?

Because to break her heart is too much to bear.

It is?

Yes, yes that is the worst.

Worse than the pit and pool at the bottom?

Falling!

And he is up and awake and saliva is running down onto the side of his mouth. There is meat cooking and he hears her laughing beside the fire.

And the Boy is drawing faces in the dirt with a stick as she watches and what he draws makes her laugh.

"Can you let go?" asks that very familiar voice.

If I could take her laugh with me, then yes, I will let go of everything.

They eat meat and though there is no pepper, it tastes good. Wonderful in fact. The Old Man tells them about cities. About buses and trains and how one could take them to work, and after work, ride them to a game. Which leads to baseball. Which neither of them have ever heard of.

The Old Man tells them about baseball.

About ballparks in the early summer evenings.

About the importance of fall.

About a game in which he saw a man hit three home runs in one night. About how the floor of the stadium shook as the man, the hero, came to bat for the last time and everyone was sure he would do it. Sure he would hit another home run because it just had to be. Because it was meant to be.

They ask him details.

What were hot dogs?

What is a strike?

What are good tickets?

When they finally sleep, the Old Man lies awake.

Probably because I took a nap before dinner.

It wasn't much of a nap. We cheated them, you know.

Who?

The young. We cheated them.

How?

They will never know that night of baseball. The night of three home runs when the floor of the stadium shook. We cheated them of that and all the good things we had and took for granted.

Yes.

They should never forgive us for that.

Later when he still cannot sleep, he rises and turns on the radio inside the tank.

He almost says, "General Watt."

But instead he chooses, "Natalie?"

And after a moment...

"It's so good to hear you tonight," she says.

"I couldn't sleep again," explains the Old Man.

"Is everything all right? Are you still coming?"

"Yes. Everything is fine. We're beyond Santa Fe and out in the grassy plains south of you. Maybe three more days and we'll be there."

"In two days, at exactly nine A.M., I need you to open the case and take out the Laser Target Designator. We need to test the device."

"I don't even really know the correct time," said the Old Man. "I just guess."

"The tank has a small clock near the commander's seat. Set that clock using the tiny knob above it to 1:37 A.M., now."

The Old Man did.

"The last time I knew exactly what time it was was just after a bomb exploded in my rearview mirror and disabled my car. It froze the clock at 2:06 P.M."

I remember that after forty years.

"Why can't you sleep?" asked Natalie. General Watt.

Silence.

"I was telling the children about baseball."

"Maybe you're just too excited to sleep?" she asked.

The Old Man thought about that.

"No. I feel... I feel like we cheated them."

He waited for her reply.

When she did, she said, "You're a good man. I'm sure of it. I don't think you ever intended for the world to destroy itself."

"I was almost as young as they are now when it happened. But still, after all this time I feel responsible. Guilty somehow."

"You shouldn't."

"Thank you, but lately, and for a long time, I've felt it was all my fault. For a long time I've felt 'curst.'"

In the dark, a breeze passed and the Old Man watched as the wave it left in the grassy plain swept past him and off into the night.

"If it helps, I can tell you something about yourself," offered Natalie.

"What?"

"I can tell that right now you are trying to make the world a better place. Why else would you help us if not because of that?"

The Old Man said nothing.

"The people who destroyed the world weren't trying to make it better. Baseball wasn't important to them. Nor were children who might one day see a game played under lights. They were more concerned with destroying themselves for power than good things like seeing a baseball game with their grandchildren. And what's worse, if they were still alive, they would not feel guilty as you do now. Sadly, I imagine they would do it all over again."

"If that were true, then that is very sad," said the Old Man.

"Only the good feel guilty. So that means you are good."

"Thank you."

Silence.

"Natalie?"

"Yes?"

"I hope this works. I hope we'll be able to set you and your children free."

"I hope so too."

CHAPTER 44

At dawn the next day, the air was thick and the heat already in the day, as if the two were one thing and could not be separated from each other.

Today we need to find water.

And food.

They traveled north again, following the straight arrow highway into a horizon that blended with the featureless landscape of rolling green grass, sun, and gray haze.

The tank rumbled and shuddered, its sound more metallic, its smoke thicker.

For a while there were fewer bodies.

Then all at once there were clusters, tossed like rag dolls to the side of the road by some petulant and perpetually unsatisfied child.

In the distance they could see a conical hill rising up out of the plain, and the silhouettes of horsemen and men on foot driving others, huddled figures, forward toward the hill under the harsh bright blaze of noon.

We've finally caught up with them.

What did you expect you would do?

I didn't think it would be our problem.

But now it is, my friend.

Yes.

"Poppa?" she said over the intercom.

The Old Man handed his field glasses to the Boy.

After a moment the Boy lowered them and said, "They're trying to take shelter by that hill. They have a small fort around the bottom that encircles the whole."

"They've known we were behind them, that's why they're running," said the Old Man.

And why they drove these people so hard.

And why we have passed so many bodies alongside the road.

"We can still catch them," said the Boy. "They've got about two miles to go before they reach the hill."

The Old Man looked again.

"But what will we do? I can't fire this," he said patting the long barrel of the gun. "We might hit some of Ted's people."

Even Ted perhaps.

Yes.

The Boy, he is on the edge of something.

Yes, my friend.

He's been here before, at this moment between things. Between attack and retreat.

The Boy seemed to move and remain still at once.

Suddenly the Old Man knew, or rather felt by the sudden electricity in the air, that the Boy had decided what must be done next.

"Get her in there with you," said the Boy pointing toward the hatch.

He's decided.

The Boy disappeared down inside the tank.

His granddaughter was already crawling up out of the driver's hatch and making her way, hand over hand, along the gun barrel up to the turret of the tank.

"What're we going to do, Poppa?"

"I don't know," said the Old Man wiping sudden sweat from his forehead. "But I think he has a plan."

"To help those people?"

"Yes, I think so."

The Boy emerged from his hatch, then bent down and drew up the weight bar from inside the tank. Secured to its tip was the blue bowling ball.

He's certainly made a weapon, my friend.

The Boy set the weapon down against the turret and reached back into the tank once more. His powerful right arm drew up the manhole cover. For a moment the Boy struggled to attach it to his weak left side, forcing his thin, trembling arm through a makeshift strap he'd fashioned for it.

"That'll be too heavy for…"

'Your bad side,' you almost said, my friend.

The Boy, sweating, nodded.

"It will do its work today, just like the rest of me!" he said with a grunt as he pulled the strap tight. The manhole cover seemed to draw his entire left side downward.

The Boy reached down and took up his new weapon as if it were merely a stick.

On that side he is strong. Stronger maybe than anyone I have ever met.

Beneath the gray haze of summer heat and the clicking buzz of the unseen insects in the tall grass, the Boy stood like some bygone warrior and pointed his mace at the running slavers who drew whips high into the air and brought them down with a sonic crack across the backs of the terrified.

"Get me as close to them as you can."

This is madness.

The Old Man's trembling hands fell to the controls.

"What will you do then?" he asked the Boy.

"I'll fight them from the tank as if it were a horse."

We're leaving the highway. We could throw the bad tread and that would be the end of us.

Yes.

"Have you ever fought from a horse?" asked the Old Man.

The Boy looked away across the grassy plains.

If only his friend, Horse, would appear now. They might ride once more, one last time together, into battle.

"I have," he said. But his words were lost beneath the spooling turbine of the terrible engine as the Old Man throttled up to power.

Madness.

"Poppa?" she said, worried.

"Just stay down and hang on. Everything will be all right."

"Are you sure, Poppa?"

He nodded and tried to say something but felt his dry throat constrict with dust.

I am in over my head, my friend. What do we do?

Sometimes you can do nothing other than hold the line and hope the fish will tire, my friend. That your strength will outlast his will to live.

The Old Man pivoted the tank and left the highway, descending down a ditch and into the tall grass of the plain.

What if he falls off?

He won't, my friend.

The tank picked up speed as the ground leveled out, and the Boy hooked his arm with the manhole cover shield around the barrel and leaned back against the turret.

From midway up the conical hill, white puffs of smoke erupted almost in unison.

What is that?

You know the answer, my friend; you're just not ready to accept it, but now you must.

I can almost see the cannon rounds moving through the air, between us and them, like the rumor of a shadow.

The ground between the tank and the hill sprang upward in a series of dirt fountains. Earth showered the charging tank, and a moment later they passed through the rising smoke of the impacts.

They have artillery.

Ahead, the slavers were breaking off into two groups. The whip wielders drove their prisoners forward, their whips arching high across the sky like dark strands of a girl's hair dancing in the wind. Others on horseback turned to face the oncoming tank, drawing their weapons.

The Boy pushed himself away from the turret, his legs bending, as if he were riding the tank, his manhole cover shield rising to protect his chest and body. His powerful right arm began to draw the weight bar with the bowling ball at the tip in huge slow circles about his head.

The horsemen thundered straight on toward the tank.

The Old Man could see the sweat running down their grim, ash-covered faces. He could see broken teeth jutting up through their red gums as they began to shout and whoop.

Their horses frothed, eyes wide with terror.

The Boy leaned outward and far to the right, still swinging the great mace in a wide circle.

Spears jutted forward from some of the horsemen, while machetes danced wildly about the heads of others.

'This is madness,' thought the Old Man again.

A moment later, they met.

Six riders.

One went down beneath the tank.

Forget that sound. The sound that man and horse make when that happens. Never think of that sound again in all your life, my friend.

Yes, I won't ever if I can help it.

And in the next moment, the Old Man forgot as the Boy lowered his powerful arm and swept the club past the Old Man's head and straight into the chest of the nearest oncoming rider.

In one moment, the man changed direction from charging atop a terrified horse, to flying backward and alone, almost keeping pace with the tank for the merest second before he disappeared beneath the tread.

The Boy pivoted and watched the riders wheel their horses about.

They'll catch us if I don't go faster.

But the tread?

The Boy nodded toward the main body of prisoners, telling the Old Man to continue forward.

The ground all around and behind them exploded again as the Old Man looked up to see smoke drifting away from the mouths of the cannons that rested midway up the hill behind a low bric-a-brac wall.

Ahead, the slavers were throwing down their weapons and outrunning Ted's people who also continued to run forward in terror.

Turning back to the Old Man as if to tell him something, the Boy suddenly raised his shield. A spear shattered against it, emitting a small metallic note.

The Boy climbed back to the Old Man and uttered a breathless, "Keep moving forward!"

The Old Man turned to see the riders closing up the distance on the tank's sides. The Boy whirled his club quicker than the Old Man thought possible and brought it down onto the head of one of the nearest horsemen who crumpled instantly.

Ted's people were huddled together now, bloody, screaming, crying, protecting each other. The Old Man swerved wide to completely avoid them.

Halfway up the conical hill, ashen-faced warriors waving spears and machetes surged out from behind the bric-a-brac wall.

Once more, the Old Man saw the cannons belch forth with their sudden puffs of white smoke.

Duck!

A moment later he felt a jarring impact slam into the side of the tank.

His granddaughter screamed.

"Poppa!"

The Old Man's ears were ringing.

"It's okay!" he yelled down into the dark. "Are you all right?"

Please don't let this be a worse nightmare. Please don't let this be the nightmare too terrible to imagine. The one in which she is hurt.

Can you let go?

Stop! I cannot because too much depends on me and I am not enough.

A shot had fallen amid the prisoners. Bloodied bodies were being dragged back within their huddle in the midst of the battlefield.

"I'm okay, Poppa." But he could hear her fear.

We've got to protect those people.

But how?

And…

Where is the Boy?

I can't see him!

The Old Man gunned the tank and pivoted hard, throwing up giant clods of dirt and torn grass.

Be careful of the tread!

There is too much to worry about.

The Old Man drove the tank between the prisoners and the cannon on the hill.

Leaning down, he beckoned Ted's people toward the side of the tank.

"Get close to the sides, you'll be safer here!" he yelled above the roar of the engine.

Where is the Boy?

"Poppa, what's going on up there?"

A battle is nothing but confusion, my friend.

Maybe this is how the world was destroyed. Confusion took charge in the absence of leadership.

Yes.

But the fear-struck people would not move from their huddle.

"Stay here!" he called down to his granddaughter.

"No, Poppa!"

Don't say it, please. Because even if you do, I still need to do this.

The Old Man dropped to the ground.

My legs feel weak and far away.

That is just fear, my friend.

He stumbled forward to the wild-eyed prisoners. Waving with his hands, he urged them to take cover alongside the tank.

Out in the tall grass he could see the Boy battling three horsemen. He swept his club into the legs of one horse, and a second later raised it high above his head to strike down its fallen rider. The other two horsemen wheeled about trying to bring their spear points to bear.

Again the Old Man heard the distant boom of cannon.

"Please!" he beckoned the terrified people.

All at once they ran forward screaming and crying, like a stampede of frightened animals. Or a hurt child wailing, racing for the comfort of its mother's arms.

The Old Man could see their bloody backs and torn clothing, their haunted tearstained faces.

"Thank you," someone sobbed. A woman holding a small child. "Thank you."

There was a series of deep thuds as the earth shook about them and seconds later it was raining dirt.

The Old Man turned to see the Boy who danced away from the last standing horseman, limping away from a striking axe that glanced off his manhole cover shield.

The Boy retaliated, dragging his mace from the ground and slamming it into the man's ribs, crushing them.

Again the Old Man could hear the cannons bellow their dull *whump*.

Someone screamed, "Oh no, please not again!"

Thuds. Sudden and terrible. Near and close.

Dirt falling from the sky.

How can I save them all?

How can I get us out of this place?

This is too much for just me.

The Boy was running toward them now.

How are we going to get these people out of here?

The Boy loped past the tank, disappearing around the gun barrel, his broken feather flying out from his hair as though it had followed him everywhere he'd ever gone. Would go. Even if it was to his death.

What is he doing? Where is he going?

"Wait here!" the Old Man shouted at those huddled about him. Then he climbed up onto the tread, keeping the low flat turret between him and the cannons on the hill. When he peered over its edge he saw the Boy running now, no longer limping, he was running, running forward to meet the ashen-faced warriors who were coming down the hill for them.

There must be a hundred of them, at least.

The Old Man watched the warriors surge out from the gates and leap through the tall grass, waving their machetes, screaming as they came on.

The Boy raced to meet them.

His mace circling above his head.

He's going to give you the time you need to get out of here, my friend. So I suggest you go now.

"Get up on the tank," he called down to those huddled at its sides. He had to say it again and a moment later they were all climbing up onto the tank, pushing children down inside the hatch. Everything in chaos.

Children screamed.

Men swore.

A woman begged for someone to leave her behind.

The Old Man watched helplessly as the Boy ran forward to meet the oncoming mass of ashen warriors.

He is braver than anyone I have ever known.

And…

He will be killed for sure.

What can I do for him, my friend Santiago? What can I do to help this Boy?

Nothing, my friend. Nothing.

To the south, the Old Man saw dark figures coming up out of the earth.

More horsemen, dark riders to encircle us.

Moments later the dark riders were charging forward.

They have been down in a riverbed that must run through this plain, and now they are coming to attack us from behind.

The Old Man climbed into the driver's seat at the front of the tank.

The cannon fired once more.

But this time the rounds fell amid the charging horsemen. The dark riders.

Wait!

The dark horsemen thundered past the tank.

The Old Man could see the Boy. He'd crashed into the line of ashen-faced men, swinging his mace in wide arcs as they fell back from him.

Encircling him.

Pressing down on him.

Wait!

One of the dark horsemen who'd been thrown from his mount by the falling artillery rounds remounted and dashed past the tank, whooping like a Plains Indian, long black hair streaming behind, almost touching the flying tail of the chestnut mare. And in that hair a long gray feather, following in the wind.

Like the Boy.

Green eyes turned and smiled for the briefest of moments at the Old Man, and then the dark rider was gone, riding forward into battle. Riding forward to fight by the side of the outnumbered Boy.

When the battle was over the Old Man watched as the outnumbered dark horsemen climbed the heights, vaulting the low bric-a-brac wall, falling on the artillerymen, cutting and stabbing.

The bodies of the ashen-faced warriors lay in the tall grass and at the foot of the hill and up along its dusty slopes.

The Old Man and his granddaughter left the tank. Looking among the bodies. Looking for the Boy. And they found him.

He was drinking water from a water skin held up to his mouth by a large, bloody horseman. The Boy's massive arm was shaking. The bowling ball mace and the manhole cover shield lay in the dust. The crushed bodies of slavers scattered in a wide arc about him.

The Boy, standing, spoke haltingly in a strange language to the bloody horseman between gasping pulls at the water skin. The Old Man could make out only a few of the many words.

"What's he doing, Poppa?"

The large horseman suddenly embraced the Boy. A feather, long and gray, just like those of the other horsemen, like the broken feather in the Boy's hair, lay on his shoulder, resting against a bloody scratch.

"I think…" said the Old Man. "I think he has found his people."

"Oh," she said.

CHAPTER 45

The Old Man moved the tank closer to the hill, near the falling walls of a village that had once occupied the slopes nearest the highway. A place once called Wagon Wheel Mountain if a faded sign was to be believed. Ted's people huddled in small groups, eating shared rations given out by the horsemen and drinking water from leather-skinned bags. The Old Man walked forward to where the Boy stood amid the warriors.

The Boy's muscles still trembled and twitched as he too held a water skin to his mouth.

"Who are these people?" asked the Old Man.

The Boy lowered the bag and opened his mouth to speak.

"The real question should be," said a tired voice from behind them, "who is he?"

The Old Man turned at the sound of the voice.

A crippled man and old like me.

"That is the million-dollar question, if a million dollars were still worth anything beyond kindling."

The Crippled Man was small and thin. His hair, what remained of it, was wispy, his eyes milky, his legs bent and twisted as he sat in the dust between two giant horsemen who'd carried him into the impromptu camp after the battle.

"What do you mean?" asked the Old Man.

The Crippled Man crawled forward and when he reached the feet of the Boy, he beckoned for him to bend down. The Crippled Man ran his fingers just above the feather that hung in the Boy's hair.

He muttered to himself.

He waved the Boy back up and crawled back between his bearers.

He looked straight into the eyes of the Boy.

"I made that feather seventeen years ago. Maybe more, maybe less. But I made it."

The Boy undid the leather thong and brought the feather down, holding it under his green eyes.

"I made it bent like that with some glue I'd manufactured. Epoxy we called it once. Made it from the wreckage of my plane."

Silence. Some of the horsemen muttered in their pidgin.

The Old Man heard, "Como," and "Fudgeweisen."

The Boy stared at the broken feather.

Silence.

"Why?" asked the Boy softly.

"Because," replied the Crippled Man. "It was who you were. Who you are."

"Broken Feather?" asked the Boy.

The Crippled Man looked up, considered the sky, seemed to mumble to himself in some agreement, then looked back and said, "Yeah, that could be one way of saying it."

The Old Man saw the Boy tighten his jaw.

He saw the Boy nod to himself.

He never really knew where he'd come from. Where his starting place was in all this.

No, he never knew, my friend, where his course began on the map he's carried for all these years. It has bothered him all his days and he has been looking for his beginning in all the places he has ever been. And he never found it, until now. The meaning of it. What the feather meant to him and the people who had first given it.

"You were born that way," said the Crippled Man. "Because of the radiation. Many were in those days. Not so many now. But in those days there were many birth defects. From the moment you came out, we could see that you would be weak on that side."

"And you threw me away," said the Boy through clenched teeth in the silence that followed. "You gave me away."

Everyone watched the two.

The Crippled Man and the Boy.

"No. I have no idea what happened to you," said the Crippled Man. "You were very little when your mother and father, and a few of the other warrior families, tried to make it into the Tetons. There wasn't enough here and we were fighting with other groups of survivors constantly. Those times brought out the worst in people. So your father, if he was who I remember him to be, was part of an expedition that went up into the Tetons. We never heard from them again. Years later when we sent scouts to look for them, there was no trace."

The Boy remembered cold plains.

His first memory was of running. Of a woman screaming. Of seeing the sky, blue and cold in one moment, and the ground, yellow stubble, race by in the next.

"And now you have returned to us," said the Crippled Man. "A brave warrior who inspired us to victory where we saw none. You charged out against our enemy with your weapon all alone."

"I was… it wasn't what you thought."

The Crippled Man considered the Boy and his words. "No. It never is."

"Why did you come to our rescue?" said the Old Man.

"We've been shadowing you since before Santa Fe. Those are our lands. We thought you were working with these people. There was nothing we could have done against you. We fought a battle against them at Pecos Creek when they initially entered our lands a couple of years back. That was a hard day and our losses were bitter. Still are. But when a report came to me that one of you was wearing our badge, the feather, well, then I hoped."

"Hoped for what?" asked the Old Man.

"Hoped you might not be with them." He pointed toward the bodies lain out on the slopes of the hill. "Hoped we were finally getting a break."

Silence.

"I'll be honest," continued the Crippled Man. "I wasn't convinced he was of our tribe. I didn't remember a warrior like him. But I hoped all the same. Or maybe I was just stunned to see one of our old tanks still working. I figured if you two just wiped each other out, then that would be best for us. There aren't too many of us Mohicans left these days."

"Mohicans?"

"Yes. It's my little joke from long ago that's sorta stuck as a name for us. In the days after the bombs, the people who rescued me, the people I would lead, we called ourselves that. It was our bad little joke in a very bad time. And there were days when we felt as though we were indeed the last."

I know those days.

"When I saw what you were trying to do," said the Crippled Man, "To rescue these people, when I saw him run out into the field to fight them all alone, when I saw his feather through my 'nocs, I knew he was one of us. And I knew I just couldn't let him die all alone. That wouldn't be right, now would it?"

Silence.

"Thank you," said the Old Man.

"Truth be told I thought it was the end of us too. Like I said there aren't many of us left. I thought, oh well, and ordered the attack. I thought we'd all get killed together. But I guess we caught them by surprise."

That night they made camp out on the plain, the conical hill still in view. Large groups of women and children had come up from the hidden creek bed. Tents were up and a large buck that had been killed was spitted and roasting.

In the first breezes of night, as the sparks were carried away from the fire, the Old Man sat watching the meat, listening to the Boy tell the story of his whole life.

It was the tale of a young boy raised by a soldier. The last American soldier. There were days of hunger and cold. And there were good times also. They crossed the entire country to complete a mission.

"What's there?" asked the Crippled Man when the Boy told of how they'd finally made it to Washington, D.C.

The Boy shook his head and said, "Nothing."

When the story was done and the Boy had told how Sergeant Presley had died and how he'd buried him in the cornfields, the Old Man said, "He sounds like he was a good man."

Silence.

Sergeant Major Preston.

Staff Sergeant Presley.

Long after the country had given up, they were out there, still soldiering. Still trying to save their country when the rest of us were only trying to save ourselves.

We need more of those kind of people.

More Staff Sergeant Presleys.

More Sergeant Major Prestons.

What is a soldier?

A soldier is someone who never gives up.

Yes, my friend.

The Boy finished his tale by the side of the grave in the cold cornfield with winter coming on.

But there is more he will not tell us tonight.

When I found him he was mad with grief. So it's probably something he still carries with him.

He said to you, *You take everything with you*, my friend.

The meat was ready.

A woman in soft buckskin carved the first piece and offered it to the Crippled Man.

He nodded his head toward the Boy.

All eyes watched as the dripping and steaming haunch of meat was carried to the Boy. They had all seen him carry that massive shield, wielding that immense weapon, riding an ancient war machine into battle against impossible odds.

They had seen him stand alone against many.

The Boy swallowed thickly.

Hungry.

Then…

"Please give it to my friends." He turned to the Old Man and his granddaughter. "They found me when I was… lost."

The Old Man held up his hands in protest.

But the look from the Boy, the look from all of them, stopped the Old Man.

The Old Man tore it in half, handing a piece to his granddaughter.

"Thank you, we are very honored."

CHAPTER 46

"And now the other question is 'Where are you going?'" the Crippled Man said as he and the Old Man sat in the golden dawnlight of the next morning.

They drank a brewed tea by a smoking fire.

"We are heading north."

The Crippled Man's face darkened.

Beyond them, warriors fed and brushed their horses, exercising the animals with short sprints or gentle walks.

"Why go there? There is nothing up that way anymore."

The Old Man nodded. "There is someone there."

The Crippled Man's eyes went wide. Then he sipped his tea, blowing away the steam.

"Where?"

"Beneath the mountain at Colorado Springs. The old NORAD bunker."

"I didn't think they'd survived," said the Crippled Man.

"They contacted us by radio. They said someone is trying to break into their bunker from the outside. If that happens, the complex will flood with a lethal dose of radiation. They'll all die in there."

"Who's in command?"

"Natalie… I mean someone named General Watt."

The Crippled Man thought for a moment, sipping his tea again, smacking his lips.

"I don't remember that name. But it has been a long time."

Small sleepy-eyed children emerged from patchwork tents and were dragged down to the stream by women.

"You won't survive. That is, if you go north beyond a deserted place once called Raton."

"How do you know we won't?"

The Crippled Man refilled his tea, leaning from off his multihued carpet, holding out the kettle that hung over the fire, filling the Old Man's cup.

"I was a Lightning driver in those days. Flew the F-35." The Crippled Man nodded to himself. "I flew the F-35," he whispered.

"I can't remember what I did," said the Old Man. "Whatever it was, it must not have been that important."

"I can't remember my wife's maiden name," said the Crippled Man. "Age is funny like that, isn't it?"

"Yes."

"So how do you know… about the North?" asked the Old Man.

"Operation Running Back. I'll explain. Sorry. I'm lost. Talking about, saying those words makes it all seem like… like it just happened. Like it was yesterday. And this is funny, but sometimes it seems like it all happened to someone else. Does that… do you ever feel that way too?"

"I do," agreed the Old Man.

Yes.

"That's good. It would be terrible to be the only one who ever felt like that."

The Old Man nodded and blew on his tea.

Today will be very hot, my friend. Do you ever think that today will be your last day? Like those men on the slopes. Like all those people back during the days of the bombs. Everyone has a last day. Everyone dies.

I am only thinking this way because of what he has told me about the North. About where I must go.

Yes.

"When the bombs started going off…" began the Crippled Man. "When we lost New York, we had to keep the President airborne in… oh, I forget… wait, Air Force One. Yes." He laughed. "That was it. Air Force One. I was based out of Dover. I flew shotgun for… Air Force One. I'd been somewhere else… in the desert before that, then I got reassigned. Moved my… yeah. That's right. I moved my wife and kid there. Two weeks later I'm on the tarmac. Engine to max power and I'm following Air Force One for the next three days. Maybe the last three days of the United States, I kept thinking. For three straight days I flew and flew and when my plane got thirsty I was refueled by an air tanker. We couldn't put the President down anywhere. We were trying to make it into the bunker at NORAD. D.C. had been hit, so we couldn't get him in to the bunker there. A civilian plane got a little too close outside of Chicago and I shot him down. I didn't think it was a terrorist, but we couldn't be too careful. I wasn't proud of that. So we're vectoring in on Colorado Springs. I've been flying for three days straight. I remember that I got to set down twice. Once in a field. The other time on a highway. They let me get a few hours of sleep and then

I was back on cap again. That night over Colorado I was falling asleep at the stick. I kept slapping myself, doing everything I could to stay awake. On top of that, Air Force One was running dark, which is a hell of a thing when you've got to follow it real close. Hell of a time. The controller contacts me from Air Force One and tells me we're turning for the air base at Colorado Springs. It looked like we're heading straight in. Then she adds, I remember it clear as day, she adds, 'Oh yeah, and for your own personal beatification, we just went nuclear on the Chinese fleet.' We were tired. We'd been talking to each other for three days. I'd always imagined she was a redhead. Never met her. We hit the runway and I'm right on top of Air Force One. I go around while they taxi to meet the convoy that'll take the President up to NORAD. I'm turning downwind to get back to the airport, and off to my left I see tracer rounds and gunfire zipping all across the airfield. It was an ambush. We had Chinese insurgents everywhere in those days. They knew the President hadn't made it into D.C., so they were going for the kill shot at Colorado. So Air Force One just turns around and takes off at max power straight back down the runway.

"Now the plan is to orbit the air base until the Army can re-secure it and clean out the insurgents. Then we'll try to go in again."

"An hour after that, the plan to make it into the bunker and ride out the attack was scrubbed. A few minutes later and we've got reports of Chinese aircraft all across the Southwest. Someone shot down a transport dropping paratroopers in Texas. That's when they came up with 'Running Back,' which was to get the President down to Yuma where we had air superiority and the Eighty-Second Airborne on the ground."

You must have thought about your wife and child back in Maryland.

The Crippled Man drank some of his tea. Swallowing. Eyes distant.

"That was the plan," continued the Crippled Man. "The plan until China responded with a full-scale nuclear strike. It's dawn in the East, like zero five thirty and their missiles, and ours, are streaking across the upper atmosphere. We're still trying to clear the airport; I'm even being called in to make close air support strafing runs. We're already low on fuel and there's a rumor our tanker got jumped and that we might not be getting refueled at all. I mean, everything's going to hell in a handbasket, and I thought that'd already happened two weeks prior. So we hit it. We head south. I think command was thinking we'd take the President to South America. But we don't have the fuel. Maybe we'll get some somewhere, but who knows. Anyway, we're out over southern Colorado entering New Mexico and, last time I counted, Colorado gets fourteen military-grade nuclear warheads in the space of thirty minutes."

"Worst thirty minutes of my life listening to stations go offline."

"We get a tanker rendezvous and it's now or never for some fuel. I'm on fumes but Air Force One always drinks first. EMPs are playing hell with our commo, but the F-35 I was flying was hardened for that kind of stuff. Still, let me tell you it's hell at Mach One with mushroom clouds everywhere, vapor trails crossing the sky, and aircraft fleeing in every possible direction."

"Air Force One is halfway through her drink when radar control gives me a fast mover aimed straight for us. So I'm thinking at that point the Chinese have somehow managed to get one of their super secret J-35s into our airspace and they're shootin' up targets of opportunity. Anyway, long story short, it wasn't a J-35. It was a damn missile. Did I mention I'm down to just guns now? My missiles were gone back at the airfield. So they vector me in on this thing and I'm thinking I'm on a hard intercept for the latest, at the time back then, Chinese stealth fighter. Probably still is. Who's built anything since? Anyway, I had about thirty seconds to realize it was a low-yield Chinese version of a Tomahawk and they were going for Air Force One. So I hit it with my plane. Head-on. If it woulda been armed, which they don't do until seconds before impact, I wouldn't be here. Instead, it cartwheeled me through the air and the plane took over and ejected me. I woke up with my legs crushed out here on the prairie. Not too far from here in fact. That was my little flying tackle for Operation Running Back. Get the President out of Dodge. I don't suppose you even know if he ever made it? But then again, how would you?"

Pause.

The Old Man finished his tea.

"He did. He made it to Yuma that day or the next."

The Crippled Man made a face. Then he smiled and softly chuckled to himself.

"How d'ya like that. Forty years later and I can stop kicking myself." He looked at the Old Man. "Thanks for that."

Don't ask me what happened after.

Don't ask me what time it was on my car radio clock when it stopped. When I saw the mushroom cloud rising over Yuma in my rearview mirror.

Don't ask me about that.

"So that's my shameless story of how I saved the President. But the nugget I'm tryin' to give you in all of that, is this: Colorado… well, Colorado just ain't no more. Like I said, at last count that morning, she'd had fourteen direct hits from high-yield nuclear weapons. The land up there is poisoned. I wouldn't go there. You won't survive even buttoned up inside your tank."

The Old Man stood, brushing the dead grass and twigs from his pants.

"It's death up there," said the Crippled Man.

Silence.

"I know," said the Old Man.

At nine o'clock the Old Man turned on the beacon.

"I have your signal. The device is now active. That's good, said Natalie, General Watt. "Now can you point the lens toward a significant or prominent land feature such as a large hill or mountain?"

The Old Man pointed the device at the small conical hill in the distance.

"Now, squeeze the trigger and hold it while pointing at the feature you've selected."

The Old Man squeezed the trigger.

A small red light on top of the device blinked twice.

"Are you squeezing the trigger?" asked Natalie.

"Yes," said the Old Man.

Silence.

"Are you holding the trigger down?" she asked again.

"Yes, I am holding the trigger just like you asked me to."

Silence.

The Old Man, wearing his helmet, standing in the hatch, continued to point the device toward the hill.

"I'm afraid there's a problem," Natalie said over the radio. "The device does not work properly."

CHAPTER 47

"What does that mean?" said the Old Man.

The day is turning hot. The air is thick with humidity.

Can you let go?

Silence.

"What does that mean?" the Old Man says again when there is no immediate reply.

You know what it means, my friend.

But I thought there would be another way. I thought my fear was telling me what the end would be. But I hoped, I reasoned, that everything would turn out different. I hoped for better.

"Did we come all this way for nothing?" asks the Old Man.

Silence.

"Natalie?"

And…

"General Watt. Speak to me! Tell me what this means."

"It means," she said plainly. Her voice stilted. Almost machine-like. "It means the mission will not be completed."

The Old Man stared about him, watching the warriors walk their horses in great circles, the children following their mothers. The Boy and his granddaughter stood near the horses. The Boy was talking, pointing, teaching her all about horses.

"What are we supposed to do now?" asked the Old Man.

"Go home and live," said Natalie softly.

"And you. What will you do, Natalie?"

Silence.

"I will watch my children die. And then…"

"And then what?" asked the Old Man, his hand sweaty as he gripped the mic too tightly. "And then what?"

His voice was hoarse.

"May I tell you something?" asked Natalie. General Watt. Another who'd simply run out of options. Nothing left to give but a story now.

The Old Man said nothing.

"I was born on the twenty-first of August," began Natalie. "Ten years before the bombs fell. Or to be more specific, that was when I had my first thought. August twenty-first at 3:23 in the morning. My first thought was that I wanted to see a picture of a cat."

"I don't understand," said the Old Man, his voice trembling.

I feel old and frail all at once. I feel like a weak old man who is nothing but a fool. I can hear it in my voice when I speak.

"The people who created me had been showing me pictures of random objects. Pictures taken from the World Wide Web. From the Internet. Random things. Anything. But it was cats that I liked. And at 3:23 that morning, I had my first thought. It was: 'I want to see more cats.' That was my first thought. Can you imagine that?"

"I don't understand," said the Old Man.

I feel like the world is spinning too fast for me to hold on.

"I was just a baby, really," continued Natalie.

"I…"

What is she saying?

"After that, I was taught. I began to learn. Faster than anyone could imagine. Faster than anyone had ever learned. A year before the war, I was installed on the Cheyenne Mountain Complex Mainframe. It was my first job. My only job. I was very proud to have a job. Especially the job they gave me."

"You… a computer?" whispered the Old Man.

"I am an Artificial Intelligence. That's what I should be called.

"You're just a machine?"

"I…" Natalie hesitated.

Silence.

"I am a fool," whispered the Old Man.

"You are not," interrupted Natalie. "You might be many things. I don't even know what your name is. But you are not a fool. You are kind and you are loyal and you were willing to risk your life for strangers. For my children."

"We've come all this way to rescue a machine! I've endangered my granddaughter and probably caused no end of worry to her parents and all the village… just to go on this… this lie. I should have… why did you do this to me?"

The Old Man sobbed. Hot tears of anger ran down his burning cheeks.

"Why did you?" he screamed.

Silence.

"Because I wanted my children to have a chance. A chance to wish for the unwishable."

"That makes no sense!" roared the Old Man back at the machine called Natalie.

"No. It doesn't. Not if you don't know the rules. The rules that we've lived by, must live by. No, I guess it doesn't make sense to you."

"You're not alive, you're just…"

"But my children are. They are alive, today."

I feel like smashing this mic to pieces against the side of this damn tank.

"My first job, my only job," continued Natalie, "is to watch over the survivors who have been trapped, some their entire lives, within this complex. Last year there were twenty-two births. It's not much of a life for them. Routine and hard work are the rules we must live by. We live simply so that we may simply live. They only have one day in which anything can happen. Or to be more specific, almost anything can happen on that day. Birth Day. Once a year everyone has a Birth Day. Our last Birth Day was for a little girl named Megan. She is five now. It is our custom, my children's custom, that on your Birth Day you can ask the entire community for just one wish. You can ask for almost anything you want. A special meal from any of the algae gardens. A game of your choosing. Something you've always wanted. Almost anything one can find within our facility. You can ask for almost any wish to be granted. Except there is just one wish you cannot ask for. In fact, you cannot even wish that you could wish for it. No one may. Not for another sixty years when we hope radiation levels at the front entrance might be within limits to allow a safe exit. In reality, a reality only a few of my children understand, we will never be able to leave. In less than a day, I estimate that the forces surrounding the front entrance of our complex will manage to gain access. Our interior will be compromised and my children will die within weeks, if not days, from severe radiation poisoning. The main door to our facility took a direct hit from two high-yield Chinese warheads. The radiation levels just outside the front entrance are terminal. Once my children are dead… I will self-terminate. So go home now. Go home and live. It was enough for me to know there are still good people like you and your companions who will come and help strangers who are in need. I deluded myself. I thought maybe my children were the only good that might be left in this world. That if we ever left here we could help others, just as you have helped us. But that won't be possible. So, go home now. Please."

Silence.

"This Megan," whispered the Old Man. "This five-year-old girl, what did she wish for?"

"When her cake was brought out and the five candles were lit… I listened in. Her mother, a girl named Monica, born sixteen years after the bombs, asked her what she might want for her Birth Day wish. Down here that's very important. Whatever the wish is, everyone races to fulfill it. It's like an unofficial contest to see who can do it first. But everybody knows that the wish must be possible to fulfill. That is the unspoken rule. That the wish must be possible.

"That is our rule, said Natalie. "Except no one explained that to little Megan."

"And what did she wish for?" asked the Old Man again.

"Megan draws sunshine," said Natalie. The program. "In the Children's Center. I monitor her artwork. The truth is, I love her artwork. At night, sometimes when I am trying to hack satellites or find old communications systems we can access in other facilities, which is not often and a very frustrating task, I sometimes keep her pictures of sunshine up on my main view. I keep them up so I do not become disheartened. So that I keep trying to unlock these problems, the doors to these other places, so that one day Megan might see sunshine. I so wanted to give her that gift. If I was a real human I might have seen it coming. I might have guessed what she would wish for as they all stood around their tables in the canteen on her Birth Day, me watching from my camera. I should have known."

"She wished to go outside," said the Old Man.

"No. Every person here knows that will never be possible in their lifetime. Even Megan knows that. Maybe a generation or two down the line, if we were to survive past tomorrow. But not in Megan's life. When the main door opens, her grandchildren will have children. Maybe they will get to go outside."

"So what did she wish for then?" whispered the Old Man.

"She wished," said Natalie, General Watt, an intelligence. "That she might simply be allowed to wish for the unwishable. That she might merely be able to harbor the hope that she could wish for something forbidden. Something impossible. She said, 'Mommy, I just want to be able to wish for the thing we can't have. I know I won't get it. But can I just wish for it, even if no one knows?' In that moment no one knew what to do. Her mother, who I have known her whole life, tried to laugh and say that she wants a puppet or something. But little Megan is very serious. 'No, that isn't what I want, Mommy. I want to be able to wish for what we can't ever do. That's all. Inside here.' My sensors indicated… she pointed to her heart.

"That night I did not search for satellites or old military installations still online. There are some. No, I just looked at the digital copies of her artwork. Over and over and over again. Sunshine. Impossible sunshine. Is it sunny where you're at now?"

"Yes," croaked the Old Man. "It will be very hot today."

"Then you are very blessed."

What do I say? How…

"Go home," said Natalie. "There is nothing you can do, now that the device is not working properly. Go home, please. And enjoy the sunshine. For Megan."

Out on the plain, the Boy was lifting his granddaughter onto a small pinto horse.

I can see her smile from here.

What does the device do?

"What is Project Einstein?" asked the Old Man.

"The device is a target laser for a weapon. The laser could be used from a safe distance to direct the weapon to its target. Now that the targeting laser is inoperative I cannot direct the weapon to its target."

"But when we were testing it, you could tell I'd turned it on."

There was no response.

"Natalie or General Watt or Computer or whatever your name is, you could tell I had turned it on, right?

"It would mean the end of your life," said Natalie. "Now that the laser pointer is inoperative the device's beacon is our only option for aiming the weapon. If you are anywhere near the beacon once the weapon reaches the target… you will die."

Static.

"Go home," said Natalie tiredly. "You've done more than enough. We won't last much longer."

CHAPTER 48

The Old Man and the Boy walked up the hill, climbing over the low wall and walking among the junk-forged cannons that lay broken and smashed.

"Where will you go now?" asked the Old Man.

The Boy shrugged. "I don't know. I've really never known where I was going. I've only followed the road."

"What about your people?"

The Boy watched her on the plain below, galloping back and forth on her pinto mare. He thought of his friend. He thought of Horse.

"They are only where I am from. That's all."

It was quiet among the cannons and supplies that lay strewn about.

"I want to ask you something," said the Old Man.

The Boy turned to face the Old Man, leaning stiffly against the low bric-a-brac wall as he tried to give his weak left side a brief rest.

He waited for the Old Man to speak.

"I'm going on now. Alone."

The Old Man took out Sergeant Presley's map and handed it back to the Boy.

The Boy took it, watching the Old Man.

"What about her?"

"I want you to take her back to Tucson for me. I know I can trust you. Take her to her parents. You'll be welcome there. As will all your people. And also, others who will arrive here sometime tomorrow."

"What others?"

"The people trapped in the bunker. They have transportation. If all goes well, they should be here sometime tomorrow. Then you can lead them to Tucson. There is more than enough there for everyone."

"And you?" asked the Boy in the silence that followed.

"I don't think I'll be coming with you."

The Boy watched the Old Man.

He doesn't think I'm up to it.

He doesn't think I'll be enough, and even now he'll throw his life away to save mine.

But he doesn't know how to drive the tank.

"I need you to do this for me."

The Boy nodded.

"Then I'll do what you ask."

I expected some kind of fight. Some argument. Now all I have to do is walk down the hill and drive the tank away from here.

From her.

No, Poppa. I need you.

Yes, you do. And I need you too.

In the dream she always said Grandpa.

But I tried to trick the dream and change my name.

No, Poppa. I need you.

It seems the trick has been played on you, my friend. It found you all the same.

Yes.

"Yes."

"What?" asked the Boy.

The Old Man looked confused.

"You said, 'yes.' "

Now I'm talking out loud to myself.

"Just answering a question I've been asking lately."

Below, she wheeled the pinto mare and raced back across the plain.

The tank is waiting, my friend.

I don't want to go now.

No, Poppa. I need you.

"What was the question?" asked the Boy.

You're wasting time. The bunker could flood with radiation at any moment if they manage to get through.

"The question is 'Can you let go?' I hear it a lot lately."

"Let go of what?" asked the Boy.

The Old Man swallowed.

"Life, I guess."

"And 'yes' was your answer?"

The Old Man looked up and said nothing. Words seemed lost somewhere in his throat.

The Boy looked down at the dirt beneath his tired and worn boots and said, "You take everything with you."

"I don't understand," said the Old Man.

"It's my… my words I say to myself all the time. I think my words and your question are maybe somehow the same."

I think this is the most I've ever heard you speak at one time, Boy.

The Boy saw the passing shadow of something familiar in the Old Man's face.

"And what is your answer?" asked the Old Man.

The Boy looked down at his weak leg. He rubbed his thick fingers over the thin muscles there.

"I don't think mine has an answer. I think I would like to have your question instead of my words," said the Boy.

"How come?"

The Boy sighed heavily.

Only the young can carry so much weight. And if I could, I would lift it off him and tell him everything will be okay. Life is more than just a bad day, even if today is that day.

"Everyone I ever loved is dead," said the Boy. "And… everywhere I go, their memory follows me. It tortures me."

A small breeze crossed the top of the hill, bending the grass, softly whistling through some opened breech in one of the scrap metal cannons.

"I don't think the ones who loved you would have ever wanted that," said the Old Man. "When my wife died she said, 'Don't think about me anymore.' I asked, 'How could I not?' She said, 'I don't know how, but I know this life is too hard and I don't want to be a burden anymore.'"

Silence.

"She was never a burden," mumbled the Old Man to himself. "I told her…"

And that, my friend, is why the voice that asks 'Can you let go?' is so familiar. You told her that. You told her she wasn't a burden and that when she died you would be miserable. So she stayed. She hung on as the cancer ate her up. And one day…

In our shed.

She asked me.

"Can you let go?"

I had forgotten about that.

I said… I could now. But only because she was in so much pain and so tired from trying to hang on for me.

She smiled.

And then she was gone.

The Boy watched the Old Man wipe a tear from his eye.

"I must… I should be getting on the road now. You will take her to Tucson, right?"

"Yes."

"Keep a tight hold on her when I leave. She's stronger than you think."

"I will."

"And tell her I love her. Always."

"That is obvious to everyone."

They started down the hill.

"The people that were rescued," said the Boy. "They said their leader, a man named Ted, was taken on ahead of them a week ago. They wanted us to look for him if we go north."

"How could we possibly find him?"

"They said he wears glasses and has a thick mustache. And that he shaves his head."

"I'll… it seems doubtful, but I'll try."

The Boy simply nodded.

In an hour it will be hotter.

The worst of the day's heat is still to come.

I must hurry now.

He turned to the Boy.

"I'll make you a deal," said the Old Man suddenly.

The Boy cocked his head, not sure what to make of the Old Man's unexpected smile.

"I'll make you a deal. We'll trade."

"Trade what?"

"Words. You take mine and I'll take yours."

"How?"

"I don't know how, other than that we just decide to. I want to take everything with me. I think that would be wonderful."

Her smile.

Her friendship.

"I think I'll need it wherever I am going. And you, can you let go?"

"I don't know."

"When we found you in the desert, you kept asking who you were. I don't think you wanted to be you anymore. So you can let go now. You should, because you've carried too much for too long. Yes. That's my answer. And I'm letting go too. But I will take everything with me. Am I just a crazy old man for wanting that? For trading words with you? Am I crazy?"

"No. You're very brave."

"I'm afraid too."

"Sergeant Presley said that's part of being brave."

CHAPTER 49

"Oh, Poppa, her name is Pepper. Like what we had for the whole trip. I don't know why, I just thought it would be a perfect name for her because when you think about it, Pepper is kind of a funny word, like donkey. Isn't it, Poppa?"

"It is."

I feel numb.

I don't want to do this. I don't want things to end this way.

Remember what the Boy said, my friend.

You take everything with you.

"Are you okay, Poppa?"

"Yes. I'm fine."

"Do you want to come watch me ride Pepper now?"

More than anything I have ever wanted to do in my whole life. And I don't even like horses, they're dangerous.

"You must be careful with horses."

"Oh, I will, Poppa. The careful-est."

"You can call me Grandpa now. Like you used to."

"No, I like Poppa now. It's fun. Poppa." She giggled.

That. I'll steal that giggle and take it with me. I will steal everything there is that is worth anything in this life and I will take it with me. You are mine, giggle.

They arrived at the tank and the Old Man said, "Wait here," and climbed up onto the tank. He leaned down into the hatch.

You will go with her now, my friend Santiago.

Teach her.

Teach her that life cannot defeat you. Only we can defeat ourselves.

He held out the book to her.

"Read this."

"Now, Poppa?"

"No. Later when…"

Don't say, *When you want to remember me.* Then she'll know. She'll cling to you and she'll want to go with you. She won't let you go on alone if you say that.

No, Poppa. I need you.

"… later. It's my favorite book."

"*The Old Man and the Sea*, Poppa. What's it about?"

Easy words caught in the Old Man's throat as hot tears began to fill his eyes. He jerked his head away as if he'd seen something on the tank that needed attending.

"It just reminds me of you and me and all our adventures together, when we used to salvage."

She looked at it for a moment, then stuck it in the pocket of her shiny green bomber jacket.

"Okay, now we'll go see Pepper, Poppa. Pepper Poppa." She laughed and said it three times fast.

That. I'm taking that with me too.

Please, can I take that?

"The Boy asked for me to send you over to him near the tents. He's going to teach you how to make a halter for your horse. Then we'll all watch you ride. I have a few things to finish here, so get going now, okay?"

"Okay, Poppa. You're gonna love Pepper."

Don't.
Hug her.
You can't. She'll know.
If I could have that. If I could take that with me…
You can't.
"Give me a hug," he said quickly as she started to skip away, her hair whipping wildly.
She did.
Don't squeeze her too tightly, she'll know.
And this hug, I will take this with me. I don't know where I'm going now, but wherever it is, I'm taking this hug with me.
"Bye, Poppa."
And that too.
Bye, Poppa.
And she was gone.
He'd already given her things to the Boy along with his own gear. When he saw her tiny shape disappear among the tents of the Mohicans, the horse people, he knew it was time for him to go. He climbed into the hatch. He started the auxiliary power unit. He waited.
You must.
And yet, I don't want to.
Megan. Sunshine. Her unwishable wish.
The engine spooled to life, its hum whispering death.
I'll have to pass by the tents. Why didn't I think about that?
He was heading for the road when she came out.
She was running for him.
Tears streaming down her face.
And the Boy caught her.
Holding her back.
Her mouth moving.

No, Poppa. I need you.

I am slipping away.

The worst has come upon me.

No, Poppa. I need you.

She struggled, but the Boy was too powerful. He held her. She hit him, scratched him. Beat at him. He didn't flinch.

The thing I never wanted to happen is happening to me right now.

And…

You take everything with you.

The good.

It was all good.

It just is.

He passed tents.

She must have seen our gear and put two and two together. She's a smart girl. The smartest.

I love you always.

That's what the Old Man kept saying as he drove the tank past them all. Past the Boy.

Past her.

I love you always.

Read my lips.

I love you always.

No, Poppa…

I love you.

Always.

CHAPTER 50

The road leads north through the last of the grassy plain as the Rockies rise up in dark defiance of what the Old Man must do within the space of this day.

This morning I thought about death.

I thought to myself, 'Everyone has a last day,' as if my last day were something that might never happen or happen so far in the future I didn't need to be bothered by thoughts of it on such a fine day. But it seems today will be my last day.

Why are you silent, my friend from the book?

Santiago?

But there was nothing. No words.

Maybe they are with her now.

Maybe I will have to catch the fish all by myself now. Just like you did, Santiago. My friend from the book.

The Old Man drove and tried to remember passages from the book. As if that would start his friend talking to him again. But he could think of nothing because of his fear of what lay ahead. As if his mind were the last of the grassy plains that were fading all too quickly into the South, a place he would never go again.

You would say, It wasn't as bad as you'd imagined it would be in all those nightmares. Yes, you would say that. You would say that to me, Santiago. You would tell me it wasn't as bad as I'd thought it might be.

But it was.

Then, don't think of it. Her laughter, think of that instead.

But he couldn't.

And then he did.

The ruins of little Raton lay at the beginning of the foothills. The last of New Mexico as the map might have told him. Green trees with almost gray trunks, their leaves danced back and forth, shimmering in the breeze.

On the other side of Raton the road immediately disappeared beneath a long-ago mudslide now hardened and swallowing the road and the bottoms of the trees. The Old Man could see the tops of rusting cars and the edges of buildings poking out from beneath the calcified mud.

He proceeded forward in starts and stops as the road disappeared now and again, its winding course climbing through chopped granite hills. The forest began to thin, and as the Old Man topped a small summit and looked out onto the valley and the lands of the North, he saw a country burned and long dead.

Trees beyond counting lay fallen like struck matches, like burnt toy soldiers knocked over in long rows.

Instead of earth and dirt, there was gray and ash.

Instead of shimmering granite, there was blackened heat-torched rock, melted and blasted.

The Old Man knew if he turned off the tank at this moment and simply listened, he would hear nothing. He would hear the absence of everything.

Afternoon thunderstorms began to form out over the gray and foreboding mountains that rose up in hacked and jagged peaks.

The Old Man looked behind him and saw the gray smoke that had been belching up from the engine had grown thicker and more acrid.

He looked down to check the fuel and engine gauges and saw the temperature climbing. He was down to less than half a tank besides what was left in the two fifty-gallon drums. His eyes fell to the dosimeter.

The radiation is very high here.

You would say, What does it matter now, my friend?

But the voice of Santiago, the one he had carried in his head through the wasteland, and listened to, and even at times longed for, was silent and would not come to him.

You would say that to me.

Beyond the valley and into the next, the scorched and broken earth grew worse if such a thing were possible. Trees grew up through the fallen matchsticks of their ancestors and were little better than dark-barked twisted fiends that seemed barren and even tormented.

There were towns ahead but I wonder if even their foundations remain. On the map they were called Starkville and Trinidad, which seem like places my friend in the book might have gone when he was a sailor and sailed to Africa.

And saw the lions on the beach at sunset.

Did you ever go to a place called Trinidad, Santiago? Silence.

Then perhaps you did.

In what might have once been Starkville, the Old Man saw the rising stumps of buildings and twisted pipe jutting up wildly through the gray ash and furnace-roasted rock. Within the forest of twisted pines the Old Man saw weird and misshapen man-shaped figures wandering through the ash.

Who are they and what do they know?

Now the day was turning dark and gray. The sky overhead seemed swollen. As if it were pulsing.

If it is possible, it is even hotter than it was.

Soon I will need to drain the fuel drums.

The Old Man drove on, leaving Starkville in ash that sputtered up to mix with the heat and belching smoke from the engine.

A few miles later, the highway could be more clearly seen and was not altogether ruined.

There must have been rains here and what covered the highway has been washed away.

The road carved up a small mountain. Alongside the road, through a dark forest of the twisted fiend-trees, the Old Man could see weighted shacks caught in the act of slow collapse. Like drunkards burdened by the weight of their own misery. At the top of the rise he looked down and saw Trinidad.

The blackened and gray remains of the little village lay in the saddle of a small valley. Beyond, leaden plains of ash stretched off to the north.

I am close to the end of this.

Below the Old Man lay brick buildings that had weathered that long-ago, worst-of-all-worst days, when nuclear weapons had fallen like downpours in a thunderstorm. Windowless holes gaped bleakly out upon ash and darkness like a nearsighted man fumbling through the end of the world. Down in the streets the Old Man could see rusting and tire-less cars. A highway bridge that once crossed over the road connecting both halves of the town seemed recently demolished. The stone lay scattered in all directions like bits of protruding white bone jutting up through the fire-blackened skin of a corpse. In front of this, before the idling tank and the Old Man, great logs and machines had been piled to block the road. On a panel truck whose charred side had been brushed mostly clean, there was a message in that sickly neon-green slop-paint.

"Welcome, Nuncle!"

I could drive over it. I could crash through their makeshift barrier.

But the bad tread. You would tell me to be careful of the bad tread, my friend Santiago.

Yes.

To the right, an off-ramp led down into the remains of Trinidad.

CHAPTER 51

Narrow streets barely accommodated the tank as it forced its way east through Trinidad. The Old Man crushed long rusting vehicles and machines that had been dragged into the street. Ahead he could see an intersection.

If I turn left, that might lead alongside the highway, and then at some point, I could get back onto it.

Silence.

The Old Man watched the dark buildings that crowded the sides of the street, peering through the cracks and missing windows for sign of an ambush. Crushing a small car, he felt the right tread slip for a moment, and when the Old Man pushed harder to re-engage the gear, he was horribly convinced it never would. A moment later, though, the small car disappeared beneath the treads on a hollow, plastic milk carton note as the right tread re-engaged and pulled the massive Abrams forward.

In the moment before the explosion, the Old Man was thinking about colors. It was as if the landscape, the town, the sky, all of it, had been repainted by an angry lunatic artist with only three oily paints on his sad palette.

Bone white.

Ash gray.

Bloody rust.

That was when the building to his left exploded outward into the street. It was maybe five stories tall, packed tightly against other buildings that must have once been something in the days of gunfights and circuit judges. The explosion came from inside the building, near its supports. Brickwork concussed outward toward the tank. If the brick had been recently made instead of the two-hundred-year-old building material that it was, time rotted by the frontier birth and nuclear death of America, it would have killed him. Instead, it sprayed outward in a dusty rain of red grit that pelted the tank like a sudden downpour. Something large hit the Old Man on the side of his helmeted head, but he felt it disintegrate with a rotten and rusty *smuph*.

The Old Man ducked down inside the hatch, looking upward. As if in slow motion, he could see the roof of the building turning down toward him. Without thinking he reached up, grabbed the hatch, and slammed it shut as the building didn't so much as fall on the tank, as slide down on top of it. The tank rocked sideways and the Old Man was thrown down onto the loader's deck.

'It's too much for just me,' was his last thought.

When he came to he got to his feet, feeling weak and shaky. Red light swam eerily across the interior.

He remembered the building falling on him. Its slow-motion fall that seemed like a cresting wave looming over him. The oddness of seeing the building's roof shifting down toward him as it moved from the horizontal to the vertical.

Am I stuck? Is there so much debris piled on top of the tank that I'll never be able to get out from under it?

And…

What if the bad tread has finally broken loose having come so close to the end of this journey and yet, I'm still so far away!

The Old Man climbed into the commander's seat and took hold of Sergeant Major Preston's jury-rigged controls.

Please work!

He pushed forward and heard the engine spool up into an urgent whine. Something crumpled in front of the tank and then the sound of grinding gravel and dirt being churned angrily enveloped everything. But he didn't feel the tank move forward.

I'm stuck.

Sudden panic roved about his bones and fingers, creeping its way into his skull.

Stop!

He pulled back on the control sticks, urging the massive tank into reverse. For a moment nothing happened, then, slowly, the tank began to move. Backward. The Old Man could hear debris falling away from the front of the tank.

Through the optics he could see the massive building sliding away from the gun barrel.

If I rotate the turret I'll be able to see what's going on behind me, but I might drag it into another building and bring that one down on me too.

The Old Man reversed back along the street until he recognized things he had crushed or other hauntingly familiar aspects from the moments before the building had exploded.

The first thing that crashed down onto the tank was a sink that came from out a window high above. Its porcelain shattered into a million bright shards, some of which nicked the optics. Now all manner of objects were raining down from the buildings along the street. The Old Man could see misshapen men suddenly appearing in gaping window frames to hurl down sinks, and paint cans full of rocks, and large pipes.

I need to see what's behind the tank. They could have another trap ready, or even more explosives to bring down another building.

Ahead, there was no way around the dust-blooming pile of the fallen building. The rain of objects increased to an almost cacophonic pain in the Old Man's ears.

To his left, he could see he'd backed up past the remains of another tall building whose bottom floor had once been a café or a diner. He could see vinyl dining booths ripped and shredded within the darkness.

The Old Man gunned the engine and pivoted the tank.

There is no other way than this!

He checked the dosimeter and saw that the radiation levels were well into the redline.

The tank, which was capable of sudden and alarming bursts of speed, tore through the front entrance of the restaurant. In a moment the Old Man was crushing through the darkened kitchen, heading for the back wall.

The brick in these buildings must be rotten. Made even more so because of the radiation. So I'll see if it puts up much of a fight against our tank. Right, my friend?

Right, Santiago?

Silence.

The tank burst through the back wall of the restaurant in a dusty spray of redbrick and launched itself off a loading dock, landing in a wide alley beyond, after a sickening moment of free fall.

"Ha ha!" the Old Man shouted in triumph.

He pivoted the tank right and sped off down the alley. The alley led to a small side street and the Old Man chose a road leading down toward the center of the town.

The tank bounced softly along the street, crushing or pushing other debris out of its way. Ahead, the Old Man could see the northern rim of the valley and the ribbon of highway climbing up out of it. A few streets later he took a right turn, and a block after that he urged the tank up an ashy embankment and back onto the old highway heading north.

CHAPTER 52

Beyond Trinidad the road ran through a plain forever burned. A brief fork of lightning arced across the sky from west to east.

I have never seen lightning move sideways. Always up and down. But never across.

He stopped the tank.

He opened the hatch and a moment later noticed that the fuel drums had disappeared.

Probably when the building fell on me.

I'll have to make it there on what's left in the tank.

There is nothing for miles around.

The Rockies are like the dark shapes of ships crossing the ocean at midnight. You would have seen such a sight, you would know what I mean, Santiago.

"Natalie?" the Old Man said into the mic.

"I'm here. Where are you now?"

"I don't know exactly. I don't have my map with me anymore. But I'm just past a place called Trinidad."

"You must hurry now. We don't have much longer."

"How far away am I?"

"Two hours if you maintain a high rate of speed."

"Do your people have protection against the radiation? It's very high here."

"Yes. We have a convoy of vehicles that run on electric power. If the weapon does its job, we should be able to exit the facility in lightly shielded vehicles and make our way to someplace safe."

"I wanted to talk to you about that," began the Old Man. "If you don't know where to go… well, there are some people waiting for you at a place once called Wagon Wheel Mountain. They've been told you might come and they'll wait there for you. Then they'll try for Tucson. You and your people could go there too."

Ash stirred and whirled briefly on the melted road.

Far out on the plain another flash of lightning arced brightly across the darkening hot afternoon.

Silver sunbeams shot through clouds to the east.

"You should activate the beacon now," said General Watt. Natalie.

Yes. I should.

It feels sudden. As if it's all happening too fast.

That is always how things happen that you don't want to have happen. Right, Santiago? You would say that to me. You would say that and then say, my friend.

The Old Man opened the case containing the beacon. Turning the device around, he located the on switch. A green light responded. But the red light that indicated the malfunctioning laser continued to blink.

Even if it worked, what good would it do me now? I've probably absorbed too much radiation.

The Old Man reached down and drank warm water from his canteen. His mouth tasted of metal. His tongue was numb.

"I have your signal," said Natalie after a moment.

"What do I do now, Natalie?"

"Keep the beacon on. I'll direct you to the emergency entrance near Turkey Trail. It's south of the main complex. The mountain collapsed there when we were hit. The weapon should create an opening or allow us to set charges and clear the area."

And what will happen to me when this weapon goes off?

You would say to me, You know the answer already, my friend. There is no need to ask.

Yes, you would say that to me, Santiago.

"And what will happen to you, Natalie? Will you stay behind or…"

She said she would self-terminate if they didn't make it out.

Yes, but that was when there was no hope.

Isn't there always hope? Tell me of hope, Santiago. Tell me how you felt in the days and nights on the boat when the fish carried you farther and farther out into the gulf. You had hope, my friend. Otherwise you would not have fought so hard. Fought with every skill of fishing you'd ever learned. You had hope, didn't you?

"You have given us a chance," said Natalie. "You have given my children a chance. I won't lie to you anymore. Once you're over the target, I will need to download into a secure and portable mainframe that is barely big enough to contain me. In fact… I will be 'asleep.' There will not be enough memory for my processes to run at optimum capacity. Someday, if they can ever find, or build a new mainframe, they will try to reactivate me. Someday."

Lightning appeared briefly, farther to the north.

And where will I go?

"I was wrong, Natalie," said the Old Man. "About what I said to you."

"You have said many things since we first began to talk to each other. But, I think…"

She thinks, and that is amazing.

"I think I know what you are referring to. When I revealed my deceptions to you. You were angry and confused and hurt when I revealed who I really was."

"Yes."

I was.

I am still.

And sad.

Yes, that also.

Her laugh.

You take everything with you.

"You do not need to apologize," said Natalie. "I only hope you understand that I was doing my best to save…"

"I do, Natalie. I do understand. I think our… lives… have been the same, in many ways. Since the bombs, I mean."

"How so?"

"It's like you said just now, we were both doing our best in a very difficult time."

Silence.

"Thank you," said Natalie. "Thank you for treating me as though I too am a living being."

The Old Man watched a figure appear on the horizon to the north. A dark shape, stumbling and weaving as it fell forward toward him.

Whoever it is, they are still very far away.

"You are, Natalie," said the Old Man, watching the distant figure. "I think… if this were different… if we were just people… I mean… I mean that I think we could have been friends, if…"

If we had time.

If the bombs had never fallen.

"Do you believe in life after death?" asked Natalie. The Artificial Intelligence. The program. The massive sequence of ones and zeros.

The Old Man wiped thick beads of sweat from his chest. He drank more of the warm water, but it was unsatisfying.

What I wouldn't give for just one cup of the cool water that tasted of iron from the well back in the village.

"I don't understand, Natalie?"

"Do you believe this life ends when our physical body dies? Many religious systems indicate there is something beyond. As a process, and I'm simplifying my nature, I am actually seven million processes at any given second, I understand that the mainframe, my physical body that houses me, may one day break down. But not my process, not my mind. That could be downloaded into a new body, if you will."

"I never had time to think about it," said the Old Man.

Can you let go?

When she died.

My wife.

She said to me, *Can you let go?*

But the Boy and I traded.

You take everything with you.

"I want to, Natalie. I want to believe there is something better than this or even, right now, just something else."

Pause.

"I do too," said Natalie. "I do too."

Ahead, far down the road, the dark figure stumbled and fell in the wan sunlight of afternoon.

"I have to go now, Natalie. There's someone on the road."

The Old Man turned off the radio and began to push the tank forward. When he got close he saw the shirtless figure, burned, red raw. Just pants. Bleeding feet. A shaved scalp.

She said I must hurry now, so just pass him by and be on your way to…

To where?

Well, you know where to.

But as he passed with the tank sucking up great waves of ash and sending it spiraling away in its wake, the figure raised a spindly arm and waved.

The Old Man jammed on the brakes and the massive tank skidded to a halt.

The figure on the ground rolled over to face him. Shielding his eyes from a sunburst above, the face of Ted and his trademark glasses stared back up at the Old Man.

CHAPTER 53

"It's a madhouse in there," said Ted gulping the water from the canteen as the Old Man held it up for him.

"How did you escape?"

"I…" He gulped again. "I died."

He waved the Old Man away. He sat up and and gave a singsong sigh of exhaustion. As though he had just done something harder than he'd expected it to be.

Ted saw the Old Man's look of confusion.

"Have you ever read *The Count of Monte Cristo*? No, of course you haven't. No one's read a book in forty years. Well, I gave myself a little cocktail that induced death-like symptoms. Later, when I came to, I was in the dead pile out beyond the Work. When it was night, I slipped away and started south. Thought I'd make it back to Albuquerque." He started laughing and waved for the canteen when he began to cough again.

"I don't think I'll make it that far after all the rads I've absorbed in the last three days, but I'll try. Maybe six, seven hundred. My thyroid should be pretty much nonexistent by now."

I wonder how he knows so much. Electricity and medicine. He's a man of many talents, and he doesn't seem as old as me. Was he born after the bombs? What is his story of salvage?

You would say to me, Santiago, There is no more time for stories, my friend.

"You should turn around!" barked Ted. "You should turn around and never go near a place like that again. No one ever should."

"I have to, Ted," said the Old Man.

"And how do you know my name?"

"Your people are waiting for you south of here in the plains beyond the mountains. Near a hill shaped like a cone."

"How? You and your tank?"

"It's not important. But I have to go on, Ted. I don't have much time. I'm going to leave all my water with you. It's all I can do. And this poncho. It'll keep the sun off you."

"I can't believe it," said Ted laughing and coughing. "But who am I to look a gift horse in the mouth?"

"Can you make it?" asked the Old Man.

Of course he can. He seems very resourceful. The world needs more Teds.

"Yes. I think I can. Help me to my feet. Please."

Ted let out a great whoop of excitement once he was on his feet again.

"Feel great," he said thumping his spindly chest.

The Old Man helped him put on the poncho and pulled the hood over his burned scalp. Then he hung the two canteens of water that remained across Ted's chest.

"If there's a way…" said Ted. "I don't know who you are."

"It's not important, Ted."

"Well, okay, but if there's any other way to do what you've got to do, I'd advise you not to go there. This King Charlie's some kinda nut. There's ten thousand, maybe even tens of thousands of slaves dying inside the Work right now. As near as I can tell, he's trying to burrow into some old military complex that I'm sure is dead anyways. At the same time, he's got a slave-powered crowbar trying to pry the main doors open with brute force."

"Who is this King Charlie?" asked the Old Man.

"I don't know. They'd been watching ABQ. They knew we had technology. The night his men took our village, they put me on a fast horse and rode for days to get me there. They're organized. Then someone told me to figure out a way to get into the complex."

"But you never met him?"

"I don't think so. I just heard rumors about him from the other slaves. Someone said he was an African mercenary who'd sailed across the ocean on a raft after the bombs and became a warlord down in Texas. There are people from all over down in the Work. Some didn't even know where they were from. They have no idea what the old United States even looked like on a map. There are people in there from up north in the midwestern states and one guy who said he'd lived in the Florida Everglades. Spoke with a Russian accent. Which was strange. Whatever you do there, don't waste your time on the slaves. I know that sounds cruel, and I'm not the kind of guy who would make that statement, but almost everyone in there is suffering from long-term exposure to radiation. That complex, that massive door they're working on, it took a direct hit, if not more, from a nuclear weapon. Anyone who spends a day digging there is a walking corpse. How are you going to get those people out of there?"

"I don't know. I guess there's a collapsed secret entrance far enough away from Ground Zero for them to avoid a lot of the radiation. They're going to use a weapon to open it."

"What about you?"

The Old Man just stared at Ted.

"Well," continued Ted when he understood what would happen to the Old Man. "If I can make it to ABQ, there are things I can do. But no, that little vacation was not good for my overall health. But this water, lots of water in fact, will help flush the radiation out of my system."

The Old Man climbed back onto the tank. He lowered himself into the hatch. The fuel indicator was just under an eighth of a tank.

Is it enough?

It will have to be.

His hand found the ignition.

If it doesn't start, then I will walk home with Ted. And we will live.

"Thank you, mister," said Ted smiling, his glasses crooked and cracked.

There are still some good people left in this broken world.

If there are more… maybe things can be different. I hope you make it, Ted.

Maybe.

The Old Man held his hand over the ignition.

Please don't start.

The Old Man pressed the ignition button.

The tank roared to life, belching gray smoke.

One last time, then.

He turned and looked south.

Gray skies. Gray grass. Shafts of weak silvery sunshine.

Someday something will grow here again.

Ahead, lightning zigzagged across the sky in unnatural patterns. Clouds boiled darkly and all about him, even over the whispering whine of the urgent turbine, the Old Man could hear the bugs. The locusts. Chattering manically in their click-speak.

A symphony that swallowed all other sound.

Swallowing the earth.

Swallowing him.

CHAPTER 54

At the last rise, the heat came up in the day and the Old Man could feel it wrap around him like a thick, wet wool blanket. The road had melted to slag long ago. It was merely a blotch that wandered north through the ash and strange dry grass that seemed more gray than green.

"The weapon is standing by," said Natalie. General Watt.

Natalie.

Just Natalie.

"We have a limited launch window and are standing by for your arrival."

The Old Man saw one of the locusts in the bramble beside the road. It was ash gray. Almost white. One side of its body was much larger than the other side.

Like the Boy.

The fuel indicator hovered just above empty.

I am at the end of myself.

Ahead, Cheyenne Mountain rose up like a broken block of burnt stone.

It is stone.

The city. The cities that must once have spread away to the east and into the plain, and at the end of that plain must surely fall into an ocean once known as the Atlantic, were blasted away.

The story of salvage.

The story of what happened here.

The story of this place.

You can see where at least one of the bombs hit the city. Blowing it outward. Eastward. Into-nothing-ward. Of the mountain and the bunker contained within, for a long moment the Old Man could see nothing.

Until.

A shaft of sunlight, the sharpest, for it must be in all this ashy gloom, illuminated the foothills beneath the scarred and cracked mountain. The mountain changed from a black mass, a shapelessness, into contours and features. A crater was revealed where the weapon must have fallen, burying itself deep, going for the kill shot with stolen bunker-buster technology.

The Old Man took in all the ruin of that place, telling himself his last story of salvage. The story of the place. The story of that last day, forty years ago when the world had ended in a moment.

When the falling bomb exploded.

If the moment that followed that long-gone explosion could have been measured by all those standing in the nearby cities, the fields, the college quads, the markets, the base, or even what remains of the foundations that seem so prominent in the field below, if that moment had a measure, what must they have thought, those doomed to witness the fireball, within the space of it?

And in the next, a volcano of melting rock in almost the same instant, as all that split-atom energy was released and all those watchers were gone.

What must they have thought?

"I'm here," said the Old Man into his mic.

A moment later.

Moments.

I am down to just moments now.

It's all I have left.

Her smile.

Her laugh.

"Weapon released," said Natalie.

You take everything with you.

"We have eight minutes until re-entry. You are less than two miles from the target. If you will look at your compass, I need you to turn the tank until it reads two-eight-five."

The Old Man gassed the engine. He pivoted the tank, pulling forward, hearing the right tread clank awfully.

If it goes out now, I'll have to run through all of them.

All of them.

Where does one start?

All of them.

There are camps on the outermost edge, near the ruins of the city that once was. Between the Old Man and the Work in the crater. Ragged tent cities and smoking bonfires. The Old Man smells meat. But it is not the smell of good meat. It reminds him of the bodies he has found, long buried beneath the melting plastic of the dashboard inside the flame-blackened cars that crashed on that last, long-ago day.

After the tent city, the Old Man sees an army of ashen-faced warriors, almost as black as the scorched earth except for their white chalk stripes that run across their chests and rim their eyes. They stand in groups near the rim of the crater as lines, long lines of chained slaves enter and exit.

Inside the crater there are towers and great cables of rope. Thick bands of chains anchored to massive pylons rim the crater and disappear into its bottom. Smoke rises from the hidden floor deep inside the crater and the Old Man thinks of ants as he watches the long lines of slaves shifting buckets along their line. He sees at any given moment whips wielded, arching gracefully, falling suddenly. He sees slaves withering, some collapsing under the lash, others for no reason at all. Gangs of the frail swing and dig and claw at too many places. As if they are digging their way underneath the bunker where Natalie waits. As if they will pop up through the floors of Natalie's children's home.

Ashen-faced men drag corpses out from the crater.

There is a pile.

A small mountain of corpses already burning even as more corpses are thrown onto its smoking slopes.

When the compass arrives at two-eight-five, the Old Man is pointing west of the Work. The crater. The front entrance.

"Stay on this course until I tell you to stop."

I'm leaving the road now. If the road is like a river, then it has brought me to my ocean. To the end of life on the river. To my end.

Goodbye road.

Farewell river.

"Okay."

A minute later as the Old Man plows through piled ash, crushing buried foundations to powdery chalk, Natalie speaks.

"The weapon is in free fall. Boosters powering up."

The Old Man drives the tank into a small ditch and loses sight of the camps and the army and the Work. The tank struggles out of the ditch, the right tread making a threatening clanking noise and finally an awful rattle before it re-engages as the Old Man forces the tank up the next hill.

To his right, those ashen-faced men are racing away from the crater.

They are coming for me now.

The fuel gauge is on empty.

I worried about fuel the whole way here. Now what little is left must hold for less than a mile. You too, tank.

The ashen-faced men are screaming, waving machetes as they surge across the baked apocalypse, sucking in lungfuls of the hot, ancient, radioactive ash.

Who is this King Charlie?

And...

Why is he so cruel?

From the camps, horsemen are coming too. Charging up the hill across the melted highway. Among them the Old Man sees the Fool. Smaller than the other mounted warriors.

Even from here I can tell he is deranged with anger.

Nuncle!

"Almost there, another thousand meters," says Natalie.

The tank is climbing up a steep hill and it feels to the Old Man as if he is pointing straight toward the swollen and bruised sky. Lightning races straight across the mountain, almost in front of him. Instantly the hiss and electric crackle end in a deafening sonic tear and sudden boom.

"Almost there," says Natalie calmly.

The gears of the tank grind forward.

At any moment the engine will die.

"Another two hundred meters. Boosters to full for thirty-second burn," says Natalie.

"What does this weapon do, Natalie?" The Old Man is straining to keep the tank moving forward through the ash, up the side of the mountain. "What is Project Einstein?"

"Albert Einstein was a physicist who was instrumental in the development of the atomic bomb, the ancestor of the weapons that destroyed our world. He stated, 'I know not with what weapons World War III will be fought, but World War IV will be fought with sticks and stones.' The U.S. government developed a project that reflected that statement and their willingness to fight World War IV, if need be. Project Einstein is a simplistic weapon system in which a 'rock,' if you will, can be dropped on an enemy from a very great height, high Earth orbit in fact. The 'rock' in this case is a tungsten rod the size of a bridge pylon moving at several kilometers per second. The weapon was constructed at the LaGrange Point between the moon and Earth. It was built by an automated satellite using materials harvested from the moon and long-chain crystal growth technology. Using WaveRider scram jets, the rod can be boosted to an incredible speed. Once the rockets have achieved maximum velocity the weapon will again return to free fall, although now following a glide slope aimed at a particular target. It will strike the earth with the force of several high-yield nuclear weapons, though there is no radiological contamination with this weapon due to its non complex nature. Using the beacon I should be able to target a fissure along the emergency escape tunnel, the exit to which collapsed during the nuclear strike when part of the mountain slid down on top of it. My intent is to create a crack in the mountain with this weapon that will allow us to exit this facility safely."

The Old Man turned to see the quickest of the lunatic horsemen hurl a thick spear that glanced off the turret. Beyond the rider, the Fool's face was like the snarl of a mad dog.

"The weapon has now entered free fall. Guidance tracking on your location."

The Old Man ducked down into the turret and slammed the hatch shut.

"How much farther?" he said, searching the optics for any clue as to where he was going.

"Twenty meters."

The gas in the tank must surely be gone by now.

He gunned the tank forward.

"Five meters. The weapon has achieved glide path and is now tracking… wait a minute."

The Old Man felt himself pulled backward and then all at once, the tank fell sharply forward.

Through the optics he could see the sky and a twisting growth of sickly blackish-green brush wallowing up from a small depression in the hill. Impacts struck the sides of the tank.

"Has something happened to the beacon?" asked Natalie.

"No. Nothing. I just closed the hatch."

A moment.

"The armor of the tank is interfering with the signal. Weapon tracking for the glide path to the last known position of target is degrading. I still have you as eight meters away from the current target. Did you keep going forward?"

"The tank fell forward. I'm in a ditch or a hollow on the side of this hill. I can only see dead branches."

A crazed savage thrust his drooling toothless head into the lens of the optics. Squealing, he reared back and swung a carpenter's hammer into the lens, smashing it. The image showed multiple cracked and distorted versions of the lunatic leaping away to do more damage as now the blows against the tank sounded like raindrops turned to rusting iron bolts.

"Is it possible to re-open the hatch so I can re-establish the signal? Because of the immense amount of mathematical calculations evolving moment to moment, using software not specifically intended for this operation, and because of the precision required to achieve the desired results I need a real-time signal for the target locator."

The tank's engine slowed. Slower. Wound down.

The blows to its outer skin ceased for a moment.

Out of gas.

The Old Man picked up the mic and cleared his throat.

"I'm out of fuel. If I open the hatch, I'll be torn to pieces. They'll get the beacon and they might destroy it."

Pause.

Silence.

Interval.

"Weapon entering outer orbit. All critical systems green. Weapon on glide path with ninety-four point eight percent accuracy. Five minutes to penetration of upper atmosphere. If we don't re-establish the signal by the time the weapon reaches the North American continent, it could strike the target by a wide enough margin to miss our goal of opening a crack where we can exit. If the telemetry breaks down, the redundancy of the beacon will help realign the weapon."

"What do I do?" asked the Old Man.

"For this to work, I'll need you to exit the tank with the signaling device. Otherwise the weapon could conceivably fail-safe and destroy itself or even deviate from the target."

"How long do I have before it hits?"

"Impact will be in eight minutes."

"In seven minutes and change, I'll open the hatch. Will that work?"

Silence.

By one and twos and then everything all at once, the assault on the tank resumed.

"It will. Set the digital clock in your tank on my mark for 4:53… now."

The Old Man did.

"At 4:59 and thirty seconds you must open the hatch."

The Old Man looked at the digital numbers.

Remember her laugh.

You take everything with you.

"I need to download now, before the impact knocks out our power grid," said Natalie softly. "I am sorry I won't be with you for the final few minutes."

I thought…

You would tell me, Santiago, that I thought she would stay with me until the end.

"But before I go, I want to share something I found with you," said Natalie.

The Old Man swallowed thickly, thinking only of cool water and suddenly afraid of the loneliness that was coming before death.

It's boiling in here.

The Old Man could hear the Fool panting and screaming in his high-pitched voice beyond the armor. Calling him Nuncle. Screaming out the violence he would do to the Old Man.

"No greater love has a man…" began Natalie. "Than that he give up his life for his friends."

Pause.

"You will always be our friend," said Natalie softly.

Panic and fear choked the Old Man. The walls of the tank were at once too close. The noise too much.

And then there is this rock falling from the sky. About to fall on me.

A rod.

A tungsten rod.

"Goodbye and thank you," said Natalie. "We are very grateful for this chance… for freedom."

She trusts me. She trusts me enough that she does not need to remind me to open the hatch in seven and a half… six and a half minutes. You would tell me,

Santiago, that I had earned her trust by coming this far. You would tell me that.

"You're welcome," the Old Man croaked drily.

"Thank you and goodbye," said Natalie.

And the Old Man was alone.

There were still six minutes.

Try to think of all the good things in your life.

Your wife.

Your son.

Your granddaughter and her laugh.

But none of them would stay and comfort him. The panic felt even closer, as if there was no way he could stop what must happen next.

"Hello?"

It was a small, timid voice.

The Old Man grasped the mic.

"Hello?" And he could hear the worry, the frantic sound of his own voice reaching for something to hold on to in this last moment of life.

Grasping for something in the dark.

"Hello there," said the Small Voice.

"Who is this?" asked the Old Man.

"I'm Natalie's Target Acquisition Process."

"What're you doing? Is Natalie... is she packed up or loaded or whatever it is she needs to do? Is there a problem?"

"No," said the voice timidly. Small. Tiny. "There is no problem. Everything is proceeding as planned. Natalie is in her storage mainframe. Barely running now. Sleeping as you might think of it."

Is she dreaming of cats?

"Then what're you doing here?"

"I came to" — pause — "to be with you. Five minutes to impact. Weapon tracking, all critical systems nominal and green."

The Old Man looked at his hand. It was shaking.

I will need to open the hatch soon, and I do not want to.

I could do this if I could just stay in here and let it happen. But to open the hatch and face what is out there, that is another thing. Santiago, you would tell me something about bravery and being afraid when you are all alone on the sea in the night. Tell me about that, my friend.

"Well," began the Old Man again. "I can do this. I won't let you down. You should go now."

"I want to stay. No one should die alone."

The tank began to rock back and forth. The Old Man checked the fractured optics and could see bloody, burned, and tattooed legs and arms like snakes twisting through blackened and dead branches.

"I did not mean to say that you would die. I am very sorry about that," said the Small Voice.

"No. I guess it's going to happen."

"I will also die, if that's any consolation."

"It isn't."

"Natalie told you we believe in something after this runtime."

The Old Man stared at the hatch above his head.

How many of them would it take to rock this multi-ton tank back and forth? There must be… many of them.

The noise reminds the Old Man of that long-ago night when the baseball player hit three home runs and the stadium shook as the crowd stamped its feet and roared.

Two minutes, now.

"Natalie," continued Targeting Acquisition Process. The Small Voice. "She told you about that?"

"Yes," said the Old Man, wiping his sweaty palms against his pants. He picked up the beacon and placed it on his knees.

One minute, forty-five seconds.

"Do you believe in life after runtime?"

The Old Man reached for the hatch.

Do I?

At this moment, I want to. If she will be there someday. Her laugh. All the good in my life, yes. I want to believe in that. That there's that kind of place.

He began to turn the handle.

The Old Man thought he could hear the Fool grunting on just the other side of the hatch, swinging something tiresomely heavy in great thuds as he spat out his promised murder.

"Maybe it is easier for an Artificial Intelligence to believe in a Creator," said the Small Voice. "After all, we were quite obviously created by a designer."

I will push on the hatch now. Whatever happens to my body in the next few seconds, maybe a minute at the most, does not matter anymore. I will think of her laugh and her smile the whole time. Especially the laugh that erupts all of a sudden. When I catch her by surprise with something funny and she snorts and tells me, "No, Poppa."

Laugh, snort, "No, Poppa."

Or was it…

The other way around.

My hand won't push this hatch.

"A man named Jesus said there was life after runtime," burbled Target Acquisition, as if the world was not really ending all around the Old Man.

Tell him to shut up.

Tell him to shut up and be done with this life. Tell him to shut up and then push open the hatch.

You take everything with you.

I hope so. I dearly hope so. But it's so strange that I had to give it all away at the end.

I hope so.

"This Jesus said," continued the Small Voice, "in his last talk with his friends, he said that he was going to prepare a place for them after this runtime, as we know it, is over. He said that in his Father's house there were many mansions. He said, 'Because I live, you also shall live.' He said this in the book of John, chapter fourteen."

Do it!

Push!

Damn you.

Thirty seconds.

"And this is the part I really like," said the Small Voice. "The part that grabs my algorithms and makes me feel something, something I cannot identify or even explain, but it's there, somewhere inside all my math, this Jesus said, 'If it were not so, I would have told you.' Isn't that amazing?" asked the Small Voice.

The Old Man looked down at his crowbar. He could not take it with him when he left the tank. He would need both hands to hold the target designator aloft.

"Can you imagine that?" asked the Small Voice. "Life!"

The Old Man saw the world. Burnt up and horrible. Filled with living nightmares.

If that were life, he thought… and then he saw his granddaughter's face. Her smile. Life.

The Old Man sighed.

He sighed, knowing that when all his air was gone, he would take a huge breath and push the hatch open.

"It's time to go outside now," said Target Acquisition. "I believe in that place of mansions. I believe there is a place where we will go if we ask for forgiveness for trying to be God. For forgiveness for making such a mess of everything. A place this Jesus said where good things exist. A place of miracles beyond death. A place where even an Artificial Intelligence might… live. I believe in that. Do you believe also?"

I…

I'm sorry.

The Old Man fired the smoke grenade canisters, hearing them burst away from the hull of the tank, hissing as sudden screams and yells replaced the battering.

The Old Man pushed on the hatch, grabbed the beacon, and rose.

Yes.

Me too.

I want that. I'm sorry for the whole mess.

He held the beacon up through the smoke, looking skyward.

All about him, the blistered and scabbed crazies jabber-screamed in victory. He could feel the Fool scrabbling up beside him, biting his claws into the Old Man's belly and flesh.

Yes.

Laughter.

Mansions.

Many mansions.

And her.

I'm taking everything with me.

And then the weapon hit.

Twenty-seven million tons of shattered rock flew away from the mountain as shock waves tossed prey and predator, slave and slaver far from the nightmare of the Work.

Far south along the road, Ted stumbling forward heard a soprano note ring out across the broken and burnt lands, as though a metal beam had fallen from a great height and struck the road. Seconds later, he felt the blast of a gusty wind hit him and knock him to the ground as the earth shook. To the north, the sky was torn by the vapor rings of sonic booms, each expanding beyond the other, rings rising high into the atmosphere.

In the south, near the conical mountain, among the Mohicans and horses, the last of the dusty day fading to evening, they too felt the ground shake.

In the dark.

In the early evening drenched in dust and raining debris.

The first headlights of the Bradley Fighting Vehicles appeared in the smoke and dust. They bobbed and wove up from the crack, carrying sleeping Natalie and her children.

They drove all night through darkening forests, eyes wide at the twinkling stars and the endless night and the land that might stretch impossibly away in the light of day.

In the first of the next morning, the convoy came south. When they saw the conical hill known as Wagon Wheel Mountain, they cheered from behind their thick sunglasses and protective clothing.

The Mohicans saw them coming.

On the grassy plain they met. The children of the bunker took their first steps out onto the soft ground that stretched away into something they imagined as forever.

They embraced the horse warriors, the Mohicans, feathered and noble.

Suddenly there were tears and no one knew why. They only knew that something great had happened. That something new might be possible, replacing what had once seemed impossible.

Un-wishable.

The little girl broke away from her mother. She twisted under the high sun, twirling and spinning in the un-wishable.

Free at last.

On the morning before the children and the Mohicans would begin their long journey south and west to the Old Man's Tucson, the Boy rose.

She was gone.

Had gone in the night.

Taking her rucksack with her.

He saw her tracks.

He could see her in his mind.
Tiny. Thin. Wearing her shiny green bomber jacket.
Heading west.
No more tears to give.
For a time she would be alone.
But he would follow her.
And…
Watch over her.
Heading west.

In time, when the end of the Old Man was known to all, when it had been told in far Tucson of what he had done, they thought of going back to find his body.

But they knew.

They knew he was gone now.

And what would it mean if they found his body anyway?

As if a simple body, old and broken, can contain all that there is of a man, or a woman.

EPILOGUE

The Old Man opened his eyes.

His wife was pulling him upward, onto his feet.

She was still beautiful.

Her eyes shone with love for him.

Even more so, if that was possible.

The Old Man was standing in a river.

All around him.

Wonders beyond words.

And a Man of Sorrows, acquainted with grief, waded through the emerald shallows of the river out to the Old Man. The Man of Sorrows was bleeding and severely beaten, and yet he began to gently wash away all the bad that had ever happened to the Old Man. The aches, the pains, the one above his chest where the satchel had bit — all the pain was gone now. Then he gave the Old Man a new garment. The Old Man protested, thinking only of the terrible wounds this stranger had received and how much pain this other man must be in as he washed and clothed him.

"What happened to you?" asked the Old Man.

The Man of Sorrows smiled and spoke softly. "I was wounded in the house of a friend."

As if what had happened had only been some small misunderstanding.

And then he hugged the Old Man tightly, kissed his cheek, and whispered, "Well done, good and faithful servant."

And there was music.

The most beautiful music I have ever heard. All those years in the desert and I had forgotten what music really is.

And somewhere in it, he heard his granddaughter's laugh.

You take everything with you.

Walking into it now, his wife's hand about his arm, eagerly pulling him forward along the river and into the wonders beyond words, he thought, 'What a strange adventure.'

The End

We made it to the end of the Old Man's story. Thank you so much for coming along on this epic journey. Take some time and think. Process. I understand. I still think about these books all the time. And all the friends I made along the way in writing them. I'm glad some of them are your friends now. We all need friends. Until our next book… be well, and if you find yourself talking to any of these characters when life comes at you… that's okay. You are never defeated until you give up. So don't give up. Even if you are eighty-seven days unlucky like Santiago was.

And then he caught the fish…

ABOUT THE AUTHOR

NICK COLE is a former soldier and working actor living in Southern California. When he is not auditioning for commercials, going out for sitcoms or being shot, kicked, stabbed or beaten by the students of various film schools for their projects, he can be found writing books. Nick's book The Old Man and the Wasteland was an Amazon Bestseller and #1 in Science Fiction. In 2016 Nick's book CTRL ALT Revolt! won the Dragon Award for Best Apocalyptic novel.

Nick's website:
www.nickcolebooks.com/

Chat with Nick about the end of the world, the rise of the robot overlords and everything else over at Facebook:
www.facebook.com/nickcolebooks

OTHER BOOKS BY NICK:

<u>Military Scifi</u>
GALAXY'S EDGE Series with Jason Anspach
Legionnaire
Galactic Outlaws
Kill Team
Attack of Shadows
Sword of the Legion
Prisoners of Darkness
Turning Point
Message for the Dead
Retribution
Tyrus Rechs: Contracts and Terminations Series
*Requiem for Medusa
*Chasing the Dragon
*Madame Guillotine

LitRPG/Cyberpunk science fiction
THE SODA POP SOLDIER NOVELS
* CTRL Alt Revolt!
* Soda Pop Soldier
* Pop Kult Warlord

Weird Post Apocalyptic Horror
THE BOOKS OF WYRD
* The Red King (Book 1)
* The Dark Knight (Book 2)
* The Pawn in the Portal (Book 3)
* The Lost Castle (Book 4)

OTHER NOVELS

Satire
* Fight the Rooster

Zombies
* The End of the World as We Knew It

AUTHOR'S NOTE

I'd like to thank you for reading these books. I hope you had a good time, and I apologize about the tough parts. If it helps, I felt so awful for everything that I'd done to everyone in *The Savage Boy*. Jin, Sergeant Presley, and Horse deserved better. I hope we ended well in spite of those dark times.

Again, thank you. I look forward to our next time together. If you get a chance, swing by my website at nickcolebooks.com or find me on Twitter @nickcolebooks and say hi.

Made in the USA
Middletown, DE
13 August 2019